The
Children
of Men

P. D. James

The Children of Men

1265 9096

Published by Random House Large Print
in association with Alfred A. Knopf
New York 1993

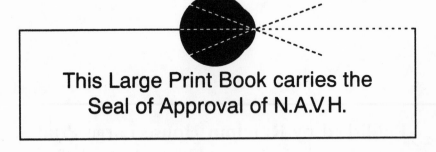

This Large Print Book carries the
Seal of Approval of N.A.V.H.

Again, to my daughters
Clare and Jane
who helped

Contents

Book One

OMEGA

January–March 2021

1

Friday 1 January 2021

Early this morning, 1 January 2021, three minutes
after midnight, the last human being to be born
on earth was killed in a pub brawl in a suburb of
Buenos Aires, aged twenty-five years, two months
and twelve days. If the first reports are to believed,
Joseph Ricardo died as he had lived. The distinction, if one can call it that, of being the last human
whose birth was officially recorded, unrelated as it
was to any personal virtue or talent, had always
been difficult for him to handle. And now he is
dead. The news was given to us here in Britain on
the nine o'clock programme of the State Radio
Service and I heard it fortuitously. I had settled
down to begin this diary of the last half of my life
when I noticed the time and thought I might as
well catch the headlines to the nine o'clock bulle-
tin. Ricardo's death was the last item mentioned,
and then only briefly, a couple of sentences delivered without emphasis in the newscaster's care-

3

fully non-committal voice. But it seemed to me, hearing it, that it was a small additional justification for beginning the diary today: the first day of a new year and my fiftieth birthday. As a child I had always liked that distinction, despite the inconvenience of having it follow Christmas too quickly so that one present—it never seemed notably superior to the one I would in any case have received—had to do for both celebrations.

As I begin writing, the three events, the New Year, my fiftieth birthday, Ricardo's death, hardly justify sullying the first pages of this new loose-leaf notebook. But I shall continue, one small additional defence against personal accidie. If there is nothing to record, I shall record the nothingness and then if, and when, I reach old age—as most of us can expect to, we have become experts at prolonging life—I shall open one of my tins of hoarded matches and light my small personal bonfire of vanities. I have no intention of leaving the diary as a record of one man's last years. Even in my most egotistical moods I am not as self-deceiving as that. What possible interest can there be in the journal of Theodore Faron, Doctor of Philosophy, Fellow of Merton College in the University of Oxford, historian of the Victorian age, divorced, childless, solitary, whose only claim to notice is that he is cousin to Xan Lyppiatt, the dictator and Warden of England.

No additional personal record is, in any case, necessary. All over the world nation states are preparing to store their testimony for the posterity which we can still occasionally convince ourselves may follow us, those creatures from another planet who may land on this green wilderness and ask what kind of sentient life once inhabited it. We are storing our books and manuscripts, the great paintings, the musical scores and instruments, the artefacts. The world's greatest libraries will in forty years' time at most be darkened and sealed. The buildings, those that are still standing, will speak for themselves. The soft stone of Oxford is unlikely to survive more than a couple of centuries. Already the University is arguing about whether it is worth refacing the crumbling Sheldonian. But I like to think of those mythical creatures landing in St. Peter's Square and entering the great Basilica, silent and echoing under the centuries of dust. Will they realize that this was once the greatest of man's temples to one of his many gods? Will they be curious about his nature, this deity who was worshipped with such pomp and splendour, intrigued by the mystery of his symbol, at once so simple, the two crossed sticks, ubiquitous in nature, yet laden with gold, gloriously jewelled and adorned? Or will their values and their thought processes be so alien to ours that nothing of awe or wonder will be able to touch them? But despite the discovery—in 1997, was it?—of a planet which the astronomers told us could support life, few of us really believe that they will come. They must be there. It is surely unreasonable to credit that only one small star in the immensity of the universe is capable of developing and supporting intelligent life. But we shall not get to them and they will not come to us.

Twenty years ago, when the world was already half-convinced that our species had lost for ever the power to reproduce, the search to find the last known human birth became a universal obsession, elevated to a matter of national pride, an international contest as ultimately pointless as it was fierce and acrimonious. To qualify, the birth had to be officially notified, the date and precise time recorded. This effectively excluded a high proportion of the human race where the day but not the hour was known, and it was accepted, but not emphasized, that the result could never be conclusive. Almost certainly, in some remote jungle, in some primitive hut, the last human being had slipped largely unnoticed into an unregarding world. But after months of checking and rechecking, Joseph Ricardo, of mixed race, born illegitimately in a Buenos Aires hospital at two minutes past three Western time on 19 October 1995, had been officially recognized. Once the result was proclaimed, he was left to exploit his celebrity as best he could while the world, as if suddenly aware of the futility of the exercise, turned its attention elsewhere. And now he is dead and I doubt whether any country will be eager to drag the other candidates from oblivion.

We are outraged and demoralized less by the impending end of our species, less even by our inability to prevent it, than by our failure to discover the cause. Western science and Western medicine haven't prepared us for the magnitude and humiliation of this ultimate failure. There have been many diseases which have been difficult to diagnose or cure and one which almost depopulated two continents before it spent itself. But we have always in the end been able to explain why. We have given names to the viruses and germs which, even today, take possession of us, much to our chagrin since it seems a personal affront that they should still assail us, like old enemies who keep up the skirmish and bring down the occasional victim when their victory is assured. Western science has been our god. In the variety of its power it has preserved, comforted, healed, warmed, fed and entertained us and we have felt free to criticize and occasionally reject it as men have always rejected their gods, but in the knowledge that, despite our apostasy, this deity, our creature and our slave, would still provide for us; the anaesthetic for the pain, the spare heart, the new lung, the antibiotic, the moving wheels and the moving pictures. The light will always come on when we press the switch and if it doesn't we can find out why. Science was never a subject I was at home with. I understood little of it at school and I understand little more now that I'm fifty. Yet it has been my god too, even if its achievements are incomprehensible to me, and I share the universal disillusionment of those whose god has died. I can clearly remember the confident words of one biologist spoken when it had finally become apparent that nowhere in the whole world was there a pregnant woman: "It may take us some time to discover the cause of this apparent universal infertility." We have had twenty-five years and we no longer even expect to succeed. Like a lecherous stud suddenly stricken with impotence, we are humiliated at the very heart of our faith in ourselves. For all our knowledge, our intelligence, our power, we can no longer do what the animals do without thought. No wonder we both worship and resent them.

The year 1995 became known as Year Omega and the term is now universal. The great public debate in the late 1990s was whether the country which discovered a cure for the universal infertility would share this with the world and on what terms. It was accepted that this was a global disaster and that it must be met by the response of a united world. We still, in the late 1990s, spoke of Omega in terms of a disease, a malfunction which would in time be diagnosed and then corrected, as man had found a cure for tuberculosis, diphtheria, polio and even in the end, although too late, for AIDS. As the years passed and the united efforts under the aegis of the United Nations came to nothing, this resolve of complete openness fell apart. Research became secret, nations' efforts a cause of fascinated, suspicious attention. The European Community acted in concert, pouring in research facilities and manpower. The European Centre for Human Fertility, outside Paris, was among the most prestigious in the world. This in turn co-operated, at least overtly, with the United States, whose efforts were if anything greater. But there was no inter-race co-operation; the prize was too great. The terms on which the secret might be shared were a cause of passionate speculation and debate. It was accepted that the cure, once found, would have to be shared; this was scientific knowledge which no race ought to, or could, keep to itself indefinitely. But across continents, national and racial boundaries, we watched each other suspiciously, obsessively, feeding on rumour and speculation. The old craft of spying returned. Old agents crawled out of comfortable retirement in Weybridge and Cheltenham and passed on their trade craft. Spying had, of course, never stopped, even after the official end of the Cold War in 1991. Man is too addicted to this intoxicating mixture of adolescent buccaneering and adult perfidy to relinquish it entirely. In the late 1990s the bureaucracy of espionage flourished as it hadn't since the end of the Cold War, producing new heroes, new villains, new mythologies. In particular we watched Japan, half-fearing that this technically brilliant people might already be on the way to finding the answer.

Ten years on we still watch, but we watch with less anxiety and without hope. The spying still goes on but it is twenty-five years now since a human being was born and in our hearts few of us believe that the cry of a new-born child will ever be heard again on our planet. Our interest in sex is waning. Romantic and idealized love has taken over from crude carnal satisfaction despite the efforts of the Warden of England, through the national porn shops, to stimulate our flagging appetites. But we have our sensual substitutes; they are available to all on the National Health Service. Our ageing bodies are pummelled, stretched, stroked, caressed, anointed, scented. We are manicured and pedicured, measured and weighed. Lady Margaret Hall has become the massage centre for Oxford and here every Tuesday afternoon I lie on the couch and look out over

the still-tended gardens, enjoying my State-provided, carefully measured hour of sensual pampering. And how assiduously, with what obsessive
concern, do we intend to retain the illusion, if not
of youth, of vigorous middle age. Golf is now the
national game. If there had been no Omega, the
conservationists would protest at the acres of
countryside, some of it our most beautiful, which
have been distorted and rearranged to provide
ever more challenging courses. All are free; this is
part of the Warden's promised pleasure. Some
have become exclusive, keeping unwelcome members out, not by prohibition, which is illegal, but
by those subtle, discriminating signals which in
Britain even the least sensitive are trained from
childhood to interpret. We need our snobberies;
equality is a political theory not a practical policy,
even in Xan's egalitarian Britain. I tried once to
play golf but found the game immediately and
totally unattractive, perhaps because of my ability
to shift divots of earth, but never the ball. Now I
run. Almost daily I pound the soft earth of Port
Meadow or the deserted footpaths of Wytham
Wood, counting the miles, subsequently measur-
ing heartbeat, weight loss, stamina. I am just as
anxious to stay alive as anyone else, just as obsessed with the functioning of my body.

Much of this I can trace to the early 1990s: the
search for alternative medicine, the perfumed oils,

the massage, the stroking and anointing, the crys-
tal-holding, the non-penetrative sex. Pornography and sexual violence on film, on television, in
books, in life, had increased and became more
explicit but less and less in the West we made love
and bred children. It seemed at the time a welcome development in a world grossly polluted by
over-population. As a historian I see it as the
beginning of the end.

We should have been warned in the early 1990s.
As early as 1991 a European Community Report
showed a slump in the number of children born in
Europe—8.2 million in 1990, with particular
drops in the Roman Catholic countries. We
thought that we knew the reasons, that the fall
was deliberate, a result of more liberal attitudes to
birth control and abortion, the postponement of
pregnancy by professional women pursuing their
careers, the wish of families for a higher standard
of living. And the fall in population was complicated by the spread of AIDS, particularly in
Africa. Some European countries began to pursue
a vigorous campaign to encourage the birth of
children, but most of us thought the fall was desir-
able, even necessary. We were polluting the planet
with our numbers; if we were breeding less it was
to be welcomed. Most of the concern was less
about a falling population than about the wish of
nations to maintain their own people, their own

culture, their own race, to breed sufficient young to maintain their economic structures. But as I remember it, no one suggested that the fertility of the human race was dramatically changing. When Omega came it came with dramatic suddenness and was received with incredulity. Overnight, it seemed, the human race had lost its power to breed. The discovery in July 1994 that even the frozen sperm stored for experiment and artificial insemination had lost its potency was a peculiar horror casting over Omega the pall of superstitious awe, of witchcraft, of divine intervention. The old gods reappeared, terrible in their power.

The world didn't give up hope until the generation born in 1995 reached sexual maturity. But when the testing was complete and not one of them could produce fertile sperm, we knew that this was indeed the end of *Homo sapiens*. It was in that year, 2008, that the suicides increased. Not mainly among the old, but among my generation, the middle-aged, the generation who would have to bear the brunt of an ageing and decaying society's humiliating but insistent needs. Xan, who had by then taken over as the Warden of England, tried to stop what was becoming an epidemic by imposing fines on the surviving nearest relations, just as the Council now pays handsome pensions to the relations of the incapacitated and dependent old who kill themselves. It had its effect; the

suicide rate fell compared with the enormous figures in other parts of the world, particularly countries whose religion was based on ancestor
worship, on the continuance of a family. But
those who lived gave way to the almost universal
negativism, what the French named *ennui univer-
sel.* It came upon us like an insidious disease;
indeed, it was a disease, with its soon-familiar
symptoms of lassitude, depression, ill-defined
malaise, a readiness to give way to minor infec-
tions, a perpetual disabling headache. I fought
against it, as did many others. Some, Xan among
them, have never been afflicted with it, protected
perhaps by a lack of imagination or, in his case,
by an egotism so powerful that no external catastrophe can prevail against it. I still occasionally
need to struggle but I now fear it less. The weapons I fight it with are also my consolations: books,
music, food, wine, nature.

These assuaging satisfactions are also bitter-
sweet reminders of the transitoriness of human
joy; but when was it ever lasting? I can still find
pleasure, more intellectual than sensual, in the
effulgence of an Oxford spring, the blossoms in
Belbroughton Road which seem lovelier every
year, sunlight moving on stone walls, horse-chest-
nut trees in full bloom, tossing in the wind, the
smell of a bean field in flower, the first snowdrops,
the fragile compactness of a tulip. Pleasure need

not be less keen because there will be centuries of springs to come, their blossom unseen by human eyes, the walls will crumble, the trees die and rot, the gardens revert to weeds and grass, because all beauty will outlive the human intelligence which records, enjoys and celebrates it. I tell myself this, but do I believe it when the pleasure now comes so rarely and, when it does, is so indistinguishable from pain? I can understand how the aristocrats and great landowners with no hope of posterity leave their estates untended. We can experience nothing but the present moment, live in no other second of time, and to understand this is as close as we can get to eternal life. But our minds reach back through centuries for the reassurance of our ancestry and, without the hope of posterity, for our race if not for ourselves, without the assurance that we being dead yet live, all pleasures of the mind and senses sometimes seem to me no more than pathetic and crumbling defences shored up against our ruins.

In our universal bereavement, like grieving parents, we have put away all painful reminders of our loss. The children's playgrounds in our parks have been dismantled. For the first twelve years after Omega the swings were looped up and secured, the slides and climbing frames left unpainted. Now they have finally gone and the asphalt playgrounds have been grassed over or sown with flowers like small mass graves. The toys have been burnt, except for the dolls, which have become for some half-demented women a substitute for children. The schools, long closed, have been boarded up or used as centres for adult education. The children's books have been systematically removed from our libraries. Only on tape and records do we now hear the voices of children, only on film or on television programmes do we see the bright, moving images of the young. Some find them unbearable to watch but most feed on them as they might a drug.

The children born in the year 1995 are called Omegas. No generation has been more studied, more examined, more agonized over, more valued or more indulged. They were our hope, our promise of salvation, and they were—they still are—exceptionally beautiful. It sometimes seems that nature in her ultimate unkindness wished to emphasize what we have lost. The boys, men of twenty-five now, are strong, individualistic, intelligent and handsome as young gods. Many are also cruel, arrogant and violent, and this has been found to be true of Omegas all over the world. The dreaded gangs of the Painted Faces who drive round the countryside at night to ambush and terrorize unwary travellers are rumoured to be Omegas. It is said that when an Omega is caught he is offered immunity if he is prepared to join the

State Security Police, whereas the rest of the gang, no more guilty, are sent on conviction to the Penal Colony on the Isle of Man, to which all those convicted of crimes of violence, burglary or repeated theft are now banished. But if we are unwise to drive unprotected on our crumbling secondary roads, our towns and cities are safe, crime effectively dealt with at last by a return to the deportation policy of the nineteenth century.

The female Omegas have a different beauty, classical, remote, listless, without animation or energy. They have their distinctive style which other women never copy, perhaps fear to copy. They wear their hair long and loose, their foreheads bound with braid or ribbon, plain or plaited. It is a style which suits only the classically beautiful face, with its high forehead and large, widely spaced eyes. Like their male counterparts, they seem incapable of human sympathy. Men and women, the Omegas are a race apart, indulged, propitiated, feared, regarded with a half-superstitious awe. In some countries, so we are told, they are ritually sacrificed in fertility rites resurrected after centuries of superficial civilization. I occasionally wonder what we in Europe will do if news reaches us that these burnt offerings have been accepted by the ancient gods and a live child has been born.

Perhaps we have made our Omegas what they

are by our own folly; a regime which combines perpetual surveillance with total indulgence is hardly conducive to healthy development. If from infancy you treat children as gods they are liable in adulthood to act as devils. I have one vivid memory of them which remains the living icon of how I see them, how they see themselves. It was last June, a hot but unsultry day of clear light with slow-moving clouds, like wisps of muslin, moving across a high, azure sky, the air sweet and cool to the cheek, a day with none of the humid languor I associate with an Oxford summer. I was visiting a fellow academic in Christ Church and had entered under Wolsey's wide, four-centred arch to cross Tom Quad when I saw them, a group of four female and four male Omegas elegantly displaying themselves on the stone plinth. The women, with their crimped aureoles of bright hair, their high bound brows, the contrived folds and loops of their diaphanous dresses, looked as though they had stepped down from the Pre-Raphaelite windows in the cathedral. The four males stood behind them, legs firmly apart, arms folded, gazing not at them but over their heads, seeming to assert an arrogant suzerainty over the whole quad. As I passed, the females turned on me their blank, incurious gaze, which nevertheless signalled an unmistakable flicker of contempt. The males briefly scowled, then averted their eyes as if from an object unworthy of further notice and gazed again over the quad. I thought then, as I do now, how glad I was that I no longer had to teach them. Most of the Omegas took a first degree, but that was all; they aren't interested in further education. The undergraduate Omegas I taught were intelligent but disruptive, ill-disciplined and bored. Their unspoken question, "What is the point of all this?," was one I was glad I wasn't required to answer. History, which interprets the past to understand the present and confront the future, is the least rewarding discipline for a dying species.

The university colleague who takes Omega with total calmness is Daniel Hurstfield, but then, as professor of statistical paleontology, his mind ranges over a different dimension of time. As with the God of the old hymn, a thousand ages in his sight are like an evening gone. Sitting beside me at a college feast in the year when I was wine secretary, he said: "What are you giving us with the grouse, Faron? That should do very nicely. Sometimes I fear you are a little inclined to be too adventurous. And I hope you have established a rational drinking-up programme. It would distress me, on my deathbed, to contemplate the barbarian Omegas making free with the college cellar."

I said: "We're thinking about it. We're still

laying down, of course, but on a reduced scale. Some of my colleagues feel we are being too pessimistic."

"Oh, I don't think you can possibly be too pessimistic. I can't think why you all seem so surprised at Omega. After all, of the four billion life forms which have existed on this planet, three billion, nine hundred and sixty million are now extinct. We don't know why. Some by wanton extinction, some through natural catastrophe, some destroyed by meteorites and asteroids. In the light of these mass extinctions it really does seem unreasonable to suppose that *Homo sapiens* should be exempt. Our species will have been one of the shortest-lived of all, a mere blink, you may say, in the eye of time. Omega apart, there may well be an asteroid of sufficient size to destroy this planet on its way to us now."

He began loudly to masticate his grouse as if the prospect afforded him the liveliest satisfaction.

2

Tuesday 5 January 2021

During those two years when, at Xan's invitation, I was a kind of observer-adviser at the Council meetings, it was usual for journalists to write that we had been brought up together, that we were as close as brothers. It wasn't true. From the age of twelve we spent the summer holidays together, but that was all. The error wasn't surprising. I half believed it myself. Even now the summer term seems in retrospect a boring concatenation of predictable days dominated by timetables, neither painful nor feared but to be endured and occasionally, briefly, enjoyed, since I was both clever and reasonably popular, until the blessed moment of release. After a couple of days at home I would be sent to Woolcombe.

Even as I write I am trying to understand what I felt for Xan then, why the bond remained so strong and for so long. It wasn't sexual, except that in nearly all close friendships there is a subcutaneous pricking of sexual attraction. We never touched, not even, I remember, in boisterous play. There was no boisterous play—Xan hated to be touched and I early recognized and respected his invisible no-man's-land, as he respected mine. It wasn't, either, the usual story of the dominant partner, the elder, if only by four months, leading the younger, his admiring disciple. He never made me feel inferior; that wasn't his way. He welcomed me without particular warmth but as if he were receiving back his twin, a part of himself. He had charm, of course; he still has. Charm is often despised but I can never see why. No one has it who isn't capable of genuinely liking others, at least at the actual moment of meeting and speaking. Charm is always genuine; it may be superficial but it isn't false. When Xan is with another person he gives the impression of intimacy, interest, of not wanting any other company. He could hear of that person's death the next day with equanimity, could probably even kill him without scruple. Now I can watch him on television as he gives his quarterly report to the nation and see the same charm.

Both our mothers are now dead. They were nursed to the end at Woolcombe, which is now a nursing home for the nominees of the Council. Xan's father was killed in a car crash in France the year after Xan became Warden of England.

There was some mystery about it; no details were ever released. I wondered about the crash at the time, still do wonder, which tells me a lot about my relationship with Xan. With part of my mind I still believe him capable of anything, half needing to believe him ruthless, invincible, beyond the bounds of ordinary behaviour, as he had seemed to be when we were boys.

The sisters' lives had taken very different paths. My aunt, by a fortunate combination of beauty, ambition and good luck, had married a middle-aged baronet, my mother a middle-grade civil servant. Xan was born at Woolcombe, one of the most beautiful manor houses in Dorset. I was born in Kingston, Surrey, in the maternity wing of the local hospital, and taken home to a semi-detached Victorian house in a long, dull road of identical houses leading up to Richmond Park. I was brought up in an atmosphere redolent of resentment. I remember my mother packing for my summer visit to Woolcombe, anxiously sorting out clean shirts, holding up my best jacket, shaking it and scrutinizing it with what seemed a personal animosity, as if simultaneously resenting what it had cost and the fact that, since it had been bought too large, to allow for growth, and was now too small for comfort, there had been no intervening period in which it had actually fitted. Her attitude to her sister's good fortune was expressed in a series of often-repeated phrases: "Just as well they don't dress for dinner. I'm not handing out for a dinner jacket, not at your age. Ridiculous!" And the inevitable question—asked with averted eyes, for she was not without shame: "They get on all right, I suppose? Of course that class of person always sleeps in separate rooms." And at the end: "Of course, it's all right for Serena." I knew even at twelve years of age that it wasn't all right for Serena.

I suspect that my mother thought a great deal more often of her sister and brother-in-law than they ever thought of her. And even my unfashionable Christian name I owe to Xan. He was called after a grandfather and great-grandfather; "Xan" had been a family name with the Lyppiatts for generations. I, too, had been named after my paternal grandfather. My mother had seen no reason why she should be outdone when it came to the eccentric naming of a child. But Sir George puzzled her. I can still hear her peevish complaint: "He doesn't look like a baronet to me." He was the only baronet either of us had met and I wondered what private image she was conjuring up—a pale, romantic Van Dyck portrait stepping down from its frame; sulky Byronic arrogance, a red-faced swashbuckling squire, loud of voice, hard rider to hounds. But I knew what she meant; he didn't look like a baronet to me either. Cer-

tainly he didn't look like the owner of Woolcombe. He had a spade-shaped face, mottled red,
with a small, moist mouth under the moustache
which looked both ridiculous and artificial, the
ruddy hair which Xan had inherited, faded to the
drab colour of dried straw, and eyes which gazed
over his acres with an expression of puzzled sadness. But he was a good shot—my mother would
have approved of that. So too was Xan. He was
not permitted to handle his father's Purdeys but
had his own couple of guns with which we would
pot rabbits, and there were two pistols which we
were allowed to use with blanks. We would set up
target cards on trees and spend hours improving
our scores. After a few days' practice I was better
than Xan both with gun and pistol. My skill surprised us both, me particularly. I hadn't expected
to like or be good at shooting; I was almost disconcerted to discover how much I enjoyed, with a
half-guilty, almost sensual pleasure, the feel of the
metal in my palm, the satisfying balance of the
weapons.

Xan had no other companions during the holidays and seemed not to need them. No friends
from Sherborne came to Woolcombe. When I
asked him about school he was elusive.

"It's all right. Better than Harrow would have
been."

"Better than Eton?"

"We don't go there any more. Great-grandfather had a tremendous row, public allegations, angry letters, dust shaken off feet. I've forgotten what it was all about."

"You never mind going back to school?"

"Why should I? Do you?"

"No, I rather like it. If I can't be here, I'd rather have school than holidays."

He was silent for a moment, then said: "The thing is this, school-masters want to understand you, that's what they think they're paid for. I keep them puzzled. Hard worker, top marks, housemaster's pet, safe for an Oxford scholarship one term; next term big, big trouble."

"What sort of trouble?"

"Not enough to get kicked out, and of course next term I'm a good boy again. It confuses them, gets them worried."

I didn't understand him either, but it didn't worry me. I didn't understand myself.

I know now, of course, why he liked having me at Woolcombe. I think I guessed almost from the beginning. He had absolutely no commitment to me, no responsibility for me, not even the commitment of friendship or the responsibility of personal choice. He hadn't chosen me. I was his cousin, I was wished on him, I was there. With me at Woolcombe he need never face the inevitable question: "Why don't you invite your friends here for the holidays?" Why should he? He had his fatherless cousin to entertain. I lifted from him, an only child, the burden of excessive parental concern. I was never particularly aware of that concern but, without me, his parents might have felt constrained to show it. From boyhood he couldn't tolerate questions, curiosity, interference in his life. I sympathized with that; I was very much the same. If there was time enough or purpose in it, it would be interesting to trace back our common ancestry to discover the roots of this obsessive self-sufficiency. I realize now that it was one of the reasons for my failed marriage. It is probably the reason why Xan has never married. It would take a force more powerful than sexual love to prise open the portcullis which defends that crenellated heart and mind.

We seldom saw his parents during those long weeks of summer. Like most adolescents, we slept late, and they had breakfasted when we got down. Our midday meal was a picnic set out for us in the kitchen, a thermos of home-made soup, bread, cheese and pâté, slabs of rich home-made fruit cake prepared by a lugubrious cook who managed illogically to grumble simultaneously at the small extra trouble we caused and at the lack of prestigious dinner parties at which she could display her skill. We got back in time to change into our suits for dinner. My uncle and aunt never entertained, at least not when I was there, and the conversation was carried on almost entirely between them while Xan and I ate, casting each other occasionally the secretive, colluding glances of the judgemental young. Their spasmodic talk was invariably about plans for us and carried on as if we weren't there.

My aunt, delicately stripping the skin from a peach, not raising her eyes: "The boys might like to see Maiden Castle."

"Not a lot to see at Maiden Castle. Jack Manning could take them out in his boat when he collects the lobsters."

"I don't think I trust Manning. There's a concert tomorrow at Poole which they might enjoy."

"What kind of concert?"

"I don't remember, I gave you the programme."

"They might like a day in London."

"Not in this lovely weather. They're much better in the open air."

When Xan was seventeen and first had the use of his father's car we would drive into Poole to pick up girls. I found these excursions terrifying and went with him only twice. It was like entering an alien world; the giggles, the girls hunting in pairs, the bold, challenging stares, the apparently inconsequential but obligatory chat. After the second time I said: "We're not pretending to feel affection. We don't even like them; they certainly don't like us. So if both parties only want sex why don't we just say so and cut out all these embarrassing preliminaries?"

"Oh, they seem to need them. Anyway, the only women you can approach like that want cash payment in advance. We can strike lucky in Poole with one film and a couple of hours' drinking."

"I don't think I'll come."

"You're probably right. I usually feel next morning that it hasn't been worth the trouble."

It was typical of him to make it sound as if my reluctance was not, as he must have known, a mixture of embarrassment, fear of failure and shame. I could hardly blame Xan for the fact that I lost my virginity in conditions of acute discomfort in a Poole car park with a redhead who made it plain, both during my fumbling preliminaries and afterwards, that she had known better ways of spending a Saturday evening. And I can hardly claim that the experience adversely affected my sex life. After all, if our sex life were determined by our first youthful experiments, most of the world would be doomed to celibacy. In no area of human experience are human beings more convinced that something better can be had if only they persevere.

Apart from the cook, I can remember few of the servants. There was a gardener, Hobhouse, with a pathological dislike of roses, particularly when

planted with other flowers. They get in everywhere, he would grumble, as if the climbers and
standard bushes which he resentfully and skil-
fully pruned had somehow mysteriously seeded
themselves. And there was Scovell, with his pretty,
pert face, whose precise function I never understood: chauffeur, gardener's boy, handyman? Xan
either ignored him or was calculatingly offensive.
I had never known him to be rude to any other
servant and would have asked him why if I hadn't
sensed, alert as always to every nuance of emotion in my cousin, that the question would be
unwise.

I didn't resent it that Xan was our grandparents' favourite. The preference seemed to me
perfectly natural. I can remember one snatch
of conversation overheard at the one Christmas when, disastrously, we were all together at
Woolcombe.

"I sometimes wonder if Theo won't go further
than Xan in the end."

"Oh no. Theo is a good-looking, intelligent
boy, but Xan is brilliant."

Xan and I colluded in that judgement. When I
got my Oxford entrance they were gratified but
surprised. When Xan was accepted at Balliol they
took it as his due. When I got my First they said
I was lucky. When Xan achieved no more than an
upper second they complained, but indulgently,

that he hadn't bothered to work.

He didn't make demands, never treated me like a poor cousin, annually provided me with food, drink and a free holiday in return for companionship or subservience. If I wanted to be alone, I could be, without complaint or comment. Usually this was in the library, a room which delighted me with its shelves filled with leather-bound books, its pilasters and carved capitals, the great stone fireplace with its carved coat of arms, the marble busts in their niches, the huge map table where I could spread my books and holiday tasks, the deep leather armchairs, the view from the tall windows across the lawn down to the river and the bridge. It was here, browsing in the county histories, that I discovered that a skirmish had been fought on that bridge in the Civil War when five young Cavaliers had held the bridge against the Roundheads until all of them had fallen. Even their names were set out, a roll-call of romantic courage: Ormerod, Freemantle, Cole, Bydder, Fairfax. I went to Xan in great excitement and dragged him into the library.

"Look, the actual date of the fight is next Wednesday, August 16. We ought to celebrate."

"How? Throw flowers in the water?"

But he was not being either dismissive or contemptuous and he was only slightly amused at my enthusiasm.

"Why not drink to them anyway? Make a ceremony of it."

We did both. We went to the bridge at sunset with a bottle of his father's claret, the two pistols, my arms filled with flowers from the walled garden. We drank the bottle between us; then Xan balanced on the parapet, firing both pistols into the air as I shouted out the names. It is one of the moments from my boyhood which have remained with me, an evening of pure joy, unshadowed, untainted by guilt or satiety or regret, immortalized for me in that image of Xan balanced against the sunset, of his flaming hair, of the pale petals of roses floating downstream under the bridge until they were lost to sight.

3

I can remember my first holiday at Woolcombe. I
followed Xan up a second flight of stairs at the
end of the corridor to a room at the top of the
house looking out over the terrace and the lawn
towards the river and the bridge. At first, sensitive
and contaminated by my mother's resentment,
I wondered if I was being put in the servants'
quarters.

Then Xan said: "I'm next door. We have our
own bathroom, it's at the end of the corridor."

I can remember every detail of that room. It
was the one I was to have every summer holiday
throughout my schooldays and until I left Oxford.
I changed, but the room never changed, and I see
in imagination a succession of schoolboys and
undergraduates, each one bearing an uncanny resemblance to myself, opening that door summer
after summer and entering by right into that inheritance. I haven't been back to Woolcombe

since my mother died eight years ago and I shall never go back now. Sometimes I have a fantasy that I shall return to Woolcombe as an old man and die in that room, pushing open the door for the last time and seeing again the single four-poster bed with its carved bedposts, the cover of faded silk patchwork; the bentwood rocking-chair with its cushion embroidered by some long-dead female Lyppiatt; the patina of the Georgian desk, a little battered but firm, steady, usable; the bookcase with the editions of nineteenth- and twentieth-century boys' books: Henty, Fenimore Cooper, Rider Haggard, Conan Doyle, Sapper, John Buchan; the bow-fronted chest of drawers with the flyblown mirror above it; and the old prints of battle scenes, terrified horses rearing before the cannons, wild-eyed cavalry officers, the dying Nelson. And I can remember best of all that day when I first entered it and, walking over to the window, looked out over the terrace, the sloping lawn, the oak trees, the sheen of the river and the small hump-backed bridge.

Xan stood at the door. He said: "We can go off somewhere tomorrow, if you like, cycling. The Bart has bought you a bicycle."

I was to learn that he seldom spoke of his father in any other way. I said: "That's kind of him."

"Not really. He had to—hadn't he?—if he wanted us to be together."

"I've got a bicycle. I always cycle to school, I could have brought it."

"The Bart thought it would be less trouble to keep one here. You don't have to use it. I like to go off for the day but you don't have to come if you don't want to. Cycling isn't compulsory. Nothing is compulsory at Woolcombe, except unhappiness."

I was to discover later that this was the kind of sardonic quasi-adult remark he liked to make. It was intended to impress me and it did. But I didn't believe him. On that first visit, innocently enchanted, it was impossible to imagine anyone suffering unhappiness in such a house. And he couldn't surely have meant himself.

I said: "I'd like to see round the house sometime." Then I blushed, afraid that I sounded like a prospective purchaser or a tourist.

"We can do that, of course. If you can wait until Saturday, Miss Maskell from the vicarage will do the honours. It'll cost you a pound but that includes the garden. It's open every other Saturday in aid of church funds. What Molly Maskell lacks in historical and artistic knowledge she makes up in imagination."

"I'd rather you showed it."

He didn't reply to that, but watched while I humped my case on to the bed and began to unpack. My mother had bought me a new case for this first visit. Miserably aware that it was too large, too smart, too heavy, I wished that I had brought my old canvas grip. I had, of course, packed too many clothes, and the wrong clothes, but he didn't comment, I don't know whether out of delicacy or tact or because he simply didn't notice. Stuffing them quickly into one of the drawers, I asked: "Isn't it strange living here?"

"It's inconvenient and it's sometimes boring, but it isn't strange. My ancestors have lived here for three hundred years." He added: "It's quite a small house."

He sounded as if he was trying to put me at ease by belittling his inheritance but when I looked at him I saw, for the first time, the look that was to become familiar to me, of a secret inner amusement which reached eyes and mouth but never broke into an open smile. I didn't know then and still don't know how much he cared for Woolcombe. It's still used as a nursing-and-retirement home for the privileged few—relations and friends of the Council, members of the Regional, District and Local Councils, people who are considered to have given some service to the State. Until my mother died Helena and I made our regular duty visits. I can still picture the two sisters sitting together on the terrace, well wrapped up against the chill, one with her terminal cancer, the other with her cardiac asthma and arthritis, envy and resentment forgotten as they faced the great equalizer of death. When I imagine the world without a living human being, I can picture—who doesn't?—the great cathedrals and temples, the palaces and the castles, existing through the uninhabited centuries, the British Library, opened just before Omega, with its carefully preserved manuscripts and books which no one will ever again open or read. But at heart I am touched only by the thought of Woolcombe; the imagined smell of its musty deserted rooms, the rotting panels in the library, the ivy creeping over its crumbling walls, a wilderness of grass and weeds obscuring the gravel, the tennis court, the formal garden; by the memory of that small back bedroom, unvisited and unchanged until the coverlet rots at last, the books turn to dust and the final picture drops from the wall.

4

Thursday 21 January 2021

My mother had artistic pretensions. No, that is arrogant and not even true. She had no pretensions to anything except a desperate respectability. But she did have some artistic talent, although I never saw her produce an original drawing. Her hobby was painting old prints, usually Victorian scenes taken from damaged bound volumes of the *Girls' Own Paper* or the *Illustrated London News*. I don't suppose it was difficult, but she did it with some skill, taking care, as she told me, to get the colours historically correct, although I don't see how she could have been sure of that. I think the nearest she got to happiness was when she was sitting at the kitchen table with her paint box and two jam jars, the angled lamp precisely focused on the print spread out on a newspaper in front of her. I used to watch her working away, the delicacy with which she dipped the finer brush into the water, the swirl of coalescing blues, yellows and whites as she mixed them on the palette. The kitchen table was large enough, if not for me to spread out all my homework, at least for me to read or write my weekly essay. I liked to look up, my brief scrutiny unresented, and watch the bright colours edging across the print, the transformation of the drab grey of the microdots into a living scene; a crowded railway terminus with bonneted women seeing off their men to the Crimean War; a Victorian family, the women in furs and bustles, decorating the church for Christmas; Queen Victoria escorted by her consort, surrounded by crinolined children, opening the Great Exhibition; boating scenes on the Isis with long-defunct college barges in the background, the moustached men in their blazers, the full-bosomed, small-waisted girls in jackets and straw hats; village churches with a straggling procession of worshippers, the squire and his lady in the foreground entering for the Easter service against a background of graves made festive with spring flowers. Perhaps it was my early fascination with these scenes which came to direct my interest as a historian to the nineteenth century, that age which now, as when I first studied it, seems like a world seen through a telescope at once so close and yet infinitely remote, fascinating in its energy, its moral seriousness, its brilliance and squalor.

My mother's hobby was not unlucrative. She

would frame the finished pictures with the help of Mr. Greenstreet, the vicar's warden from the local church they both regularly, and I reluctantly, attended, and would sell them to antique shops. I shall never now know what part Mr. Greenstreet played in her life, apart from his neat-fingered facility with wood and glue, or might have played except for my ubiquitous presence, any more than I can know how much my mother was paid for the pictures and whether, as I now suspect, it was this extra income which provided me with the school trips, the cricket bats, the extra books which I was never grudged. I did my bit to contribute; it was I who found the prints. I would rummage through boxes in junk shops in Kingston and further afield on my way home from school or on Saturdays, sometimes cycling fifteen or twenty miles to a shop which yielded the best spoils. Most were cheap and I bought them from my pocket money. The best I stole, becoming adept at removing centrepieces from bound books without damage, extracting prints from their mounts and slipping them into my school atlas. I needed these acts of vandalism, as I suspect most young boys needed their minor delinquencies. I was never suspected, I the uniformed, respectful, grammar-school boy who took his lesser findings to the till and paid without hurry or apparent anxiety and who occasionally bought the cheaper second-hand books from the boxes of miscellanea outside the shop door. I enjoyed these solitary excursions, the risk, the thrill of discovering a treasure, the triumph of returning with my spoils. My mother said little except to ask what I had spent and to reimburse me. If she suspected that some of the prints were worth more than I told her I had paid, she never questioned, but I knew that she was pleased. I didn't love her but I did steal for her. I learned early and at that kitchen table that there are ways of avoiding, without guilt, the commitments of love.

I know, or think I know, when my terror of taking responsibility for other people's lives or happiness began, although I may be deceiving myself; I have always been clever at devising excuses for my personal shortcomings. I like to trace its roots to 1983, the year my father lost his fight against cancer of the stomach. That was how, listening to the grown-ups, I heard it described. "He's lost his fight," they said. And I can see now that it was a fight, carried on with some courage even if he hadn't much option. My parents tried to spare me the worst of knowledge. "We try to keep things from the boy" was another frequently overheard phrase. But keeping things from the boy meant telling me nothing except that my father was ill, would have to see a specialist, would go into hospital for an operation, would soon be home again, would have to go back into hospital. Sometimes I wasn't even told that; I would return from school to find him no longer there and my mother feverishly cleaning the house, with a face set like stone. Keeping things from the boy meant that I lived without siblings in an atmosphere of uncomprehended menace in which the three of us were moving inexorably forward to some unimagined disaster which, when it came, would be my fault. Children are always ready to believe that adult catastrophes are their fault. My mother never spoke the word "cancer" to me, never referred to his illness except incidentally. "Your father's a little tired this morning." "Your father has to go back into hospital today." "Get those schoolbooks out of the sitting-room and go upstairs before the doctor comes. He'll be wanting to talk to me."

She would speak with eyes averted, as if there was something embarrassing, even indecent, about the disease, which made it an unsuitable subject for a child. Or was this a deeper secrecy, a shared suffering, which had become an essential part of their marriage and from which I was as rightly excluded as I was from their marriage bed? I wonder now whether my father's silence, which seemed at the time a rejection, was deliberate. Were we alienated less by pain and weariness, the slow draining away of hope, than by his wish not to increase the anguish of separation? But he can't have been so very fond of me. I wasn't an easy child to love. And how could we have communicated? The world of the terminally ill is the world of neither the living nor the dead. I have watched others since I watched my father, and always with a sense of their strangeness. They sit and speak, and are spoken to, and listen, and even smile, but in spirit they have already moved away from us and there is no way we can enter their shadowy no-man's-land.

I can't now remember the day he died except for one incident: my mother sitting at the kitchen table, weeping at last tears of anger and frustration. When, clumsy and embarrassed, I tried to put my arms round her, she wailed: "Why do I always have such rotten luck?" It seemed then to that twelve-year-old, as it seems now, an inadequate response to personal tragedy, and its banality influenced my attitude to my mother for the rest of my childhood. That was unjust and judgemental, but children are unjust and judgemental to their parents.

Although I have forgotten, or perhaps deliberately put out of mind, all but one memory of the day my father died, I can recall every hour of the day he was cremated: the thin drizzle that made the crematorium gardens look like a pointilliste painting; the waiting in the mock cloister until an earlier cremation was over and we could file in and take our places in those stark pine pews; the smell of my new suit; the wreaths stacked up against the chapel wall; the smallness of the coffin—it seemed impossible to believe that it actually held my father's body. My mother's anxiety that all should go well was increased by the fear that her baronet brother-in-law would attend. He didn't, and neither did Xan, who was at his prep school. But my aunt came, too smartly dressed, and the only woman not predominantly in black, giving my mother a not-unwelcome cause for complaint. It was after the baked meats of the funeral feast that the two sisters agreed I should spend the next summer holiday at Woolcombe and the pattern for all subsequent summer holidays was established.

But my main memory of the day is its atmosphere of suppressed excitement and a strong disapproval which I felt was focused on me. It was then that I first heard the phrase reiterated by friends and neighbours who, in their unaccustomed black, I hardly knew: "You'll have to be the man of the family now, Theo. Your mother will look to you." I couldn't then say what for nearly forty years I have known to be true. I don't want anyone to look to me, not for protection, not for happiness, not for love, not for anything.

I wish that my remembrance of my father was

happier, that I had a clear view, or at least some view, of the essential man which I could take hold of, make part of me; I wish that I could name even three qualities which characterized him. Thinking about him now for the first time in years, there are no adjectives which I can honestly conjure up, not even that he was gentle, kind, intelligent, loving. He may have been all of these things, I just don't know. All I know about him is that he was dying. His cancer wasn't quick or merciful—when is it merciful?—and he took nearly three years to die. It seems that most of my childhood was subsumed in those years by the look and the sound and the smell of his death. He was his cancer. I could see nothing else then and I can see nothing else now. And for years my memory of him, less memory than reincarnation, was one of horror. A few weeks before his death he cut his left index finger opening a tin and the wound became infected. Through the bulky lint-and-gauze bandage applied by my mother seeped blood and pus. It seemed not to worry him; he would eat with his right hand, leaving his left resting on the table, gently regarding it, with an air of slight surprise, as if it were separate from his body, nothing to do with him. But I couldn't take my eyes from it, hunger fighting with nausea. To me it was an obscene object of horror. Perhaps I projected on to his bandaged finger all my unacknowledged fear of his mortal illness. For months after his death I was visited by a recurrent nightmare in which I would see him at the foot of my bed pointing at me a bleeding yellow stump, not of a finger but of a whole hand. He never spoke; he stood mute in his striped pyjamas. His look was sometimes an appeal for something I couldn't give, but more often gravely accusatory, as was that pointing. It seems now unjust that he should for so long have been remembered only with horror, with dripping pus and blood. The form of the nightmare, too, puzzles me now that, with my amateur adult knowledge of psychology, I attempt to analyse it. It would be more explicable had I been a girl. The attempt to analyse was, of course, an attempt at exorcism. In part it must have succeeded. After I killed Natalie he visited me weekly; now he never comes. I am glad that he has finally gone, taking with him his pain, his blood, his pus. But I wish that he had left me a different memory.

5

Friday 22 January 2021

Today is my daughter's birthday, would have been my daughter's birthday if I hadn't run her over and killed her. That was in 1994, when she was fifteen months old. Helena and I were living then in an Edwardian semi-detached house in Lathbury Road, too large and too expensive for us, but Helena, as soon as she knew she was pregnant, had insisted on a house with a garden and a south-facing nursery. I can't remember now the exact circumstances of the accident, whether I was supposed to be keeping an eye on Natalie or thought that she was with her mother. All that must have come out at the inquest; but the inquest, that official allocation of responsibility, has been erased from memory. I do remember that I was leaving the house to go into College and backing the car, which Helena had clumsily parked the previous day, so that I could more easily manoeuvre it through the narrow garden gate. There was no garage at Lathbury Road but we had standing for two cars in front of the house. I must have left the front door open and Natalie, who had walked since she was thirteen months, toddled out after me. That minor culpability must have been established at the inquest, too. But some things I do remember: the gentle bump under my rear left wheel like a ramp but softer, more yielding, more tender than any ramp. The immediate knowledge, certain, absolute, terrifying, of what it was. And the five seconds of total silence before the screaming began. I knew that it was Helena screaming and yet part of my mind couldn't believe that what I was hearing was a human sound. And I remember the humiliation. I couldn't move, couldn't get out of the car, couldn't even stretch out my hand to the door. And then George Hawkins, our neighbour, was banging on the glass and shouting, "Get out you bastard, get out!" And I can remember the irrelevance of my thought, seeing that gross, anger-distorted face pressing against the glass: He never liked me. And I can't pretend that it didn't happen. I can't pretend it was someone else. I can't pretend I wasn't responsible.

Horror and guilt subsumed grief. Perhaps if Helena had been able to say, "It's worse for you, darling," or "It's as bad for you, darling," we might have salvaged something from the wreckage of a marriage which from the start hadn't been particularly seaworthy. But of course she couldn't; that wasn't what she believed. She thought that I cared less, and she was right. She thought that I cared less because I loved less, and she was right about that too. I was glad to be a father. When Helena told me she was pregnant I felt what I presume are the usual emotions of irrational pride, tenderness and amazement. I did feel affection for my child, although I would have felt more had she been prettier—she was a miniature caricature of Helena's father—more affectionate, more responsive, less inclined to whine. I'm glad that no other eyes will read these words. She has been dead for almost twenty-seven years and I still think of her with complaint. But Helena was obsessed by her, totally enchanted, enslaved, and I know that what spoiled Natalie for me was jealousy. I would have got over it in time, or at least come to terms with it. But I wasn't given time. I don't think Helena ever believed that I'd run Natalie over on purpose, at least not when she was rational; even at her most bitter she managed to prevent herself from saying the unforgivable words, as a woman burdened with a sick and cantankerous husband, out of superstition or a remnant of kindness, will bite back the words, "I wish you were dead." But, given the chance, she would rather have had Natalie alive than me. I'm not blaming her for that. It seemed perfectly reasonable at the time and it seems so now.

I would lie distanced in the king-sized bed waiting for her to fall asleep, knowing that it might be hours before she did, worrying about next day's over-filled diary, about how, with the prospect of endless broken nights, I would be able to cope, reiterating into the darkness my litany of justification—"For Christ's sake, it was an accident. I didn't mean to do it. I'm not the only father to have run down his child. She was supposed to be looking after Natalie, the child was her responsibility, she made it plain enough it wasn't mine. The least she could have done was to look after her properly." But angry self-justification was as banal and irrelevant as a child's excuse for breaking a vase.

We both knew that we had to leave Lathbury Road. Helena said: "We can't stay here. We should look for a house near the centre of the city. After all, that's always what you've wanted. You've never really liked this place."

The allegation was there but unspoken: you're glad that we're moving, glad that her death has made it possible.

Six months after the funeral we moved to St. John Street, to a tall Georgian house with a front door on the street, where parking is difficult. Lathbury Road was a family house; this is a house for the unencumbered, if agile, and the solitary. The move suited me because I liked being close to the city centre, and Georgian architecture, even speculative Georgian requiring constant maintenance, has a greater cachet than Edwardian. We hadn't made love since Natalie's death but now Helena moved into her own room. It was never discussed between us but I knew that she was saying that there would be no second chance, that I had killed not only her beloved daughter but all hope of another child, of the son she suspected I had really wanted. But that was in October 1994 and the choice was no longer there. We didn't stay permanently apart, of course. Sex and marriage are more complicated than that. From time to time I would cross the few feet of carpeted floor between her room and mine. She neither welcomed me nor rejected me. But there was a wider, more permanent gulf between us and that I made no effort to cross.

This narrow, five-storeyed house is too large for me, but with our falling population I'm hardly likely to be criticized for not sharing my overprovision. There are no undergraduates clamouring for a bed-sitting-room, no young homeless families to prick the social conscience of the more privileged. I use it all, mounting from floor to floor through the routine of my day, as if methodically stamping my ownership on vinyl, on carpet and rugs and polished wood. The dining-room and kitchen are in the basement, the latter with a wide arc of stone steps leading to the garden. Above them, two small sitting-rooms have been converted into one which also serves as a library, a television-and-music room and a convenient place in which to see my students. On the first floor is a large L-shaped drawing-room. This too has been converted from two smaller rooms, the two discordant fireplaces proclaiming its former use. From the back window I can look out over the small walled garden with its single silver birch tree. At the front, two elegant windows, ceiling-high, with a balcony beyond, face St. John Street.

Anyone pacing between the two windows would have little difficulty describing the room's owner. Obviously an academic; three walls are lined with bookshelves from ceiling to floor. A historian; the books themselves make that plain. A man concerned primarily with the nineteenth century; not only the books but the pictures and ornaments proclaim this obsession: the Stafford-shire commemorative figures, the Victorian genre oil paintings, the William Morris wallpaper. The room, too, of a man who likes his comfort and who lives alone. There are no family photographs, no board games, no disarray, no dust, no feminine clutter, little evidence, indeed, that the room is ever used. And a visitor might guess, too, that nothing here is inherited, everything acquired. There are none of those unique or eccentric artefacts, valued or tolerated because they are heirlooms, no family portraits, undistinguished oils given their place to proclaim ancestry. It is the room of a man who has risen in the world, surrounding himself with the symbols both of his achievements and his minor obsessions. Mrs. Kavanagh, the wife of one of the college scouts, comes in three times a week to clean for me and does it well enough. I have no wish to employ the Sojourners to whom, as ex-adviser to the Warden of England, I am entitled.

The room I like best is at the top of the house, a small attic room with a charming fireplace in wrought iron and decorated tiles, furnished only with a desk and chair and containing the necessities for making coffee. An uncurtained window looks out over the campanile of St. Barnabas Church to the far green slope of Wytham Wood. It is here I write my diary, prepare my lectures and seminars, write my historical papers. The front door is four storeys down, inconvenient for answering the doorbell; but I have ensured that there are no unexpected visitors in my self-sufficient life.

Last year, in March, Helena left me for Rupert Clavering, thirteen years younger than she, who combines the appearance of an over-enthusiastic rugby player with, one is forced to believe, the sensitivity of an artist. He designs posters and dust jackets and does them very well. I recall something she said during our pre-divorce discussions, which I was at pains to keep unacrimonious and unemotional: that I had slept with her only at carefully regulated intervals because I wanted my affairs with my students to be driven by more discriminating needs than the relief of crude sexual deprivation. Those weren't, of course, her words, but that was her meaning. I think she surprised both of us by her perception.

6

The task of writing his journal—and Theo thought of it as a task, not a pleasure—had become part of his over-organized life, a nightly addition to a weekly routine half imposed by circumstance, half deliberately devised in an attempt to impose order and purpose on the shapelessness of existence. The Council of England had decreed that all citizens should, in addition to their ordinary jobs, undertake two weekly training sessions in skills which would help them to survive if and when they became part of the remnant of civilization. The choice was voluntary. Xan had always known the wisdom of giving people a choice in matters where choice was unimportant. Theo had elected to do one stint in the John Radcliffe Hospital, not because he felt at home in its antiseptic hierarchy or imagined that his ministrations to the sick and aged flesh which both terrified and repelled him was any more gratifying to the recipients than it was to him, but because he thought the knowledge gained might be the most personally useful, and it was no bad idea to know where, should the need arise, he could with some cunning lay his hands on drugs. The second two-hour session he spent more agreeably on house maintenance, finding the good humour and crude critical comments of the artisans who taught there a welcome relief from the more refined disparagements of academe. His paid job was teaching the full- and part-time mature students who, with the few former undergraduates doing research or taking higher degrees, were the University's justification for its existence. On two nights a week, Tuesday and Friday, he dined in Hall. On Wednesday he invariably attended the three o'clock service of Evensong in Magdalen Chapel. A small number of colleges with more than usually eccentric collegers or an obstinate determination to ignore reality still used their chapels for worship, some even reverting to the old Book of Common Prayer. But the choir at Magdalen was among the best regarded and Theo went to listen to the singing, not to take part in an archaic act of worship.

It happened on the fourth Wednesday in January. Walking to Magdalen as was his custom, he had turned from St. John Street into Beaumont Street and was nearing the entrance to the Ashmolean Museum when a woman approached him wheeling a pram. The thin drizzle had stopped and as she drew alongside him she paused to fold back the mackintosh cover and push down the pram hood. The doll was revealed, propped upright against the cushions, the two arms, hands mittened, resting on the quilted coverlet, a parody of childhood, at once pathetic and sinister. Shocked and repelled, Theo found that he couldn't keep his eyes off it. The glossy irises, unnaturally large, bluer than those of any human eye, a gleaming azure, seemed to fix on him their unseeing stare which yet horribly suggested a dormant intelligence, alien and monstrous. The eyelashes, dark brown, lay like spiders on the delicately tinted porcelain cheeks and an adult abundance of yellow crimped hair sprung from beneath the close-fitting lace-trimmed bonnet.

It had been years since he had last seen a doll thus paraded, but they had been common twenty years ago, had indeed become something of a craze. Doll-making was the only section of the toy industry which, with the production of prams, had for a decade flourished; it had produced dolls for the whole range of frustrated maternal desire, some cheap and tawdry but some of remarkable craftsmanship and beauty which, but for the Omega which originated them, could have become cherished heirlooms. The more expensive ones—some he remembered costing well over

£2,000—could be bought in different sizes: the new-born, the six-month-old baby, the year-old, the eighteen-month-old child able to stand and walk, intricately powered. He remembered now that they were called Six-Monthlies. At one time it wasn't possible to walk down the High Street without being encumbered by their prams, by groups of admiring quasi-mothers. He seemed to remember that there had even been pseudo-births and that broken dolls were buried with ceremony in consecrated ground. Wasn't it one of the minor ecclesiastical disputes of the early 2000s whether churches could legitimately be used for these charades and even whether ordained priests could take part?

Aware of his gaze, the woman smiled, an idiot smile, inviting connivance, congratulations. As their eyes met and he dropped his, so that she shouldn't see his small pity and his greater contempt, she jerked the pram back, then put out a shielding arm as if to ward off his masculine importunities. A more responsive passer-by stopped and spoke to her. A middle-aged woman in well-fitting tweeds, hair carefully groomed, came up to the pram, smiled at the doll's owner and began a congratulatory patter. The first woman, simpering with pleasure, leaned forward, smoothed the satin quilted pram cover, adjusted the bonnet, tucked in a stray lock of hair. The second tickled the doll beneath its chin as she might a cat, still murmuring her baby talk.

Theo, more depressed and disgusted by the charade than surely such harmless play-acting justified, was turning away when it happened. The second woman suddenly seized the doll, tore it from the coverings and, without a word, swung it twice round her head by the legs and dashed it against the stone wall with tremendous force. The face shattered and shards of porcelain fell tinkling to the pavement. The owner was for two seconds absolutely silent. And then she screamed. The sound was horrible, the scream of the tortured, the bereaved, a terrified, high-pitched squealing, inhuman yet all too human, unstoppable. She stood there, hat askew, head thrown back to the heavens, her mouth stretched into a gape from which poured her agony, her grief, her anger. She seemed at first unaware that the attacker still stood there, watching her with silent contempt. Then the woman turned and walked briskly through the open gates, across the courtyard and into the Ashmolean. Suddenly aware that the attacker had escaped, the doll-owner galumphed after her, still screaming, then, apparently realizing the hopelessness of it, returned to the pram. She had grown quieter now and, sinking to her knees, began gathering up the broken pieces, sobbing and moaning gently, trying to match them as she might a jigsaw puzzle. Two gleaming eyes, horribly real, joined by a spring, rolled towards Theo. He had a second's impulse to pick them up, to help, to speak at least a few words of comfort. He could have pointed out that she could buy another child. It was a consolation he hadn't been able to offer his wife. But his hesitation was only momentary. He walked briskly on. No one else went near her. Middle-aged women, those who had reached adulthood in the year of Omega, were notoriously unstable.

He reached the chapel just as the service was about to begin. The choir of eight men and eight women filed in, bringing with them a memory of earlier choirs, boy choristers entering grave-faced with that almost imperceptible childish swagger, crossed arms holding the service sheets to their narrow chests, their smooth faces lit as if with an internal candle, their hair brushed to gleaming caps, their faces preternaturally solemn above the starched collars. Theo banished the image, wondering why it was so persistent when he had never even cared for children. Now he fixed his eyes on the chaplain, remembering the incident some months previously when he had arrived early for Evensong. Somehow a young deer from the Magdalen meadow had made its way into the chapel and was standing peaceably beside the altar as if this were its natural habitat. The chaplain,

harshly shouting, had rushed at it, seizing and
hurling prayer books, thumping its silken sides.
The animal, puzzled, docile, had for a moment
endured the assault and then, delicate-footed, had
pranced its way out of the chapel.

The chaplain had turned to Theo, tears stream-
ing down his face. "Christ, why can't they wait?
Bloody animals. They'll have it all soon enough.
Why can't they wait?"

As Theo looked now at his serious, self-
important face it seemed, in this candle-lit peace,
no more than a bizarre scene from a half-
remembered nightmare.

The congregation, as usual, numbered fewer
than thirty and many of those present, regulars
like himself, were known to Theo. But there was
one newcomer, a young woman, seated in the stall
immediately opposite his own, whose gaze, from
time to time, it was difficult to avoid although she
gave no sign of recognition. The chapel was dimly
lit and through the flicker of candles her face
gleamed with a gentle, almost transparent light, at
one moment seen clearly, then as elusive and insubstantial as a wraith. But it was not unknown to
him; somehow he'd seen her before, not just with
a momentary glance, but face to face and for a
stretch of time. He tried to force and then trick his
memory into recall, fixing his eyes on her bent
head during the confession, appearing to stare

past her with pious concentration during the reading of the first lesson, but constantly aware of her, casting over her image memory's barbed net. By the end of the second lesson he was becoming irritated by his failure and then, as the choir, mostly middle-aged, arranged their music sheets and gazed at the conductor, waiting for the organ to begin and his small surpliced figure to raise his paw-like hands and begin their delicate paddling of the air, Theo remembered. She had been briefly a member of Colin Seabrook's class on Victorian Life and Times, with its subtitle Women in the Victorian Novel, which he had taken for Colin eighteen months previously. Seabrook's wife had had a cancer operation; there was a chance of a holiday together if Colin could find a substitute for this one four-session class. He could recall their conversation, his half-hearted protest.

"Shouldn't you get a member of the English Faculty to do it for you?"

"No, old boy, I've tried. They've all got excuses. Don't like evening work. Too busy. Not their period—don't think it's only historians who go in for that crap. Can do one session but not four. It's only one hour, Thursdays, six to seven. And you won't have to bother with preparation, I've only set four books and you probably know them by heart: *Middlemarch, Portrait of a Lady, Vanity Fair, Cranford.* Only fourteen in the class, fifty-year-old women mainly. They should be fussing round their grandchildren, so they've time on their hands, you know how it is. Charming ladies, if a little conventional in their taste. You'll love them. And they'll be tickled pink to have you. The comfort of culture, that's what they're after. Your cousin, our esteemed Warden, is very keen on the comfort of culture. All they want is to escape temporarily into a more agreeable and permanent world. We all do it, dear boy, only you and I call it scholarship."

But there had been fifteen students, not fourteen. She had come in two minutes late and had quietly taken her seat at the back of the group. Then as now he had seen her head outlined against carved wood and lit by candles. When the last intake of undergraduates had gone down, hallowed college rooms had been opened to mature, part-time students, and the class had been held in an agreeable, panelled lecture room at Queen's College. She had listened, apparently attentively, to his preliminary discourse on Henry James and had at first taken no part in the ensuing general discussion until a large woman in the front row began extravagantly praising Isabel Archer's moral qualities and sentimentally lamenting her undeserved fate.

The girl had suddenly said: "I don't see why you should particularly pity someone who was given so much and made such poor use of it. She could have married Lord Warburton and done a great deal of good to his tenants, to the poor. All right, she didn't love him, so there was an excuse and she had higher ambitions for herself than marriage to Lord Warburton. But what? She had no creative talent, no job, no training. When her cousin made her rich, what did she do? Gad round the world with Madame Merle, of all people. And then she marries that conceited hypocrite and goes in for Thursday salons gorgeously dressed. What happened to all the idealism? I've got more time for Henrietta Stackpole."

The woman had protested: "Oh, but she's so vulgar!"

"That's what Mrs. Touchett thinks, so does the author. But at least she has talent, which Isabel hasn't, and she uses it to earn her living, and support her widowed sister." She added: "Isabel Archer and Dorothea both discard eligible suitors to marry self-important fools, but one sympathizes more with Dorothea. Perhaps this is because George Eliot respects her heroine and, at heart, Henry James despises his."

She might, Theo had suspected, have been relieving boredom by deliberate provocation. But, whatever her motive, the ensuing argument had been noisy and lively and for once the remaining thirty minutes had passed quickly and agreeably.

He had been sorry and a little aggrieved when, the following Thursday, watched for, she had failed to appear.

The connection made and curiosity appeased, he could sit back in peace and listen to the second anthem. It had been the custom at Magdalen for the last ten years to play a recorded anthem during Evensong. Theo saw from the printed service sheet that this afternoon there was to be the first of a series of fifteenth-century English anthems, beginning with two by William Byrd, "Teach Me, O Lord" and "Exult Thyself, O God." There was a brief anticipatory silence as the *informator choristarum* bent down to switch on the tape. The voices of boys, sweet, clear, asexual, unheard since the last boy chorister's voice had broken, soared and filled the chapel. He glanced across at the girl, but she was sitting motionless, her head thrown back, her eyes fixed on the rib vaulting of the roof, so that all he could see was the candle-lit curve of her neck. But at the end of the row was a figure he suddenly recognized: old Martindale, who had been an English fellow on the eve of retirement when he himself was in his first year. Now he sat perfectly still, his old face uplifted, the candlelight glinting on the tears which ran down his cheeks in a stream so that the deep furrows looked as if they were hung with pearls. Old Marty, unmarried, celibate, who all his life had loved the beauty of boys. Why, Theo wondered, did he and his like come week after week to seek this masochistic pleasure? They could listen to the recorded voices of children perfectly well at home, so why did it have to be here, where past and present fused in beauty and candlelight to reinforce regret? Why did he himself come? But he knew the answer to that question. Feel, he told himself, feel, feel, feel. Even if what you feel is pain, only let yourself feel.

The woman left the chapel before him, moving swiftly, almost surreptitiously. But when he stepped out into the cool air, he was surprised to find her obviously waiting.

She came up beside him and said: "Could I please speak to you? It's important."

From the ante-chapel the bright light streamed out into the late-afternoon dusk and for the first time he saw her clearly. Her hair, dark and luscious, a rich brown with flecks of gold, was brushed back and disciplined into a short, thick pleat. A fringe fell over a high, freckled forehead. She was light-skinned for someone so dark-haired, a honey-coloured woman, long-necked with high cheekbones, wide-set eyes whose colour he couldn't determine under strong straight brows, a long narrow nose, slightly humped, and a wide, beautifully shaped mouth. It was a pre-

Raphaelite face. Rossetti would have liked to have painted her. She was dressed in the current fashion for all but Omegas—a short, fitted jacket and, beneath it, a woollen skirt reaching to mid-calf below which he could see the highly coloured socks which had become this year's craze. Hers were bright yellow. She carried a leather sling bag over her left shoulder. She was gloveless and he could see that her left hand was deformed. The middle and forefinger were fused into a nail-less stump and the back of the hand was grossly swollen. She held it cradled in her right as if comforting or supporting it. There was no effort to hide it. She might even have been proclaiming her deformity to a world which had become increasingly intolerant of physical defects. But at least, he thought, she had one compensation. No one who was in any way physically deformed, or mentally or physically unhealthy, was on the list of women from whom the new race would be bred if ever a fertile male was discovered. She was, at least, saved from the six-monthly, time-consuming, humiliating re-examinations to which all healthy females under forty-five were subjected.

She spoke again, more quietly: "It won't take long. But please, I have to talk to you, Dr. Faron."

"If you need to." He was intrigued, but he

couldn't make his voice welcoming.

"Perhaps we could walk round the new cloisters."

They turned together in silence. She said: "You don't know me."

"No, but I remember you. You were at the second of the classes I took for Dr. Seabrook. You certainly enlivened the discussion."

"I'm afraid I was rather vehement." She added, as if it were important to explain: "I do very much admire *The Portrait of a Lady.*"

"But presumably you haven't arranged this interview to reassure me about your literary taste."

As soon as the words were spoken he regretted them. She flushed, and he sensed an instinctive recoil, a loss of confidence in herself, and perhaps in him. The naïvety of her remark had disconcerted him, but he need not have responded with such hurtful irony. Her unease was infectious. He hoped that she wasn't proposing to embarrass him with personal revelations or emotional demands. It was difficult to reconcile that articulate confident debater with her present almost adolescent gaucherie. It was pointless to try to make amends and for half a minute they walked in silence.

Then he said: "I was sorry when you didn't reappear. The class seemed very dull the following week."

"I would have come again, but my hours were changed to the evening shift. I had to work." She didn't explain at what or where, but added: "My name is Julian. I know yours, of course."

"Julian. That's unusual for a woman. Were you named after Julian of Norwich?"

"No, I don't think my parents had ever heard of her. My father went to register the birth and he gave the name as Julie Ann. That's what my parents had chosen. The registrar must have misheard, or perhaps Father didn't speak very clearly. It was three weeks before my mother noticed the mistake and she thought it was too late to change it. Anyway, I think she rather liked the name, so I was christened Julian."

"But I suppose people call you Julie."

"What people?"

"Your friends, your family."

"I haven't any family. My parents were killed in the race riots in 2002. But why should they call me Julie? Julie isn't my name."

She was perfectly polite, unaggressive. He might have supposed that she was puzzled by his comment but puzzlement was surely unjustified. His remark had been inept, unthinking, condescending perhaps, but it hadn't been ridiculous. And if this encounter was the preliminary to a request that he should give a talk about the social history of the nineteenth century it was an unusual one.

He asked: "Why do you want to speak to me?"

Now that the moment had come he sensed her reluctance to begin, not, he thought, out of embarrassment or regret that she had initiated the encounter, but because what she had to say was important and she needed to find the right words.

She paused and looked at him. "Things are happening in England—in Britain—that are wrong. I belong to a small group of friends who think we ought to try to stop them. You used to be a member of the Council of England. You're the Warden's cousin. We thought that before we acted you might talk to him. We're not really sure that you can help, but two of us, Luke—he's a priest—and I, thought you might be able to. The leader of the group is my husband, Rolf. He agreed that I should talk to you."

"Why you? Why hasn't he come himself?"

"I suppose he thought—they thought—that I'm the one who might be able to persuade you."

"Persuade me to what?"

"Just to meet us, so that we can explain what we have to do."

"Why can't you explain now? Then I can decide whether I'm prepared to meet you. What group are you talking about?"

"Just a group of five. We haven't really got started yet. We may not need to if there is a hope of persuading the Warden to act."

He said carefully: "I was never a full member of the Council, only personal adviser to the Warden of England. I haven't attended for over three years, I don't see the Warden any longer. The relationship means nothing to either of us. My influence is probably no greater than yours."

"But you could see him. We can't."

"You could try. He's not totally inaccessible. People are able to telephone him, sometimes to speak to him. Naturally he has to protect himself."

"Against the people? But seeing him, even speaking to him, would be to let him and the State Security Police know we exist, perhaps even who we are. It wouldn't be safe for us to try."

"Do you really believe that?"

"Oh yes," she said sadly. "Don't you?"

"No, I don't think I do. But if you're right, then you're taking an extraordinary risk. What makes you think you can trust me? You're surely not proposing to place your safety in my hands on the evidence of one seminar on Victorian literature? Have any of the rest of the group even met me?"

"No. But two of us, Luke and I, have read some of your books."

He said drily: "It's unwise to judge an academic's personal probity from his written work."

"It was the only way we had. We know it's a risk but it's one we have to take. Please meet us.

Please at least hear what we have to say."

The appeal in her voice was unmistakable, simple and direct, and, suddenly, he thought he understood why. It had been her idea to approach him. She had come with only the reluctant acquiescence of the rest of the group, perhaps even against the wish of its leader. The risk she was taking was her own. If he refused her, she would return empty-handed and humiliated. He found that he couldn't do it.

He said, knowing even as he spoke that it was a mistake: "All right. I'll talk to you. Where and when do you next meet?"

"On Sunday at ten o'clock in St. Margaret's Church at Binsey. Do you know it?"

"Yes, I know Binsey."

"At ten o'clock. In the church."

She had got what she had come for and she didn't linger. He could scarcely catch her murmured, "Thank you. Thank you." Then she slipped from his side so quickly and quietly that she might have been a shadow among the many moving shadows of the cloister.

He loitered for a minute so that there would be no chance of overtaking her and then in silence and solitude made his way home.

7

Saturday 30 January 2021

At seven o'clock this morning Jasper Palmer-
Smith telephoned and asked me to visit him. The
matter was urgent. He gave no explanation, but,
then, he seldom does. I said I could be with him
immediately after lunch. These summonses, increasingly peremptory, are also becoming more
common. He used to demand my presence about
once every quarter; now it is about once a month.
He taught me history and he was a marvellous
teacher, at least of clever students. As an undergraduate I had never admitted to liking him, but
had said with casual tolerance, "Jasper's not so
bad. I get on all right with him." And I did, for an
understandable if not particularly creditable reason: I was his favourite pupil of my year. He
always had a favourite. The relationship was almost entirely academic. He is neither gay nor particularly fond of the young; indeed, his dislike of
children has been legendary and they were always

kept well out of sight and sound on the rare occa-
sions when he condescended to accept a private
dinner invitation. But each year he would select
an undergraduate, invariably male, for his approval and patronage. We assumed that the crite-
ria he demanded were intelligence first, looks
second and wit third. He took time over the
choice but, once made, it was irrevocable. It was
a relationship without anxiety for the favourite,
since, once approved, he could do no wrong. It
was free, too, of peer resentment or envy, since
JPS was too unpopular to be courted, and it was
in fairness admitted that the favourite had no part
in his selection. Admittedly one was expected to
gain a First; all the favourites did. At the time I
was chosen I was conceited and confident enough
to see this as a probability but one which need not
worry me for at least another two years. But I did
work hard for him, wanted to please him, to justify his choice. To be selected from the crowd is
always gratifying to self-esteem; one feels the need
to make some return, a fact which accounts for a
number of otherwise surprising marriages. Perhaps that was the basis of his own marriage to a
mathematics fellow from New College five years
older than he. They seemed, in company at least,
to get on well enough together, but in general
women disliked him intensely. During the early
1990s, when there was an upsurge of allegations

about sexual harassment, he instituted an unsuccessful campaign to ensure that a chaperone was provided at all tutorials of female students on the grounds that otherwise he and his male colleagues were at risk from unjustified allegations. No one was more adept at demolishing a woman's self-confidence while treating her with meticulous, indeed almost insulting, consideration and courtesy.

He was a caricature of the popular idea of an Oxford don: high forehead, receding hairline, thin, slightly hooked nose, tight-lipped. He walked with his chin jutting forward as if confronting a strong gale, shoulders hunched, his faded gown billowing. One expected to see him pictured, high-collared as a *Vanity Fair* creation, holding one of his own books with slender-tipped, fastidious fingers.

He occasionally confided in me and treated me as if grooming me as his successor. That, of course, was nonsense; he gave me much but some things were not within his gift. But the impression his current favourite had of being in some sense a crown prince has made me wonder subsequently whether this wasn't his way of confronting age, time, the inevitable blunting of the mind's keen edge, his personal illusion of immortality.

He had often proclaimed his view of Omega, a reassuring litany of comfort shared by a number of his colleagues, particularly those who had laid down a good supply of wine or had access to their college cellar.

"It doesn't worry me particularly. I'm not saying I hadn't a moment of regret when I first knew Hilda was barren; the genes asserting their atavistic imperatives, I suppose. On the whole I'm glad; you can't mourn for unborn grandchildren when there never was a hope of them. This planet is doomed anyway. Eventually the sun will explode or cool and one small insignificant particle of the universe will disappear with only a tremble. If man is doomed to perish, then universal infertility is as painless a way as any. And there are, after all, personal compensations. For the last sixty years we have sycophantically pandered to the most ignorant, the most criminal and the most selfish section of society. Now, for the rest of our lives, we're going to be spared the intrusive barbarism of the young, their noise, their pounding, repetitive, computer-produced so-called music, their violence, their egotism disguised as idealism. My God, we might even succeed in getting rid of Christmas, that annual celebration of parental guilt and juvenile greed. I intend that my life shall be comfortable, and, when it no longer is, then I shall wash down my final pill with a bottle of claret."

His personal plan for survival in comfort until

the last natural moment was one thousands of people had adopted in those early years before Xan took power, when the great fear was of a total breakdown of order. Removal from the city—in his case from Clarendon Square—to a small country house or cottage in wooded country with a garden for food production, a nearby stream with water fresh enough to be drunk after boiling, an open fireplace and store of wood, tins of food carefully selected, enough matches to last for years, a medicine chest with drugs and syringes, above all strong doors and locks against the possibility that the less prudent might one day turn envious eyes on their husbandry. But in recent years Jasper has become obsessive. The wood store in the garden has been replaced by a brick-built structure with a metal door activated by remote control. There is a high wall round the garden and the door to the cellar is padlocked.

Usually when I visit, the wrought-iron gates are unlocked in anticipation of my arrival and I can open them and leave the car in the short driveway. This afternoon they were locked and I had to ring. When Jasper came to let me in I was shocked by the difference a month had made in his appearance. He was still upright, his step still firm, but as he came closer I saw that the skin stretched tightly over the strong bones of the face was greyer and there was a fiercer anxiety in the sunken eyes,

almost a gleam of paranoia, which I hadn't noticed before. Ageing is inevitable but it is not con-
sistent. There are plateaux of time stretching over
years when the faces of friends and acquaintances
look virtually unchanged. Then time accelerates
and within a week the metamorphosis takes place.
It seemed to me that Jasper had aged ten years in
a little over six weeks.

I followed him into the large sitting-room at the
back of the house, with its French windows looking out over the terrace and the garden. Here, as
in his study, the walls were completely covered
with bookshelves. It was, as always, obsessively
tidy, furniture, books, ornaments precisely in
place. But I detected, for the first time, the small
tell-tale signs of incipient neglect, the smeared
windows, a few crumbs on the carpet, a thin layer
of dust on the mantelshelf. There was an electric
fire in the grate but the room was chilly. Jasper
offered me a drink and, although mid-afternoon is
not my favourite time for drinking wine, I accepted. I saw that the side-table was more liberally
supplied with bottles than on my last visit. Jasper
is one of the few people I know who use their best
claret as an all-day, all-purpose tipple.

Hilda was sitting by the fire, a cardigan round
her shoulders. She stared ahead, without a welcome or even a look, and made no sign when I
greeted her other than a brief nod of the head. The

change in her was even more marked than in Jasper. For years, so it seemed to me, she had looked always the same: the angular but upright figure, the well-cut tweed skirt with the three centre box pleats, the high-necked silk shirt and cashmere cardigan, the thick grey hair intricately and smoothly twisted into a high bun. Now the front of the cardigan, half-slipped from her shoulders, was stiff with congealed food, her tights, hanging in loose folds above uncleaned shoes, were grubby and her hair hung in strands about a face set rigidly in lines of rebarbative disapproval. I wondered, as I had on previous visits, what exactly was wrong with her. It could hardly be Alzheimer's disease, which has been largely controlled since the late 1990s. But there are other kinds of senility which even our obsessive scientific concern with the problems of ageing has still been unable to alleviate. Perhaps she is just old, just tired, just sick to death of me. I suppose, in old age, there is advantage in retreating into a world of one's own, but not if the place one finds is hell.

I wondered why I had been asked to call but didn't like to ask directly. Finally Jasper said: "There's something I wanted to discuss with you. I'm thinking of moving back into Oxford. It was that last television broadcast by the Warden that decided me. Apparently the eventual plan is for everyone to move into towns so that facilities and services can be concentrated. He said that the people who wished to remain in remote districts were free to do so but that he wouldn't be able to guarantee supplies of power or petrol for transport. We're rather isolated here."

I said: "What does Hilda think about it?"

Jasper didn't even bother to glance at her. "Hilda is hardly in a position to object. I'm the one who does the caring. If it's easier for me, it's what we ought to do. I was thinking that it might suit us both—I mean you and me—if I joined you in St. John Street. You don't really need that large house. There's plenty of room at the top for a separate flat. I'd pay for the conversion, of course."

The idea appalled me. I hope I concealed my repugnance. I paused as if considering the idea, then said: "I don't think it would really suit you. You'd very much miss the garden. And the stairs would be difficult for Hilda."

There was a silence; then Jasper said: "You've heard of the Quietus, I suppose, the mass suicide of the old?"

"Only what I read briefly in the newspapers, or see on television."

I remembered one picture, I think the only one ever shown on television: white-clad elderly being wheeled or helped on to the low barge-like ship, the high, reedy singing voices, the boat slowly pulling away into the twilight, a seductively peaceful scene, cunningly shot and lit.

I said: "I'm not attracted to gregarious death. Suicide should be like sex, a private activity. If we want to kill ourselves, the means are always at hand, so why not do it comfortably in one's own bed? I would prefer to make my quietus with a bare bodkin."

Jasper said: "Oh, I don't know, there are people who like to make an occasion of these rites of passage. It's happening in one form or another all over the world. I suppose there's comfort in numbers, in ceremony. And their survivors get this pension from the State. Not exactly a pittance either, is it? No, I think I can see the attraction. Hilda was talking about it the other day."

I thought that unlikely. I could imagine what the Hilda I had known would have thought of such a public exhibition of sacrifice and emotion. She had been a formidable academic in her day, cleverer, people said, than her husband, her sharp tongue venomous in his defence. After her marriage she taught and published less, talent and personality diminished by the appalling subservience of love.

Before leaving, I said: "It looks as if you could do with extra help. Why not apply for a couple of Sojourners? Surely you'd qualify."

He dismissed the idea. "I don't think I want strangers here, particularly not Sojourners. I don't trust those people. It's asking to get murdered under my own roof. And most of them don't know what a day's work means. They're better used mending the roads, cleaning the sewers and collecting the rubbish, jobs where they can be kept under supervision."

I said: "The domestic workers are very carefully selected."

"Perhaps, but I don't want them."

I managed to get away without making any promises. On the drive back to Oxford I pondered how to frustrate Jasper's determination. He was, after all, used to getting his own way. It looks as if the thirty-year-old bill for benefits received, the special coaching, the expensive dinners, the theatre and opera tickets, is belatedly being presented. But the thought of sharing St. John Street, of the violation of privacy, of my increasing responsibility for a difficult old man, repels me. I owe Jasper a great deal, but I don't owe him that.

Driving into the city, I saw a queue about a hundred yards long outside the Examination Schools. It was an orderly, well-dressed crowd, old and middle-aged, but with more women than men. They stood waiting quietly and patiently with that air of complicity, controlled anticipation and lack of anxiety which characterizes a queue where everyone has a ticket, entry is assured and there is a sanguine expectation that the entertainment will be worth the wait. For a moment I was puzzled, then remembered: Rosie McClure, the evangelist, is in town. I should have realized at once; the advertisements have been prominent enough. Rosie is the latest and most successful of the television performers who sell salvation and do very well out of a commodity which is always in demand and which costs them nothing to supply. For the first two years after Omega we had Roaring Roger and his sidekick, Soapy Sam, and Roger still has a following for his weekly TV slot. He was—still is—a natural and powerful orator, a huge man, white-bearded, consciously moulding himself on the popular idea of an Old Testament prophet, pouring out his comminations in a powerful voice curiously given increased authority by its trace of a Northern Ireland accent. His message is simple if unoriginal: Man's infertility is God's punishment for his disobedience, his sinfulness. Only repentance can appease the Almighty's rightful displeasure, and repentance is best demonstrated by a generous contribution towards Roaring Roger's campaign expenses. He himself never touts for cash; that remains the job of Soapy Sam. They were initially an extraordinarily effective pair and their large house on Kingston Hill is the solid manifestation

of their success. In the first five years after Omega
the message had some validity, as Roger ful-
minated against inner-city violence, old women
attacked and raped, children sexually abused,
marriage reduced to no more than a monetary
contract, divorce the norm, dishonesty rife and
the sexual instinct perverted. Text after damning
Old Testament text fell from his lips as he held
aloft his well-thumbed Bible. But the product had
a short shelf-life. It is difficult to fulminate suc-
cessfully against sexual licence in a world over-
come by ennui, to condemn the sexual abuse of
children when there are no more children, to
denounce inner-city violence when the cities
are increasingly becoming the peaceful reposi-
tories of the docile aged. Roger has never ful-
minated against the violence and selfishness of
the Omegas; he has a well-developed sense of
self-preservation.

Now, with his decline, we have Rosie McClure.
Sweet Rosie has come into her own. She is origi-
nally from Alabama but left the United States in
2019, probably because her brand of religious he-
donism is over-supplied there. The gospel according to Rosie is simple: God is love and everything
is justified by love. She has resurrected an old pop
song of the Beatles, a group of young Liverpool
boys in the 1960s, "All You Need Is Love," and
it is this repetitive jingle, not a hymn, which pre-

cedes her rallies. The Last Coming is not in the future but now, as the faithful are gathered in, one by one, at the end of their natural lives and translated to glory. Rosie is remarkably specific about the joys to come. Like all religious evangelists, she realizes that there is little satisfaction in the contemplation of heaven for oneself if one cannot simultaneously contemplate the horrors of hell for others. But hell as described by Rosie is less a place of torment than the equivalent of an ill-conducted and uncomfortable fourth-rate hotel where incompatible guests are forced to endure each other's company for eternity and do their own washing-up with inadequate facilities although, presumably, with no lack of boiling water. She is equally specific about the joys of heaven. "In my Father's house are many mansions," and Rosie assures her adherents that there will be mansions to suit all tastes and all degrees of virtue, the highest pinnacle of bliss being reserved for the chosen few. But everyone who heeds Rosie's call to love will find an agreeable place, an eternal Costa del Sol liberally supplied with food, drink, sun and sexual pleasure. Evil has no place in Rosie's philosophy. The worst accusation is that people have fallen into error because they have not understood the law of love. The answer to pain is an anaesthetic or an aspirin, to loneliness the assurance of God's personal concern, to bereavement the certainty of reunion. No man is called to practise inordinate self-denial, since God, being Love, desires only that His children shall be happy.

Emphasis is placed on the pampering and gratification of this temporal body, and Rosie is not above giving a few beauty hints during her sermons. These are spectacularly arranged, the white-clad choir of a hundred ranked under the strobe lights, the brass band and the Gospel singers. The congregation join in the cheerful choruses, laugh, cry and fling their arms like demented marionettes. Rosie herself changes her spectacular dresses at least three times during each rally. Love, proclaims Rosie, all you need is love. And no one need feel deprived of a love object. It needn't be a human being; it can be an animal—a cat, a dog; it can be a garden; it can be a flower; it can be a tree. The whole natural world is one, linked by love, upheld by love, redeemed by love. One would suppose that Rosie had never seen a cat with a mouse. By the end of the rally the happy converts are generally throwing themselves into each other's arms and casting notes into the collection buckets with reckless enthusiasm.

During the mid-1990s the recognized churches, particularly the Church of England, moved from the theology of sin and redemption to a less uncompromising doctrine: corporate social responsibility coupled with a sentimental humanism. Rosie has gone further and has virtually abolished the Second Person of the Trinity together with His cross, substituting a golden orb of the sun in glory, like a garish Victorian pub sign. The change was immediately popular. Even to un-believers like myself, the cross, stigma of the bar-barism of officialdom and of man's ineluctable cruelty, has never been a comfortable symbol.

8

Just before nine-thirty on Sunday morning Theo set off to walk across Port Meadow to Binsey. He had given his word to Julian and it was a matter of pride not to renege. But he admitted to himself that there was a less estimable reason for fulfilling his promise. They knew who he was and where to find him. Better be bothered once, meet the group and get it over, than spend the next few months in the embarrassing expectation of meeting Julian every time he went to chapel or shopped in the covered market. The day was bright, the air cold but dry under a clear sky of deepening blue; the grass, still crisp from an early morning frost, crackled under his feet. The river was a crinkled ribbon reflecting the sky, and as he crossed the bridge and paused to look down, a noisy gaggle of ducks and two geese came clamouring, wide-beaked, as if there could still be children to fling them crusts and then run screaming in half-simulated fear from their noisy importunities. The hamlet was deserted. The few farmhouses to the right of the wide green were still standing but most of their windows were boarded up. In places the boarding had been smashed and through the splinters and spears of jagged glass edging the window frames he could glimpse the remnants of peeling wallpaper, flowered patterns once chosen with anxious care but now in tattered fragments, frail transitory banners of departed life. On one of the roofs slates were beginning to slide, revealing the rotting timbers, and the gardens were wildernesses of shoulder-high grass and weeds.

The Perch Inn, as he knew, had long been closed, as custom had dwindled. Across Port Meadow to Binsey had been one of his favourite Sunday-morning walks, with the inn as its destination. It seemed to him now that he passed through the hamlet like the ghost of that former self, seeing with unfamiliar eyes the narrow half-mile avenue of chestnuts which led north-west from Binsey to St. Margaret's Church. He tried to remember when he had last taken this walk. Was it seven years ago, or ten? He could recall neither the occasion nor his companion if there had been one. But the avenue had changed. The chestnuts were still standing but the lane, dark under the intertwined boughs of the trees, had narrowed to a footpath musty with fallen leaves and tangled with an untamed profusion of elderberry and ash. The Local Council had, he knew, designated certain footpaths for clearage but gradually the number of those preserved had fallen. The old were too weak for the work, the middle-aged, on whom the burden of maintaining the life of the State largely depended, were too busy, the young cared little for the preservation of the countryside. Why preserve what would be theirs in abundance? They would all too soon inherit a world of unpopulated uplands, unpolluted streams, encroaching woods and forests and deserted estuaries. They were seldom seen in the country and, indeed, seemed frightened by it. Woods, in particular, had become places of menace which many feared to enter, as if terrified that, once lost among those dark unyielding trunks and forgotten paths, they would never again emerge into the light. And it wasn't only the young. More and more people were seeking the company of their own kind, deserting the lonelier villages even before prudence or official decree made it necessary, and moving to those designated urban districts where the Warden had promised that light and power would be provided, if possible, until the end.

The solitary house which he remembered still stood in its garden to the right of the church and Theo saw to his surprise that it was at least partly occupied. The windows were curtained, there was a thin trail of smoke from the chimney and to the left of the path some attempt had been made to clear the earth of the knee-high grasses and to cultivate a vegetable garden. A few shrivelled runner beans still hung from the supporting sticks and there were uneven rows of cabbages and yellowing, half-picked Brussels sprouts. During his visits as an undergraduate he remembered regretting that the peace of the church and the house, which it was difficult to believe were so close to the city, had been spoiled by the loud, ceaseless roar from the M40 motorway. Now that nuisance was hardly noticeable and the house seemed wrapped in an ageless calm.

It was broken when the door burst open and an elderly man in a faded cassock precipitated himself out and came squawking and stumbling down the path, waving his arms as if to repel recalcitrant beasts. He called out in a quavering voice: "No service! No service today. I've got a christening at eleven o'clock."

Theo said: "I'm not attending a service, I'm just visiting."

"That's all they ever do. Or so they say. But I shall want the font at eleven. All out then. Everyone out except the christening party."

"I don't expect to be here as late as that. Are you the parish priest?"

He came close and glared at Theo with fierce paranoid eyes. Theo thought that he had never seen anyone so old, the skull stretching the paper-thin, mottled skin of his face as if death couldn't wait to claim him.

The old man said: "They had a black Mass here last Wednesday, singing and shouting all night. That's not right. I can't stop it, but I don't approve. And they don't clear up after themselves— blood, feathers, wine all over the floor. And black candle-grease. You can't get it out. It won't come out, you know. And it's all left for me to do. They don't think. It isn't fair. It isn't right."

Theo said: "Why don't you keep the church locked?"

The old man became conspiratorial. "Because they've taken the key, that's why. And I know who's got it. Oh yes, I know." He turned and stumbled, muttering, towards the house, wheeling round at the door to shout a final warning. "Out at eleven o'clock. Unless you're coming to the christening. All out by eleven."

Theo made his way to the church. It was a small stone building and with its short twin-belled turret it looked very like an unpretentious stone house with a single chimney stack. The church-yard was as overgrown as a long-neglected field. The grass was tall and pale, as hay and ivy had leached over the gravestones, obliterating the names. Somewhere in this tangled wilderness was the well of St. Frideswide, once a place of pilgrimage. A modern pilgrim would have difficulty in finding it. But the church was obviously visited. On either side of the porch was a terra-cotta pot containing a single rose bush, the stems now denuded but still bearing a few starved winter-blighted buds.

Julian was waiting for him in the porch. She didn't hold out her hand or smile, but said, "Thank you for coming, we're all here," and pushed open the door. He followed her into the dim interior and was met by a strong wave of incense overlaying a more feral smell. When he had first come here, more than twenty-five years ago, he had been transported by the silence of its ageless peace, seeming to hear upon the air the echo of long-forgotten plainsong, of old imperatives and desperate prayers. All that had gone. Once it had been a place where silence was more than the absence of noise. Now it was a stone building; nothing more.

He had expected the group to be waiting for him, standing or sitting together in the dim rustic emptiness. But he saw that they had separated themselves and had been walking in different parts of the church as if some argument or a restless need for solitude had forced them apart. There were four of them, three men and a tall

woman standing beside the altar. As he and Julian
entered they came quietly together and grouped
themselves in the aisle facing him.

He had no doubt which one was Julian's husband and their leader even before he came forward and, it seemed, deliberately confronted him.
They stood facing each other like two adversaries
weighing each other up. Neither smiled or put out
a hand.

He was very dark, with a handsome, rather
sulky face, the restless, suspicious eyes bright and
deep-set, the brows strong and straight as brush
strokes accentuating the jutting cheekbones. The
heavy eyelids were spiked with a few black hairs
so that the lashes and eyebrows looked joined.
The ears were large and prominent, the lobes
pointed, pixie ears at odds with the uncompromising set of the mouth and the strong clenched jaw.
It was not the face of a man at peace with himself
or his world, but why should he be, missing by
only a few years the distinction and privileges of
being an Omega? His generation, like theirs, had
been observed, studied, cosseted, indulged, preserved for that moment when they would be male
adults and produce the hoped-for fertile sperm. It
was a generation programmed for failure, the ultimate disappointment to the parents who had bred
them and the race which had invested in them so
much careful nurturing and so much hope.

When he spoke his voice was higher than Theo had expected, harsh-toned and with a trace of an accent which he couldn't identify. Without waiting for Julian to make any introductions he said: "There's no need for you to know our surnames. We'll use forenames only. I'm Rolf and I'm the leader of the group. Julian is my wife. Meet Miriam, Luke and Gascoigne. Gascoigne is his forename. His gran chose it for him in 1990, God knows why. Miriam used to be a midwife and Luke is a priest. You don't need to know what any of us do now."

The woman was the only one to come forward and grasp Theo's hand. She was black, probably Jamaican, and the oldest of the group, older than himself, Theo guessed, perhaps in her mid- or late fifties. Her high bush of short, tightly curled hair was dusted with white. The contrast between the black and white was so stark that the head looked powdered, giving her a look both hieratic and decorative. She was tall and gracefully built with a long, fine-featured face, the coffee-coloured skin hardly lined, denying the whiteness of the hair. She was wearing slim black trousers tucked into boots, a high-necked brown jersey and sheepskin jerkin, an elegant, almost exotic contrast to the rough serviceable country clothes of the three men. She greeted Theo with a firm handshake and a speculative, half-humorous colluding glance, as if they were already conspirators.

At first sight there was nothing remarkable about the boy—he looked like a boy although he couldn't be younger than thirty-one—whom they called Gascoigne. He was short, almost tubby, crop-haired and with a round, amiable face, wide-eyed, snub-nosed—a child's face which had grown with age but not essentially altered since he had first looked out of his pram at a world which his air of puzzled innocence suggested he still found odd but not unfriendly.

The man called Luke, whom he remembered Julian too had described as a priest, was older than Gascoigne, probably over forty. He was tall, with a pale, sensitive face and an etiolated body, the large knobbled hands drooping from delicate wrists, as if in childhood he had outgrown his strength and had never managed to achieve robust adulthood. His fair hair lay like a silk fringe on the high forehead; his grey eyes were widely spaced and gentle. He looked an unlikely conspirator, his obvious frailty in stark contrast to Rolf's dark masculinity. He gave Theo a brief smile which transformed his slightly melancholy face, but did not speak.

Rolf said: "Julian explained to you why we agreed to see you." He made it sound as if Theo were the supplicant.

"You want me to use my influence with the

Warden of England. I have to tell you that I have
no influence. I gave up any such right when I
relinquished my appointment as his adviser. I'll
listen to what you have to say but I don't think
there's anything I can do to influence either the
Council or the Warden of England. There never
was. That's partly why I resigned."

Rolf said: "You're his cousin, his only living
relative. You were more or less brought up together. The rumour is that you're the only one in
England he's ever listened to."

"Then the rumour is wrong." Theo added:
"What sort of group are you? Do you always
meet here in this church? Are you some kind of
religious organization?"

It was Miriam who answered. "No. As Rolf
explained, Luke is a priest, although he hasn't a
full-time job or a parish. Julian and he are Christians, the rest of us aren't. We meet in churches
because they're available, they're open, they're
free and they're usually empty, at least the ones
we choose are. We may have to give this one up.
Other people are beginning to use it."

Rolf broke in, his voice impatient, over-em-
phatic. "Religion and Christianity have nothing
to do with it. Nothing!"

As if she hadn't heard him, Miriam went on:
"All sorts of eccentrics meet in churches. We're
just one set of oddballs among many. No one asks

any questions. If they do, we're the Cranmer Club. We meet to read and study the old Book of Common Prayer."

Gascoigne said: "That's our cover." He spoke with the satisfaction of a child who has learned some of the grown-ups' secrets.

Theo turned to him. "Is it? So what do you reply when the State Security Police ask you to recite the Collect for the first Sunday in Advent?" Seeing Gascoigne's embarrassed incomprehension, he added: "Hardly a convincing cover."

Julian said quietly: "You may not sympathize with us but you don't have to despise us. The cover isn't meant to convince the SSP. If they started taking an interest in us no cover would protect us. They'd break us in ten minutes. We know that. The cover gives us a reason, an excuse for meeting regularly and in churches. We don't publicize it. It's there if anyone asks, if we need it."

Gascoigne said: "I know the prayers are called Collects. Do you know the one you asked me?" He wasn't being accusatory, merely interested.

Theo said: "I was brought up with the old Book. The church my mother took me to as a boy must have been one of the last to use it. I'm a historian. I have an interest in the Victorian church, in old liturgies, defunct forms of worship."

Rolf said impatiently: "All this is irrelevant. As Julian says, if the SSP take us they're not going to waste time examining us on the old catechism. We're not in any danger yet; not unless you betray us. What have we done so far? Nothing but talk. Before we do act two of us thought it might be sensible to make an appeal to the Warden of England, your cousin."

Miriam said: "Three of us. It was a majority. I went along with Luke and Julian. I thought it was worth a try."

Rolf again ignored her. "It wasn't my idea to get you here. I'm being honest with you. I've no reason to trust you and I don't particularly want you."

Theo replied: "And I didn't particularly want to come, so we meet on equal footing. You want me to speak to the Warden. Why don't you do that yourselves?"

"Because he wouldn't listen. He may listen to you."

"And if I agree to see him, and if he does listen, what do you want me to say?"

Now that the question was so baldly put it seemed that they were temporarily nonplussed. They looked at each other as if wondering which one would begin.

It was Rolf who answered: "The Warden was elected when he first took power, but that was fifteen years ago. He hasn't called an election since. He claims to rule by the people's will, but what he is is a despot and a tyrant."

Theo said drily: "It would be a brave messenger who was prepared to tell him that."

Gascoigne said: "And the Grenadiers are his private army. It's him they take an oath to. They don't serve the State any more, they serve him. He's got no right to use that name. My granddad was a private in the Grenadiers. He said they were the best regiment in the British Army."

Rolf ignored him. "And there are things he could do even without waiting for a general election. He could end the semen-testing programme. It's time-wasting and degrading, and it's hopeless anyway. And he could let the Local and Regional Councils choose their own Chairmen. That would at least be the beginning of democracy."

Luke said: "It isn't only the semen testing. He should stop the compulsory gynaecological examinations. They degrade women. And we want him to put an end to the Quietus. I know that all the old people are supposed to be volunteers. Maybe it started out like that. Maybe some of them still are. But would they want to die if we gave them hope?"

Theo was tempted to ask "Hope of what?"

Julian broke in. "And we want something done

about the Sojourners. Do you think it's right that there's an edict prohibiting our Omegas from emigrating? We import Omegas and others from less affluent countries to do our dirty work, clean the sewers, clear away the rubbish, look after the incontinent, the aged."

Theo said: "They're anxious enough to come, presumably because they get a better quality of life."

Julian said: "They come to eat. Then, when they get old—sixty is the age limit, isn't it?—they're sent back whether they want to go or not."

"That's an evil their own countries could redress. They could begin by managing their affairs better. Anyway, their numbers aren't great. There's a quota, the intake is carefully controlled."

"Not only a quota, stringent requirements. They have to be strong, healthy, without criminal convictions. We take the best and then chuck them back when they're no longer wanted. And who gets them? Not the people who need them most. The Council and their friends. And who looks after the foreigners when they're here? They work for a pittance, they live in camps, the women separate from the men. We don't even give them citizenship; it's a form of legalized slavery."

Theo said: "I don't think you'll start a revolution on the issue of the Sojourners, or on the Quietus for that matter. People don't care enough."

Julian said: "We want to help them to care."

"Why should they? They live without hope on a dying planet. What they want is security, comfort, pleasure. The Warden of England can promise the first two, which is more than most foreign governments are managing to do."

Rolf had been listening to their exchange without speaking. Then he said suddenly: "What's he like, the Warden of England? What sort of man is he? You should know, you were brought up with him."

"That doesn't give me an open entry to his mind."

"All that power, more than anyone has ever had before—in this country anyway—all in his hands. Does he enjoy it?"

"Presumably. He doesn't seem anxious to let it go." He added: "If you want democracy, you have somehow to revitalize the Local Council. It begins there."

Rolf said: "It ends there too. It's how the Warden exercises control at that level. And have you seen our local chairman, Reggie Dimsdale? He's seventy, querulous, shit-scared, only doing the job because it gets him a double petrol allowance and a couple of foreign Omegas to look after his bloody great barn of a house and wipe his bum for him when he gets incontinent. No Quietus for him."

"He was elected to the Council. They were all elected."

"By whom? Did you vote? Who cares? People are just relieved that someone will do the job. And you know how it works. The Chairman of the Local Council can't be appointed without the approval of the District Council. That needs the approval of the Regional Council. He or she has to be approved by the Council of England. The Warden controls the system from top to bottom, you must know that. He controls it, too, in Scotland and Wales. Each has its own Warden, but who appoints them? Xan Lyppiatt would call himself the Warden of Great Britain except that, for him, it hasn't got quite the same romantic appeal."

The remark, thought Theo, showed perception. He recalled an old conversation with Xan. "Hardly 'Prime Minister,' I think. I don't want to appropriate someone else's title, particularly when it carries such a weight of tradition and obligation. I might be expected to call an election every five years. And not 'Lord Protector.' The last one was hardly an unqualified success. 'Warden' will do very well. But Warden of Great Britain and Northern Ireland? That hardly has the romantic ring I'm aiming for."

Julian said: "We'll get nowhere with the Local Council. You live in Oxford, you're a citizen like everyone else. You must read the kind of stuff they paste up after the meetings, the things they discuss. The maintenance of the golf courses and bowling greens. Are the clubhouse facilities adequate? Decisions about job allocations, petrol-allowance complaints, applications to employ a Sojourner. Auditions for the local amateur choir. Are there enough people wanting violin lessons to make it worthwhile for the Council to employ a full-time professional? Sometimes they even discuss street policing, not that it's really necessary now that the threat of deportation to the Man Penal Colony is hanging over prospective burglars."

Luke said gently: "Protection, comfort, pleasure. There has to be something more."

"It's what people care about, what they want. What more should the Council be offering?"

"Compassion, justice, love."

"No state has ever concerned itself with love, and no state ever can."

Julian said: "But it can concern itself with justice."

Rolf was impatient: "Justice, compassion, love. They're all words. What we're talking about is power. The Warden is a dictator masquerading as a democratic leader. He ought to be made to be responsible to the will of the people."

Theo said: "Ah, the will of the people. That's a fine sounding phrase. At present, the will of the people seems to be for protection, comfort, pleasure." He thought: I know what offends you—the fact that Xan enjoys such power, not the way he exercises it. The little group had no real cohesion and, he suspected, no common purpose. Gascoigne was fuelled by indignation about the appropriation of the name Grenadier, Miriam by some motive which was, as yet, unclear, Julian and Luke by religious idealism, Rolf by jealousy and ambition. As a historian he could have pointed out a dozen parallels.

Julian said: "Tell him about your brother, Miriam. Tell him about Henry. But let's sit down before you begin."

They settled themselves in a pew, crouching forward to listen to Miriam's low voice, looking, thought Theo, like a huddled ill-assorted bunch of half-reluctant worshippers.

"Henry got sent to the island eighteen months ago. Robbery with violence. It wasn't much violence, not real violence. He robbed an Omega and pushed her over. It was no more than a shove but she fell to the ground and she told the court that Henry had kicked her in the ribs while she was lying there. That isn't true. I'm not saying Henry didn't push her. He's been grief and trouble since childhood. But he didn't kick that Omega, not when she was down. He snatched her handbag and pushed her over and then he ran. It happened in London, just before midnight. He ran round the corner of Ladbroke Grove straight into the arms of the State Security Police. He's had bad luck all his life."

"Were you in court?"

"My mother and I, both of us. My father died two years ago. We got Henry a lawyer—paid him too—but he wasn't really interested. Took our money and did nothing. We could see that he agreed with the prosecution that Henry ought to be sent to the island. After all, it was an Omega he robbed. That counted against him. And, then, he's black."

Rolf said impatiently: "Don't start all that crap about racial discrimination. It was the push that did it for him, not his colour. You can't be sent to the Penal Colony except for a crime of violence against the person or for a second conviction for burglary. Henry had no convictions for burglary but two for theft."

Miriam said: "Shoplifting. Nothing really bad. He stole a scarf for Mum's birthday and a bar of chocolate. But that was when he was a kid. For God's sake Rolf, he was twelve! It was over twenty years ago."

Theo said: "If he knocked the victim down, he was guilty of a crime of violence whether or not he kicked her."

"But he didn't. He pushed her aside and she fell. It wasn't deliberate."

"The jury must have thought otherwise."

"There wasn't a jury. You know how difficult it is to get people to serve. They're not interested. Won't bother. He was tried under the new arrangements, a judge and two magistrates. They've got power to send people to the island. And it's for life. There's no remission, you never get out. A life sentence in that hell for one push which he didn't mean. It killed my mother. Henry was her only son and she knew she'd never see him again. She just turned her face to the wall after that. But I'm glad she did die. At least she never knew the worst that happened to him."

She looked at Theo and said simply: "You see, I did know. He came home."

"You mean he escaped from the island? I thought that was impossible."

"Henry did it. He found a broken dinghy, one that the security force had overlooked when they got the island ready for the convicts. Every boat which wasn't worth taking away they burnt, but one was hidden or got overlooked, or perhaps they thought it was too damaged to be useful. Henry was always good with his hands. He repaired it in secret and he made two oars. Then, four weeks ago, January the third it was, he waited until it was dark and pushed off."

"It was incredibly foolhardy."

"No, it was sensible. He knew that he'd either make it or drown, and drowning was better than staying on that island. And he got home, he got back. I live—well, never mind where I live. It's in a cottage on the edge of a village. He arrived after midnight. I'd had a heavy day at work and I meant to go to bed early. I was tired but restless, so I made myself a cup of tea when I got in and then I fell asleep in my chair. I only slept for about twenty minutes but when I awoke I found I wasn't ready for bed. You know how it is. You get beyond tiredness. It's almost too much of an effort to undress.

"It was a dark night, starless, and the wind was rising. Usually I like the sound of the wind when I'm snug at home, but that night it was different, not comforting, wailing and hissing in the chimney, menacing. I got the blues, the black dog on my shoulder, thinking of Mother dead and Henry lost for ever. I thought I'd better shake myself out of it and get up to bed. And then I heard the knocking on the door. There is a bell but he didn't use that. He just used the knocker twice, and feebly, but I heard. I went to the peep-hole but I could see nothing, only blackness. It was after

midnight now and I couldn't think who could be
calling and so late. But I put on the chain and
opened the door. There was a dark shape, col-
lapsed against the wall. He had only the strength
to knock twice before he fell unconscious. I
managed to drag him in and to revive him. I gave
him some soup and brandy and after an hour he
could talk. He wanted to talk so I let him, cradling
him in my arms."

Theo asked: "What sort of state was he in?"

It was Rolf who replied: "Filthy, stinking,
bloody and desperately thin. He'd walked from
the Cumbrian coast."

Miriam went on: "I washed him and bandaged
his feet and managed to get him to bed. He was
terrified to sleep alone, so I lay down beside him
fully dressed. I couldn't sleep. It was then he
began talking. He talked for over an hour. I didn't
speak. I just held him and listened. Then, at last,
he was silent and I knew he was asleep. I lay there,
holding him, listening to his breathing, his muttering. Sometimes he gave a groan and then he
would suddenly shriek and sit up, but I managed
to soothe him as if he were a baby and he would
sleep again. I lay beside him and wept silently for
the things he'd told me. Oh, but I was angry too.
I burned with anger like a hot coal in my breast.

"The island is a living hell. Those who went
there human are nearly all dead and the rest are

devils. There's starvation. I know they have seeds, grain, machinery, but these are mostly town offenders not used to growing things, not used to working with their hands. All the stored food has been eaten now, gardens and fields stripped. Now, when people die, some get eaten too. I swear it. It has happened. The island is run by a gang of the strongest convicts. They enjoy cruelty and on Man they can beat and torture and torment and there's no one to stop them and no one to see. Those who are gentle, who care, who ought not to be there, don't last long. Some of the women are the worst. Henry told me things I can't repeat and I shall never forget.

"And then next morning they came for him. They didn't burst in, they didn't make very much noise. They just surrounded the cottage quietly and knocked at the door."

Theo asked: "Who were they?"

"Six Grenadiers and six men from the State Security Police. One beaten exhausted man and they sent twelve to take him. The SSP were the worst. I think they were Omegas. They didn't say anything to me at first, they just went upstairs and dragged him down. When he saw them he gave a shriek. I'll never forget that shriek. Never, never . . . Then they turned on me, but an officer, he was one of the Grenadiers, told them to leave me alone. He said, " 'She's his sister, naturally he came here. She had no choice but to help him.' "

Julian said: "We thought afterwards that he must have had a sister himself, someone he knew would never let him down, would always be there."

Rolf said impatiently: "Or else he thought he could show a little humanity and get paid for it by Miriam one way or the other."

Miriam shook her head. "No, it wasn't like that. He was trying to be kind. I asked him what would happen to Henry. He didn't reply, but one of the SSP said, 'What do you expect? But you'll get his ashes.' It was the captain of the SSP who told me that they could have picked him up when he landed but that they followed him all the way from Cumbria to Oxford. Partly to see where he'd go, I suppose, partly because they wanted to wait until he felt safe before they arrested him."

Rolf said with bitter anger: "It was that re-finement of cruelty which gave them an extra kick."

"A week later the package arrived. It was heavy, like two pounds of sugar, and the same shape, done up in brown paper with a typed label. Inside was this plastic bag filled with white grit. It looked like garden fertilizer, nothing to do with Henry. There was just a typed note, no signature. 'Killed while attempting to escape.' Nothing else. I dug a hole in the garden. I remember that it was raining and when I poured the white grit into the hole it was as if the whole garden was crying. But I didn't cry. Henry's sufferings were over. Anything was better than being sent back to that island."

Rolf said: "There'd be no question of sending him back, of course. They wouldn't want anyone to know that it's possible to get away. And it won't be, not now. They'll start patrolling the coast."

Julian touched Theo's arm and looked him full in the face. "They shouldn't treat human beings like that. No matter what they've done, what they are, they shouldn't treat people like that. We have to stop it."

Theo said: "Obviously there are social evils, but they are nothing to what is happening in other parts of the world. It's a question of what the country is prepared to tolerate as the price of sound government."

Julian asked: "What do you mean by sound government?"

"Good public order, no corruption in high places, freedom from fear of war and crime, a reasonably equitable distribution of wealth and resources, concern for the individual life."

Luke said: "Then we haven't got sound government."

"We may have the best that is possible in the

circumstances. There was wide public support for setting up the Man Penal Colony. No government can act in advance of the moral will of the people."

Julian said: "Then we have to change the moral will. We have to change people."

Theo laughed. "Oh, that's the kind of rebellion you have in mind? Not the system but human hearts and minds. You're the most dangerous revolutionaries of all, or would be if you had the slightest idea how to begin, the slightest chance of succeeding."

Julian asked, as if seriously interested in his answer: "How would you begin?"

"I wouldn't. History tells me what happens to people who do. You have one reminder on that chain round your neck."

She put up her distorted left hand and briefly touched the cross. Beside that swollen flesh it seemed a very small and fragile talisman.

Rolf said: "You can always find excuses for doing nothing. The fact is that the Warden runs Britain as his private fiefdom. The Grenadiers are his private army and the State Security Police are his spies and executioners."

"You've no proof of that."

"Who killed Miriam's brother? Was that execution after a proper trial or secret murder? What we want is real democracy."

"With you at the head of it?"

"I'd make a better job of it than he does."

"I imagine that's exactly what he thought when he took over from the last Prime Minister."

Julian said: "So you won't speak to the Warden?"

Rolf broke in. "Of course he won't. He never intended to. It was a waste of time getting him here. Pointless, stupid and dangerous."

Theo said quietly: "I haven't said I won't see him. But I've got to take him more than hearsay, particularly as I can't even tell him where and how I've got my information. Before I give you a decision I want to see a Quietus. When is the next one due to be held? Does anyone know?"

It was Julian who replied. "They've stopped advertising them, but of course the news does get round in advance. There's a female Quietus in Southwold this Wednesday, in three days' time. It's off the pier, north of the town. D'you know the town? It's about eight miles south of Lowestoft."

"That's not very convenient."

Rolf said: "Not for you, maybe. But it is for them. No railway so they won't get crowds, a long drive so people wonder if it's worth the petrol just to see Granny despatched in a white nightie to the sound of 'Abide With Me.' Oh, and there's just the one access by road. They can control how many people attend, keep an eye on them. If there's trouble they can pick up the people responsible."

Julian asked: "How long must we wait before you report back?"

"I'll decide whether to see the Warden immediately after the Quietus. Then we'd better wait for a week and arrange a meeting."

Rolf said: "Leave it for a fortnight. If you do see the Warden, they may put a watch on you."

Julian asked: "How will you let us know whether you've agreed to see him?"

"I'll leave a message after I've seen the Quietus. Do you know the Cast Museum in Pusey Lane?"

Rolf said: "No."

Luke said eagerly: "I do. It's part of the Ashmolean, an exhibition of plaster casts and marble copies of Greek and Roman statues. We used to be taken there during art class at school. I haven't been there for years. I didn't even know that the Ashmolean was keeping it open."

Theo said: "There's no particular reason to close it. It doesn't require much supervision. A few elderly scholars occasionally drift in. The opening hours are on the board outside."

Rolf was suspicious. "Why there?"

"Because I like to visit it occasionally and the attendant is used to seeing me. Because it provides a number of accessible hiding places. Mainly because it's convenient for me. Nothing else about this enterprise is."

Luke said: "Where exactly will you leave the message?"

"On the ground floor, the right-hand wall, under the head of the *Diadoumenos*. The catalogue number is C38 and you'll find that on the bust. If you can't remember the name, you can remember the number, presumably. If you can't, then write it down."

Julian said: "It's Luke's age, that makes it easy. Will we have to lift the statue?"

"It's not a statue, merely a head, and you needn't touch it. There's a very narrow gap between the base and the shelf. I'll leave my answer on a card. It won't be incriminating, a simple yes or no. You could telephone me for it, but no doubt you believe that might be unwise."

Rolf said: "We try never to telephone. Even though we haven't got started yet, we take normal precautions. Everyone knows that the lines are tapped."

Julian asked: "And if your answer is yes, and the Warden agrees to see you, when will you let us know what he says, what he promises to do?"

Rolf broke in: "Better leave it for at least two weeks. Report on Wednesday, fourteen days after the Quietus. I'll meet you on foot anywhere in Oxford, an open space might be best."

Theo said: "Open spaces can be watched through binoculars. Two people, obviously meeting, in the middle of a park, meadow or university park draw attention to themselves. A public building is safe. I'll meet Julian in the Pitt Rivers Museum."

Rolf said: "You appear to like museums."

"They have the advantage of being places where people can legitimately loiter."

Rolf said: "Then I'll meet you at twelve o'clock in the Pitt Rivers."

"Not you; Julian. You used Julian to make the first approach to me. It was Julian who brought me here today. I'll be in the Pitt Rivers at midday on the Wednesday two weeks after the Quietus and I shall expect her to come alone."

It was just before eleven when Theo left them in the church. He stood for a moment in the porch, glanced at his watch and looked out over the unkept graveyard. He wished that he hadn't come, hadn't got involved in this futile and embarrassing enterprise. He was more affected by Miriam's story than he cared to admit. He wished he had never heard it. But what was he expected to do, what could anyone do? It was too late now. He didn't believe that the group was in any danger. Some of their concern had seemed close to paranoia. And he had hoped for a temporary reprieve from responsibility, that there would be no Quietus for months. Wednesday was a bad day for him. It would mean rearranging his diary at short notice. He hadn't seen Xan for three years. If they were to meet again, it was humiliating and disagreeable to see himself in the role of supplicant. He was as irritated with himself as with the group. He might despise them as a gang of amateur malcontents, but they had outwitted him, had sent the one member whom they knew he would find it difficult to refuse. Why he should have found it difficult was a question he was not at present willing to explore. He would go to the Quietus as he had promised and leave them a message in the Cast Museum. He hoped that the message could justifiably be the single word NO.

The christening party was coming up the path, the old man, now wearing a stole, shepherding them with small cries of encouragement. There were two middle-aged women and two older men, the men soberly dressed in blue suits, the women wearing flowered hats, incongruous above their winter coats. Each of the women was carrying a white bundle wrapped in a shawl beneath which fell the lace-trimmed pleated folds of christening robes. Theo made to pass them, eyes tactfully averted, but the two women almost barred his way and, smiling the meaningless smile of the half-demented, thrust forward the bundles, inviting his admiration. The two kittens, ears flattened beneath the ribboned bonnets, looked both ridiculous and endearing. Their eyes were wide-open, uncomprehending opal pools, and they seemed worried at their confinement. He wondered if they had been drugged, then decided that they had probably been handled, caressed and carried like babies since birth and were accustomed to it. He wondered, too, about the priest. Whether validly ordained or an impostor—and there were plenty about—he was hardly engaged in an orthodox rite. The Church of England, no longer with a common doctrine or a common liturgy, was so fragmented that there was no knowing what some sects might not have come to believe, but he doubted whether the christening of animals was encouraged. The new Archbishop, who described herself as a Christian Rationalist, would, he suspected, have prohibited infant baptism on the grounds of superstition, had infant baptism still been possible. But she could hardly control what was happening in every redundant church. The kittens presumably would not welcome a douche of cold water over their heads, but no one else was likely to object. The charade was a fitting conclusion to a morning of folly. He set off walking vigorously towards sanity and that empty inviolate house he called home.

9

On the morning of the Quietus, Theo awoke to a weight of vague unease, not heavy enough to be called anxiety, but a mild unfocused depression, like the last tatters of an unremembered but disagreeable dream. And then, even before he put out his hand to the light switch, he knew what the day held. It had been his habit all his life to devise small pleasures as palliatives to unpleasant duties. Normally he would now begin planning his route with care: a good pub for an early lunch, an interesting church to visit, a detour to take in an attractive village. But there could be no compensation on this journey whose end and purpose was death. He had better get there as quickly as possible, see what he had promised to see, return home, tell Julian there was nothing that he or the group could do, and attempt to put the whole unsought and unwelcome experience out of his mind. That meant rejecting the more interesting route, via Bedford, Cambridge and Stowmarket, in favour of the M40 to the M25, then northeast to the Suffolk coast by the A12. It would be a faster if less direct and certainly duller route, but, then, he wasn't expecting to enjoy the drive.

But he made good progress. The A12 was in much better condition than he had expected, considering that the east-coast ports were now almost derelict. He made excellent time, arriving at Blythburgh, on the estuary, just before two. The tide was receding but beyond the reeds and mud flats the water stretched like a silken scarf and a fitful early-afternoon sun struck gold in the windows of Blythburgh Church.

It had been more than twenty-seven years since he was last here. Then he and Helena had taken a weekend break at the Swan in Southwold when Natalie was only six months old. They had only been able to afford a second-hand Ford in those days. Natalie's carry-cot had been firmly strapped to the back seat and the boot filled with the paraphernalia of babyhood: large packets of disposable nappies, sterilizing equipment for the bottles, tins of baby food. When they reached Blythburgh, Natalie had begun to cry and Helena had said that she was hungry and should be fed now without waiting to get to the hotel. Why couldn't they stop at the White Hart at Blythburgh? The innkeeper would be sure to have facilities for heating milk. They could both have a pub lunch and she could feed Natalie. But the car park, he saw, was crowded and he disliked the trouble and disruption which the child and Helena's demands would cause. His insistence on pressing on for the few extra miles to Southwold had been ill-received. Helena, attempting ineffectually to pacify the child, had scarcely glanced at the gleaming water, at the great church, moored like a majestic ship among the reed beds. The weekend break had begun with the usual resentment and had continued with half-repressed ill-humour. It was, of course, his fault. He had been more ready to hurt his wife's feelings and deprive his daughter than to inconvenience a pub bar full of strangers. He wished there could be one memory of his dead child which wasn't tainted with guilt and regret.

He decided almost on impulse to lunch at the pub. Today his was the only car parked there. And inside the low-raftered room the black hearth of blazing logs which he remembered had been replaced with a two-bar electric fire. He was the only customer. The publican, very old, served him with a local beer. It was excellent, but the only food on offer was pre-cooked pies which the man heated in the microwave oven. It was an inadequate preparation for the ordeal ahead.

He took the remembered turn on to the Southwold road. The Suffolk countryside, crimped and barren under the winter sky, looked unchanged, but the road itself had deteriorated, making the drive as bumpy and hazardous as a cross-country rally. But when he reached the outskirts of Reydon he saw small gangs of Sojourners with their overseers, obviously preparing to make a start on repairing the surface. The dark faces glanced at him as he slowed and drove carefully past. Their presence surprised him. Southwold had surely not been designated as a future approved population centre. Why, then, was it important to ensure reasonable access?

And now he was driving past the wind shield of trees and the grounds and buildings of St. Felix School. A large board at the gate proclaimed that it was now the East Suffolk Craft Centre. Presumably it was open only during the summer, or at weekends, for he saw no one on the broad, unkempt lawns. He drove over Bight Bridge and entered the little town, its painted houses seeming to sleep in a post-prandial stupor. Thirty years ago its inhabitants had been mainly elderly: old soldiers walking their dogs, retired couples, bright-eyed and weather-beaten, walking arm in arm along the front. An atmosphere of ordered calm, all passion spent. Now it was almost deserted. On the bench outside the Crown Hotel two old men sat side by side staring into the distance, brown gnarled hands crossed over the handles of their walking sticks.

He decided to park in the yard of the Swan and have coffee before making his way to the north beach, but the inn was closed. As he was getting back into his car a middle-aged woman wearing a flowered apron came out of the side door and locked it behind her.

He said: "I was hoping to have coffee. Is the hotel closed permanently?"

She was pleasant-faced but nervous, and looked around before replying. "Just today, sir. A mark of respect. It's the Quietus, you see, or perhaps you didn't know."

"Yes," he said, "I did know."

Wishing to break the profound sense of isolation which lay heavily on buildings and streets, he said: "I was last here thirty years ago. It hasn't changed very much."

She laid one hand on the car window and said: "Oh, but it has, sir, it has changed. But the Swan is still a hotel. Not so many customers, of course, now people are moving out of the town. You see, it's scheduled for evacuation. The government won't be able to guarantee us power and services at the end. People are moving to Ipswich or Norwich." Why all the hurry, he wondered irritably.

Surely Xan could keep this place going for another twenty years.

In the end he parked the car on the small green at the end of Trinity Street and began walking along the cliff-top path towards the pier.

The mud-grey sea heaved sluggishly under a sky the colour of thin milk, faintly luminous at the horizon as if the fickle sun were about once more to break through. Above this pale transparency there hung great bunches of darker-grey and black cloud, like a half-raised curtain. Thirty feet below him he could see the stippled underbelly of the waves as they rose and spent themselves with weary inevitability, as if weighted with sand and pebbles. The rail of the promenade, once so pristine and white, was rusted and in parts broken, and the grassy slope between the promenade and the beach huts looked as if it hadn't been cropped for years. Once he would have seen below him the long shining row of wooden chalets with their endearingly ridiculous names, ranged like brightly painted dolls' houses facing the sea. Now there were gaps like missing teeth in a decaying jaw and those remaining were ramshackle, their paint peeling, precariously roped by staves driven into the bank, waiting for the next storm to sweep them away. At his feet the dry grasses, waist-high, beaded with dry seed pods, stirred fitfully in the

breeze which was never entirely absent from this
easterly coast.

Apparently the embarkation was to take place
not from the pier itself but from a specially
erected wooden jetty alongside it. He could see in
the distance the two low boats, their decks fes-
tooned with garlands of flowers, and, on the end
of the pier overlooking the jetty, a small group of
figures some of whom he thought were in uniform. About eighty yards in front of him three
coaches were drawn up on the promenade. As he
approached, the passengers began to get down.
First came a small group of bandsmen dressed in
red jackets and black trousers. They stood chat-
ting in a disorderly little group, the sun glinting on
the brass of their instruments. One of them gave
his neighbour a playful cuff. For a few seconds
they pretended to spar, then, bored with the
horseplay, lit cigarettes and stared out to sea. And
now came the elderly people, some able to de-
scend unaided, others leaning on nurses. The lug-
gage hold of one of the coaches was unlocked and
a number of wheelchairs dragged out. Last of all
the most frail were helped from the coach and into
the wheelchairs.

Theo kept his distance and watched as the thin
line of bent figures straggled down the sloping
path which bisected the cliff, towards the beach
huts on the lower promenade. Suddenly he real-

ized what was happening. They were using the huts for the old women to change into their white robes, huts which for so many decades had echoed with the laughter of children, and whose names, not thought of for nearly thirty years, now came unbidden to his mind, the silly, happy celebrations of family holidays: Pete's Place, Ocean View, Spray Cottage, Happy Hut. He stood grasping the rusty rail at the top of the cliff, watching as, two by two, the old women were helped up the steps and into the huts. The members of the band had watched but made no movement. Now they conferred a little together, stubbed out their cigarettes, picked up their instruments and made their own way down the cliff. They formed themselves into a line and stood waiting. The silence was almost eerie. Behind him the row of Victorian houses, shuttered, empty, stood like shabby memorials of happier days. Below him the beach was deserted; only the squawk of gulls disturbed the calm.

And now the old women were being helped down from the huts and arranged in line. They were all wearing long white robes, perhaps nightdresses, with what looked like woollen shawls and white capes over them, a necessary comfort in the keen wind. He was glad of the warmth of his own tweed coat. Each woman was carrying a small posy of flowers so that they looked like a bevy of dishevelled bridesmaids. He found himself wondering who had placed the flowers ready, who had unlocked the huts, left the nightdresses folded for that purpose. The whole event, which seemed so haphazard, so spontaneous, must have been carefully organized. And he noticed for the first time that the huts on this part of the lower promenade had been repaired and newly painted.

The band began playing as the procession shuffled slowly along the lower promenade towards the pier. As the first blare of brass broke the silence he felt a sense of outrage, a dreadful pity. They were playing cheerful songs, melodies from the time of his grandparents, the songs of the Second World War, which he recognized but whose names he could not at first recall. Then some of the titles fell into his mind: "Bye Bye, Blackbird," "Somebody Stole My Girl," "Somewhere over the Rainbow." As they approached the pier the music changed and he recognized the strains of a hymn, "Abide with Me." After the first verse had been played and the tune began again, there rose from beneath him a querulous mewing like the sound of sea birds and he realized that the old people were singing. As he watched some of the women began swaying to the music, holding out their white skirts and clumsily pirouetting. It occurred to Theo that they could have been drugged.

Keeping pace with the last couple in the line, he followed them towards the pier. And now the scene was plain beneath him. There was a crowd of only about twenty, some perhaps relatives and friends, but most members of the State Security Police. The two low boats might once, he thought, have been small barges. Only the hulls remained and these had been fitted with rows of benches. There were two soldiers in each of the boats and, as the old women entered, they bent down, presumably either to shackle their ankles or to attach weights. The motorboat, moored at the pier itself, made the plan clear. Once out of sight of land the soldiers would knock away the plugs and then board the motorboat and return to shore. The band on shore was still playing, this time Elgar's "Nimrod." The singing had ceased and no sound reached him except the ceaseless crash of the waves on the shingle and an occasional quiet word of command blown to him on the thin breeze.

He told himself that he had seen enough. He would be justified now in returning to the car. He wanted nothing more than to drive furiously away from this little town which spoke to him only of helplessness, of decay, of emptiness and death. But he had promised Julian that he would see a Quietus and that must mean watching until the boats were out of sight. As if to reinforce his intention, he walked down the concrete steps from the upper promenade to the beach. No one came forward to order him away. The little group of officials, the nurses, the soldiers, even the bandsmen, concerned with their part in the macabre ceremony, seemed not even to notice that he was there.

Suddenly there was a commotion. One of the women being helped on to the nearer boat gave a cry and began a violent thrashing of her arms. The nurse with her was taken by surprise and, before she could move, the woman had leapt from the jetty into the water and was struggling ashore. Instinctively Theo cast off his heavy coat and ran towards her, scrunching over the pebbles and shingle, feeling the icy bite of the sea freezing his ankles. She was only about twenty yards from him now and he could see her plainly, the wild white hair, the nightdress sticking to her body, the swinging, pendulous breasts, the arms with their weals of crêpy skin. A crashing wave tore the nightdress from her shoulder and he saw the breast swaying obscenely like a giant jellyfish. She was still screaming, a high, piercing whistle like a tortured animal. And almost at once he recognized her. It was Hilda Palmer-Smith. Buffeted, he struggled towards her, holding out both hands.

And then it happened. His outstretched hands were about to grasp her wrists when one of the soldiers leapt into the water from the jetty and, with the butt of his pistol, struck her viciously on the side of the head. She fell forward into the sea, arms whirling. There was a brief stain of red before the next wave came, engulfed her, lifted her, receded and left her spreadeagled in the foam. She tried to rise but again he struck. Theo had reached her by now and clutched one of her hands. Almost immediately he felt his shoulders seized and he was flung aside. He heard a voice, quiet, authoritative, almost gentle: "Let it be, sir. Let it be."

Another wave, larger than the last, engulfed her and knocked him off his feet. It receded and, struggling up, he saw her again, stretched out, the nightdress rucked up over the thin legs, all of the lower body exposed. He gave a groan and again staggered towards her, but this time he, too, felt a blow on the side of his head and fell. He was aware of the harshness of pebbles grinding into his face, of the overwhelming smell of salt sea water, of a pounding in his ears. His hands scrabbled at the shingle, trying to get a hold. But sand and shingle were sucked away beneath him. And then another wave struck and he felt himself dragged back into deeper water. Only half-conscious, he tried to raise his head, tried to breathe, knowing that he was close to drowning. And then came the third wave, which lifted him bodily and flung him among the stones of the beach.

But they hadn't intended him to drown. Shivering with cold, spluttering and retching, he was aware of strong hands under his shoulders, of being lifted out of the water as lightly as if he were a child. Someone was dragging him face-downwards up the beach. He could feel his toe-caps rasping the patches of wet sand and the drag of the shingle on his soaking trouser-legs. His arms dangled powerlessly, the knuckles bruised and grazed by the larger stones on the upper ridges of the shore. And all the time he could smell the strong sea-smell of the beach and hear the rhythmic thudding of the surf. Then the dragging stopped, and he was dumped ungently on soft, dry sand. He felt the weight of his coat as it was thrown over his body. He was dimly aware of a dark shape passing over him, and then he was alone.

He tried to raise his head, aware for the first time of a throbbing pain, expanding and contracting like a living thing pulsating in his skull. Each time he managed to lift his head it swayed weakly from side to side, then thudded again into the sand. But at the third try he managed to raise it a few inches and opened his eyes. The lids were weighted with caked sand, sand that covered his face and blocked his mouth, while strands of slimy weeds webbed his fingers and hung in his hair. He felt like a man dug from some watery grave with all the trappings of his death still on him. But in the moment before he lapsed into unconsciousness he was able to see that someone had dragged him into the narrow space between two beach huts. They were raised on low stilts and he could see beneath the floors the detritus of long-forgotten holidays half-buried in the dirty sand: the gleam of silver paper, an old plastic bottle, the rotting canvas and splintered struts of a deck chair, and a child's broken spade. He shuffled painfully to get closer and reached out his hand, as if to lay hold on it would be to lay hold on safety and peace. But the effort was too great and, closing his smarting eyes, he sank with a sigh into the darkness.

When he awoke he thought at first that it was totally dark. Turning on his back he looked up into a sky faintly speckled with stars and saw before him the pale luminosity of the sea. He remembered where he was and what had happened. His head still ached, but now only with a dull, persistent pain. Passing his hand over his skull, he felt a lump as large as a hen's egg, but it seemed to him there was no great damage done. He had no idea of the time and it was impossible to see the hands of his watch. He rubbed his cramped limbs into life, shook the sand from his coat and, putting it on, stumbled down to the edge of the sea, where he knelt and bathed his face. The water was icy cold. The sea was calmer now and there was a shimmering path of light under a fugitive moon. The gently heaving water stretched before him completely empty and he thought of the drowned, still shackled in rows, ribbed by the ship's timbers, of white hair gracefully rising and falling in the tide. After returning to the beach huts, he rested for a few minutes on one of the steps, gathering his strength. He checked his jacket pockets. His leather notecase was soaking wet, but at least it was there and the contents were intact.

He made his way up the steps to the promenade. There were only a few street lights but they were sufficient for him to see the dial of his watch. It was seven o'clock. He had been unconscious, and presumably then asleep, for less than four hours. As he came up to Trinity Street he saw with relief that the car was still there, but there was no other sign of life. He stood irresolute. He was beginning to shiver and he felt a longing for hot food and drink. The thought of driving back to Oxford in his present state appalled him, but his need to get out of Southwold was almost as imperative as his hunger and thirst. It was while he was standing irresolute that he heard the closing of a door and looked round. A woman with a small dog on a lead was emerging from one of the

Victorian terraced houses fronting the little green. It was the only house in which he could see a light, and he noticed that the ground-floor window displayed a large notice, BED AND BREAKFAST.

On impulse he walked over to her and said: "I'm afraid I've had an accident. I'm very wet. I don't think I'm fit to drive home tonight. Have you a vacancy? My name is Faron, Theo Faron."

She was older than he expected, with a round, windburned face, gently creased like a balloon from which the air has been expelled, bright beady eyes and a small mouth, delicately shaped and once pretty but now, as he looked down on her, restlessly munching as if still relishing the aftertaste of her last meal.

She seemed unsurprised and, better still, unfrightened at his request and when she spoke her voice was pleasant. "I have a room vacant if you would just wait until I have taken Chloe for her evening duties. There's a special little place reserved for the dogs. We take care not to soil the beach. Mothers used to complain if the beach wasn't clean for the children and—old habits remain. I'm EMO—Evening Meal Optional. Would you be wanting that?"

She looked up at him and for the first time he saw a trace of anxiety in the bright eyes. He said he very much wanted it.

She returned within three minutes and he followed her down the narrow hall, then into a back sitting-room. It was small, almost claustrophobic, crammed with old-fashioned furniture. He had an impression of fading chintz, of a mantelshelf crowded with small china animals, of patchwork cushions on the low fireside chairs, of photographs in silver frames and the smell of lavender. It seemed to him that the room was a sanctum, its flower-papered walls enclosing the comfort and security which in his anxiety-fraught childhood he had never known.

She said: "I'm afraid I haven't very much in the refrigerator tonight, but I could give you soup and an omelette."

"That would be wonderful."

"The soup isn't home-made, I'm afraid, but I mix two tins to make it more interesting and add a little something, chopped parsley or an onion. I think you will find it palatable. Did you want it in the dining-room, or here in the sitting-room, in front of the fire? That might be cosier for you."

"I'd like to have it here."

He settled himself in a low button-backed chair, stretching his legs out in front of the electric fire, watching the steam rise from his drying trousers. The food came quickly, the soup first—a mixture, he detected, of mushroom and chicken sprinkled with parsley. It was hot, and surprisingly good, and the roll and butter accompanying it were fresh. Then she brought in a herb omelette. She asked if he would like tea, coffee or cocoa. What he wanted was alcohol, but that seemed not to be on offer. He settled for tea and she left him to drink it alone, as she had left him for the whole of the meal.

When he had finished, she reappeared, as if she had been waiting at the door, and said: "I've put you in the back room. Sometimes it's nice to get away from the sound of the sea. And don't worry about the bed being aired. I'm most particular about airing the beds. I've put in two bottles. You can kick them out if you're too hot. I've turned on the immersion heater so there's plenty of hot water if you want a bath."

His limbs ached from the hours lying on the damp sand and the prospect of stretching them out in hot water was appealing. But, hunger and thirst appeased, tiredness took over. It was too much trouble even to run the bath.

He said: "I'll bath in the morning, if I may."

The room was on the second floor and at the back as she had promised. Standing aside as he entered, she said: "I'm afraid I haven't any pyjamas large enough for you but there's a very old dressing-gown which you could use. It used to belong to my husband."

She seemed unsurprised and unworried that he had brought none of his own. An electric fire had been plugged in close to the Victorian grate. She bent to switch it off before leaving and he realized that what she was charging wouldn't cover all-night heating. But he didn't need it. Hardly had she closed the door after her than he tore off his clothes, drew back the bed-coverings and slid into warmth and comfort and oblivion.

Breakfast next morning was served to him in the ground-floor dining-room, at the front of the house. It was set with five tables, each with a pristine white table-cloth and a small vase of artificial flowers, but there were no other guests.

The room, with its cluttered emptiness, its air of promising more than could be provided, sparked a memory of the last holiday he had taken with his parents. He had been eleven and they had spent a week at Brighton staying in a bed-and-breakfast boarding house on the cliff top towards Kemp Town. It had rained nearly every day and his memory of the holiday was of the smell of wet raincoats, of the three of them huddled in shelters looking out at the grey heaving sea, of walking the streets in search of affordable entertainment until it was half past six and they could return for the evening meal. They had eaten in just such a room as this, the family groups, unused to being waited on, sitting in mute embarrassed patience until the proprietress, determinedly cheerful, came in with the laden trays of meat and two vegetables.

Throughout the holiday he had been resentful and bored. It occurred to him now, for the first time, how little joy his parents had had in their lives and how little he, their only child, had contributed to that meagre store.

She waited on him eagerly, providing a full breakfast of bacon, eggs and fried potatoes, obviously torn between her desire to watch him enjoy it and the realization that he would prefer to eat alone. He ate quickly, anxious to get away.

As he paid her he said: "It was good of you to take me in, a solitary man and without an overnight bag. Some people might have been reluctant."

"Oh no, I wasn't at all surprised to see you. I wasn't worried. You were an answer to prayer."

"I don't think I've ever been called that before."

"Oh, but you were. I haven't had a B and B for four months now and one feels so useless. There's nothing worse than feeling useless when you're old. So I prayed that God would show me what I ought to do, whether there was any point in carrying on. And He sent you. I always find, don't you, that when you're in real trouble, faced with problems which seem too much for you, and just ask, He does answer."

"No," he said, counting out the coins, "no, I can't say that's been my experience."

She went on as if she hadn't heard him: "I realize, of course, that I shall have to give up eventually. The little town is dying. We aren't scheduled as a population centre. So the newly retired don't come here any more and the young leave. But we shall be all right. The Warden has promised that everyone at the end will be cared for. I expect I'll be moved to a little flat in Norwich."

He thought: Her God provides the occasional overnight customer, but it is the Warden she relies on for the essentials. On impulse he asked: "Did you see the Quietus here yesterday?"

"Quietus?"

"The one held here. The boats at the pier."

She said, her voice firm: "I think you must be mistaken, Mr. Faron. There was no Quietus. We have none of that kind of thing in Southwold."

After that he sensed that she was as anxious to see him go as he was to leave. He thanked her again. She hadn't told him her name and he didn't ask. He was tempted to say: "I've been very comfortable. I must come back and spend a short holiday with you." But he knew that he would never return and her kindness deserved better of him than a casual lie.

10

Next morning he wrote the single word YES on a postcard and folded it carefully and precisely, running his thumb along the crease. The act of writing those three letters seemed portentous in ways he couldn't as yet foresee, a commitment to more than his promised visit to Xan.

Shortly after ten o'clock he made his way over the narrow cobbles of Pusey Lane to the museum. A single custodian was on duty, seated as usual at a wooden table opposite the door. He was very old and he was sound asleep. His right arm, curved on the table-top, cradled a high-domed, speckled head spiked with bristles of grey hairs. His left hand looked mummified, a collection of bones loosely held together by a stained glove of mottled skin. Close to it lay an open paperback, Plato's *Theaetetus*. He was probably a scholar, one of the unpaid band who volunteered to take turns and to keep the museum open. His presence, asleep or awake, was unnecessary; no one was going to risk deportation to the Isle of Man for the few medallions in the display case, and who could or would want to carry out the great *Victory of Samafaya* or the *Wings of the Nike of Samothrace?*

Theo had been reading history, yet it was Xan who had introduced him to the Cast Museum, entering it light-footed, as joyously expectant as a child with a new nursery of toys showing off its treasures. Theo, too, had fallen under its spell. Even in the museum their tastes differed. Xan liked best the rigour and the stern unemotional faces of the early-classical male statues on the ground floor. Theo preferred the lower room, with its examples of the softer, flowing Hellenistic lines. Nothing, he saw, was changed. Casts and statues stood ranked under the light of the high windows, like the closely packed lumber of a discarded civilization, the armless torsos with their grave faces and arrogant lips, the elegantly dressed curls above bound foreheads, eyeless gods secretly smiling, as if they were privy to a truth more profound than the spurious message of these ice-cold limbs: that civilizations rise and fall but man endures.

As far as he knew, once he had gone down Xan had never revisited the museum, but to Theo it had become a place of refuge over the years. In those dreadful months following Natalie's death and his move to St. John Street, it had provided a convenient escape from his wife's grief and resentment. He could sit on one of the hard utilitarian chairs, reading or thinking in this silent air, seldom disturbed by a human voice. From time to time small groups of school children or individual students would come into the museum and then he would close his book and leave. The special atmosphere which the place held for him depended on his being alone.

Before doing what he had come to do, he walked round the museum, partly from a half-superstitious feeling that, even in this silence and emptiness, he should act like a casual visitor, partly from the need to revisit old delights and see if they could still touch him: the Attic gravestone of the young mother from the fourth century B.C., the servant holding the swaddled baby, the tombstone of a little girl with doves, grief speaking across nearly three thousand years. He looked and thought and remembered.

When he came up again to the ground floor he saw that the attendant was still asleep. The head of the *Diadoumenos* was still in its place in the ground floor gallery but he looked at it with less emotion than when he had first seen it thirty-two years ago. Now the pleasure was detached, intellectual; then he had run his finger over the forehead, had traced the line from nose to throat, shaken with that mixture of awe, reverence and excitement which, in those heady days, great art could always produce in him.

Taking the folded postcard from his pocket, he inserted it between the base of the marble and the shelf, its edge just visible to a keen and searching eye. Whoever Rolf sent to retrieve it should be able to dislodge it with the tip of a fingernail, a coin, a pencil. He had no fear of anyone else finding it and, even if they did, the message could tell them nothing. Checking that the edge of the card could be seen, he felt again the mixture of irritation and embarrassment which he had first felt in the church at Binsey. But now the conviction that he was becoming unwillingly involved in an enterprise as ridiculous as it was futile was less powerful. The image of Hilda's half-naked body rolling in the surf, of that thin, wailing procession, the crack of a gun on bone; these imposed dignity and seriousness on even the most childish games. He had only to shut his eyes to hear again the crash of the falling wave, its long withdrawing sigh.

There was some dignity and much safety in the self-selected role of spectator, but, faced with some abominations, a man had no option but to step onto the stage. He would see Xan. But was he motivated less by outrage at the horror of the

Quietus than by the memory of his own humiliation, the carefully judged blow, his body hauled
up the beach and dumped as if it were an unwanted carcase?

As he was passing the table on his way to the
door the aged custodian stirred and sat up. Perhaps the footfall had penetrated his half-sleeping
mind with a warning of duty neglected. His first
gaze at Theo was one of fear almost amounting to
terror. And then Theo recognized him. He was
Digby Yule, a retired classics don from Merton.

Theo introduced himself. "It's good to see you,
sir. How are you?"

The question seemed to increase Yule's ner-
vousness. His right hand began an apparently un-
controlled drumming of the table-top. He said:
"Oh, very well, yes, very well, thank you, Faron.
I'm managing all right. I do for myself, you know.
I live in lodgings off the Iffley Road but I manage
very well. I do everything for myself. The landlady isn't an easy woman—well, she has her own
problems—but I'm no trouble to her. I'm no trouble to anyone."

What was he afraid of, Theo wondered. The
whispered call to the SSP that here was another
citizen who had become a burden on others? His
senses seemed to have become preternaturally
sharp. He could smell the faint tang of disinfectant, see the flakes of soapy foam on stubble and

chin, note that the half-inch of shirt-cuff protruding from the shabby jacket sleeves was clean but unironed. Then it occurred to him that it was in his power to say: "If you're not comfortable where you are there's plenty of room with me in St. John Street. I'm on my own now. It would be pleasant for me to have some company."

But he told himself firmly that it wouldn't be pleasant, that the offer would be seen as both presumptuous and condescending, that the old man wouldn't be able to cope with the stairs, those convenient stairs which excused him from the obligations of benevolence. Hilda wouldn't have been able to cope with the stairs either. But Hilda was dead.

Yule was saying: "I just come here twice a week. Monday and Friday, you know. I'm standing in for a colleague. It's good to have something useful to do and I like the quality of the silence. It's different from the silence in any other Oxford building."

Theo thought: Perhaps he will die here quietly, sitting at this table. What better place to go? And then he had an image of the old man left there, still at the table, of the last custodian locking and bolting the door, of the endless, unbroken silent years, of the frail body mummified or rotting at last under the marble gaze of those blank unseeing eyes.

11

Tuesday 9 February 2021

Today I saw Xan for the first time in three years. There was no difficulty in getting an appointment, although it wasn't his face that appeared on the televiewer, but one of his aides, a Grenadier with sergeant's stripes. Xan is guarded, cooked for, driven, serviced by a small company of his private army; even from the beginning no women secretaries or personal assistants, no women housekeepers or cooks were employed at the court of the Warden. I used to wonder whether this was to avoid even the hint of sexual scandal or whether the loyalty Xan demanded was essentially masculine: hierarchical, unquestioning, unemotional.

He sent a car for me. I told the Grenadier that I would prefer to drive to London myself, but he merely said with unemphatic finality: "The Warden will send a car and driver, sir. He will be at the door at nine-thirty."

Somehow I had expected that it would still be George, who was my regular driver when I was Xan's adviser. I liked George. He had a cheerful, engaging face with protruding ears, a wide mouth and a rather broad, retroussé nose. He seldom spoke, and never unless I began the conversation. I suspected that all drivers worked under that prohibition. But there emanated from him—or so I liked to believe—a spirit of general goodwill, perhaps even of approval, which made our drives together a restful and anxiety-free interlude between the frustrations of Council meetings and the unhappiness of home. This driver was leaner, aggressively smart in his apparently new uniform, and the eyes which met mine gave nothing away, not even dislike.

I said: "Is George no longer driving?"

"George is dead, sir. An accident on the A4. My name is Hedges. I shall be your driver on both journeys."

It was difficult to think of George, that skilled and meticulously careful driver, being involved in a fatal accident, but I asked no more questions. Something told me that curiosity would be unsatisfied and further inquiry unwise.

There was no point in attempting to rehearse the interview to come or in speculating how Xan would receive me after three years' silence. We hadn't parted in anger or bitterness but I knew that what I had done had in his eyes been inexcusable. I wondered whether it was also unforgivable. He was used to getting what he wanted. He had wanted me at his side, and I had defected. But now he had agreed to see me. In less than an hour I should know whether he wanted the breach to be permanent. I wondered whether he had told any other members of the Council that I'd asked for an interview. I neither expected nor wished to see them, that part of my life is over, but I thought of them as the car sped smoothly, almost silently, towards London.

There are four of them. Martin Woolvington, in charge of Industry and Production; Harriet Marwood, responsible for Health, Science and Recreation; Felicia Rankin, whose Home Affairs portfolio, something of a ragbag, includes Housing and Transport; and Carl Inglebach, Minister for Justice and State Security. The allocation of responsibility is more a convenient way of dividing the workload than the conferring of absolute authority. No one, at least while I attended the Council meetings, was inhibited from encroaching on another's field of interest, and decisions were taken by the whole Council by a majority vote in which, as Xan's adviser, I had no part. Was it, I wondered now, this humiliating exclusion rather than any awareness of my ineffectiveness which had made my position intolerable?

Influence was no substitute for power.

Martin Woolvington's use to Xan and the justification for his place on the Council is no longer
in doubt and must have strengthened since my
defection. He is the member with whom Xan is
most intimate, the one he probably comes closest
to calling a friend. They were in the same regiment, serving as subalterns together, and Woolvington was one of the first men Xan appointed to
serve on the Council. Industry and Production is
one of the heaviest portfolios, including, as it
does, agriculture, food and power, and the direction of labour. In a Council notable for high intelligence, Woolvington's appointment at first
surprised me. But he isn't stupid; the British Army
had ceased to value stupidity among its com-
manders long before the 1990s, and Martin more
than justifies his place by a practical, non-intellec-
tual intelligence and an extraordinary capacity for
hard work. He says little in Council but his contri-
butions are invariably apposite and sensible. His
loyalty to Xan is absolute. During Council meetings he was the only one who doodled. Doodling,
I had always thought, was a sign of minor stress,
a need to keep the hands busy, a useful expedient
for avoiding meeting the eyes of others. Martin's
doodling was unique. The impression he gave was
of a reluctance to waste time. He could listen with
half his mind and draw up on paper his battle

lines, plan his manoeuvres; could still draw his meticulous toy soldiers, usually in the uniform of the Napoleonic Wars. He would leave his papers on the table when he left and I was astounded at the detail and the skill of the drawings. I rather liked him, because he was invariably courteous and displayed none of the covert resentment at my presence which, morbidly sensitive to atmosphere, I thought I detected in all the others. But I never felt that I understood him and I doubt whether it ever occurred to him to try to understand me. If the Warden wanted me there, that was good enough for him. He is little more than medium height, with fair wavy hair and a sensitive, aesthetic face which reminded me strongly of a photograph I had seen of a 1930s film star, Leslie Howard. The resemblance, once detected, reinforced itself, imbuing him in my eyes with a sensibility and dramatic intensity which were foreign to his essentially pragmatic nature.

I never felt at ease with Felicia Rankin. If Xan had wanted a colleague who was both a young woman and a distinguished lawyer, he had less acerbic choices available to him. I have never been able to understand why he chose Felicia. Her appearance is extraordinary. She is invariably televised and photographed in profile or half-face and, seen thus, gives the impression of calm, conventional loveliness: the classic bone structure, the high arched eyebrows, the blond hair swept back into a chignon. When seen full-faced, the symmetry vanishes. It is as if her head has been fashioned from distinct halves, both attractive but put together in a discordance which, in certain lights, is close to deformity. The right eye is larger than the left, the forehead above it bulges slightly, the right ear is larger than its fellow. But the eyes are remarkable, huge with clear grey irises. Looking at them when her face was in repose, I used to wonder what it felt like to be cheated so spectacularly of beauty by so minute a margin. Sometimes in Council I found it difficult to keep my eyes from her and she would suddenly turn her head and catch my quickly averted eyes with her own bold contemptuous glance. I wondered now how much my morbid obsession with her looks had fuelled our mutual antipathy.

Harriet Marwood, at sixty-eight the oldest member, is responsible for Health, Science and Recreation, but her main function on the Council was obvious to me after the first meeting I attended and is indeed obvious to the whole country. Harriet is the wise old woman of the tribe, the universal grandmother, reassuring, comforting, always there, upholding her own outdated standard of manners and taking it for granted that the grandchildren will conform. When she appears on television screens to explain the latest instruction it's impossible not to believe that all is for the best. She could make a law requiring universal suicide seem eminently reasonable; half the country, I suspect, would immediately comply. Here is the wisdom of age, certain, uncompromising, caring. Before Omega she was head of a girls' public school and teaching was her passion. Even as headmistress she had continued to teach the sixth form. But it was the young she wanted to teach. She despised my compromise of taking a job in adult education, spooning out the pabulum of popular history and even more popular literature to the bored middle-aged. The energy, the enthusiasm she had given as a young woman to teaching is now given to the Council. They are her pupils, her children, and, by a process of extension, so is the whole country. I suspect that Xan finds her useful in ways I can't guess. I also think her extremely dangerous.

People who bother to cogitate about the personalities of the Council say that Carl Inglebach is the brain, that the brilliant planning and administration of the tightly knit organization which holds the country together has been formulated within that high domed head, that without his administrative genius the Warden of England would be ineffectual. It's the kind of thing that gets said about the powerful and he may have encouraged it, although I doubt that. He is impervious to public opinion. His creed is simple. There are things about which nothing can be done and to try to change them is a waste of time. There are things that ought to be changed and, the decision once made, the change should be put in hand without procrastination or clemency. He is the most sinister member of the Council and, after the Warden, the most powerful.

I didn't speak to my driver until we reached the Shepherd's Bush roundabout, when I leaned forward, tapped the window between us and said: "I'd like you to drive through Hyde Park then down Constitution Hill and Birdcage Walk if you will."

He said, without a motion of his shoulders or any expression in his voice: "That, sir, is the route the Warden has instructed me to take."

We drove in front of the palace, its windows shuttered, the flagpole without its standard, the sentry boxes empty, the great gates closed and padlocked. St. James's Park looked more unkempt than when I had last seen it. This was one of the parks which the Council had decreed should be properly maintained and there was, in fact, a distant group of toiling figures wearing the yellow-and-brown overalls of Sojourners, picking up rubbish and apparently clipping the edges of the still-bare flowerbeds. A wintry sun lit the surface of the lake on which the bright plumage of two mandarin ducks stood out like painted toys. Under the trees lay a thin powder of last week's snow and I saw, with interest but with no lifting of the heart, that the nearer patch of white was a drift of the first snowdrops.

There was very little traffic in Parliament Square and the iron gates to the entrance of the Palace of Westminster were closed. Here once a year Parliament meets, the Members elected by the District and Regional Councils. No bills are debated, no legislation is enacted, Britain is governed by decree of the Council of England. The official function of Parliament is to discuss, advise, receive information and make recommendations. Each of the five members of the Council reports personally in what the media describe as the annual message to the nation. The session lasts only for a month and the agenda is set by the Council. The subjects discussed are innocuous. Resolutions by a two-thirds majority go to the Council of England, who can reject or accept as they will. The system has the merit of simplicity and gives the illusion of democracy to people who no longer have the energy to care how or by whom they are governed as long as they get what the Warden has promised: freedom from fear, freedom from want, freedom from boredom.

For the first few years after Omega, the King, still uncrowned, opened Parliament with the old splendour, but driving through almost empty streets. From being the potent symbol of continuity and tradition, he has become an unemployable archaic reminder of what we have lost. Now he still opens Parliament, but quietly, wearing a lounge suit, stealing in and out of London almost unnoticed.

I could remember a conversation I'd had with Xan the week before I resigned my post. "Why don't you get the King crowned? I thought you were anxious to maintain normality."

"What would be the point of it? People aren't interested. They would resent the huge expense of a ceremony which has become meaningless."

"We hardly ever hear of him. Where is he, under house arrest?"

Xan had given his inward laugh. "Hardly house. Palace or castle arrest, if you like. He's comfortable enough. Anyway I don't think that the Archbishop of Canterbury would agree to crown him."

And I remembered my reply. "That's hardly surprising. You knew when you appointed Margaret Shivenham to Canterbury that she was a fervent republican."

Just inside the railings of the park, walking in line along the grass, came a company of flagellants. They were naked to the waist, wearing, even in the cold of February, nothing but yellow loincloths and sandals on their bare feet. As they walked they swung back the heavy knotted cords to lacerate already bleeding backs. Even through the car window I could hear the whistle of the leather, the thud of the whips on naked flesh. I looked at the back of the driver's head, the half moon of meticulously cropped dark hair under the cap, the single mole above the collar which had irritatingly held my gaze for most of the silent journey.

Now, determined to get some response from him, I said: "I thought this kind of public display had been made illegal."

"Only on the public highway or pavement, sir. I imagine they feel they're entitled to walk through a park."

I asked: "Do you find the spectacle offensive? I gather that was why the flagellants were banned. People dislike the sight of blood."

"I find it ridiculous, sir. If God exists and He's decided He's had enough of us, He isn't going to change His mind because a rabble of no-hopers dress up in yellow and go wailing through the park."

"Do you believe in Him? Do you believe He exists?"

We had drawn up now at the door of the old Foreign Office. Before getting out to open the door for me he looked round and gazed into my face. "Perhaps His experiment went spectacularly wrong, sir. Perhaps He's just baffled. Seeing the mess, not knowing how to put it right. Perhaps not wanting to put it right. Perhaps He only had enough power left for one final intervention. So He made it. Whoever He is, whatever He is, I hope He burns in His own hell."

He spoke with extraordinary bitterness, and then his face assumed its cold, immobile mask. He stood to attention and opened the door of the car.

12

The Grenadier on duty inside the door was one Theo recognized. He said, "Good morning, sir," and smiled almost as if there had been no lapse of three years and Theo was entering as of right to take his appointed place. Another Grenadier, this time unknown to him, came forward and saluted. Together they mounted the ornate staircase.

Xan had rejected Number Ten Downing Street as both his office and residence, and had chosen instead the old Foreign and Commonwealth building overlooking St. James's Park. Here he had his private flat on the top floor, where, as Theo knew, he lived in an ordered and comfortable simplicity which is only achievable when buttressed by money and staff. The room at the front of the building, used twenty-five years ago by the Foreign Secretary, had from the first been both Xan's office and the Council chamber.

Without knocking, the Grenadier opened the

door and loudly announced his name.

He found himself facing, not Xan, but the full Council. They were sitting at the same small oval table he remembered, but along one side only and closer than was usual. Xan was in the middle, flanked by Felicia and Harriet, with Martin on the far left, Carl on his right. A single vacant chair had been placed immediately opposite Xan. It was a calculated ploy obviously intended to disconcert him, and momentarily it succeeded. He knew that the five pairs of watching eyes hadn't missed his involuntary hesitation at the door, the flush of annoyance and embarrassment. But surprise gave way to a spurt of anger and the anger was helpful. They had taken the initiative, but there was no reason why they should retain it.

Xan's hands were lying lightly on the table, the fingers curved. Theo saw the ring with a shock of recognition and knew that he was meant to recognize it. It could hardly have been concealed. Xan was wearing on the third finger of his left hand the Coronation Ring, the wedding ring of England, the great sapphire surrounded with diamonds and surmounted with a cross of rubies. He looked down at it, smiled, and said: "An idea of Harriet's. It would look appallingly vulgar if one didn't know that it was real. The people need their baubles. Don't worry, I'm not proposing to have

myself anointed by Margaret Shivenham in Westminster Abbey. I doubt whether I could get
through the ceremony with the appropriate grav-
ity. She looks so ridiculous in her mitre. You're
thinking that there was a time when I wouldn't
have worn it."

Theo said: "A time when you wouldn't have
felt the need to wear it." He could have added:
"Nor the need to tell me that it was Harriet's
idea."

Xan motioned towards the empty chair. Theo
took it and said: "I asked for a personal interview
with the Warden of England and I understood
that was what I was getting. I'm not applying for
a job, nor am I a candidate for a viva voce."

Xan said: "It's three years since we met or
spoke. We thought you might like to meet old—
what would you say, Felicia?—friends, comrades,
colleagues?"

Felicia said: "I would say acquaintances. I
never understood Dr. Faron's precise function
when he was Warden's Adviser and it hasn't
become clearer with his absence and the passing
of three years."

Woolvington looked up from his doodling. The
Council must have been sitting for some time. He
had already massed a company of foot soldiers.
He said: "It never was clear. The Warden asked

for him and that was good enough for me. He didn't contribute very much, as I remember, but neither did he hinder."

Xan smiled, but the smile didn't reach his eyes. "That's in the past. Welcome back. Say what you've come to say. We're all friends here." He made the banal words sound like a threat.

There was no point in circumlocution. Theo said: "I was at the Quietus at Southwold last Wednesday. What I saw was murder. Half of the suicides looked drugged and those who did know what was happening didn't all go willingly. I saw women dragged on to the boat and shackled. One was clubbed to death on the beach. Are we culling our old people now like unwanted animals? Is this murderous parade what the Council means by security, comfort, pleasure? Is this death with dignity? I'm here because I thought you ought to know what's being done in the Council's name."

He told himself: I'm being too vehement. I'm antagonizing them before I've really started. Keep it calm.

Felicia said: "That particular Quietus was mismanaged. Things got out of control. I've asked for a report. It's possible that some of the guards exceeded their duties."

Theo said: "Someone exceeded his duties. Hasn't that always been the excuse? And why do we need armed guards and shackles if these people are going willingly to their death?"

Felicia explained again with barely controlled impatience: "That particular Quietus was mismanaged. Appropriate action will be taken against those responsible. The Council notes your concern, your rational, indeed laudable, concern. Is that all?"

Xan appeared not to have heard her question. He said: "When my turn comes I propose to take my lethal capsule comfortably in bed at home and preferably on my own. I've never quite seen the point of the Quietus, although you seemed keen on them, Felicia."

Felicia said: "They began spontaneously. About twenty eighty-year-olds in a home in Sussex decided to organize a coach party to Eastbourne, then, hand in hand, jumped over Beachy Head. It became something of a fashion. Then one or two Local Councils thought they ought to meet an obvious need and organize the thing properly. Jumping off cliffs may be an easy way out for the old people but someone has the unpleasant job of clearing away the bodies. One or two of them actually survived for a short time, I believe. The whole thing was messy and unsatisfactory. Towing them out to sea was obviously more sensible."

Harriet leaned forward, her voice persuasive, reasonable: "People need their rites of passage and they want company at the end. You have the strength to die alone, Warden, but most people find it comforting to feel the touch of a human hand."

Theo said: "The woman I saw die didn't get the touch of a human hand except, briefly, mine. What she got was a pistol crack on her skull."

Woolvington did not bother to look up from his doodling. He muttered: "We all die alone. We shall endure death as once we endured birth. You can't share either experience."

Harriet Marwood turned to Theo. "The Quietus is, of course, absolutely voluntary. There are all the proper safeguards. They have to sign a form—in duplicate, is it, Felicia?"

Felicia said curtly: "In triplicate. One copy for the Local Council, one to the nearest relation so that they can claim the blood money, and one is retained by the old person and collected when they board the boat. That goes to the Office of Census and Population."

Xan said: "As you see, Felicia has it all under control. Is that all, Theo?"

"No. The Man Penal Colony. Do you know what's happening there? The murders, the starvation, the complete breakdown of law and order."

Xan said: "We do. The question is, how do you know?"

Theo didn't reply, but in his heightened awareness the question sounded a clear warning bell.

Felicia said: "I seem to remember that you were present at our meeting in your somewhat ambiguous capacity when the setting up of the Man Penal Colony was under discussion. You made no objection except on behalf of the then resident population, whom we proposed to resettle on the mainland. They have been resettled, comfortably and advantageously, in their chosen parts of the country. We get no complaints."

"I assumed that the Colony would be properly run, that the basic necessities for a reasonable life would be provided."

"They are. Shelter, water and seeds to grow food."

"I assumed, also, that the Colony would be policed, governed. Even in the nineteenth century, when convicts were deported to Australia, the settlements had a governor, some liberal, some draconian, but all responsible for the maintenance of peace and order. The settlements weren't left to the mercy of the strongest and most criminal of the convicts."

Felicia said: "Weren't they? That's a matter of opinion. But we're not dealing with the same situation. You know the logic of the penal system. If people choose to assault, rob, terrify, abuse and exploit others, let them live with people of the same mind. If that's the kind of society they want, then give it to them. If there is any virtue in them, then they'll organize themselves sensibly and live at peace with each other. If not, their society will degenerate into the chaos they're so ready to impose on others. The choice is entirely theirs."

Harriet broke in: "As for employing a governor or prison officers to enforce order, where will you find these people? Have you come here to volunteer? And if you won't, who will? People have had enough of criminals and criminality. They aren't prepared today to live their lives in fear. You were born in 1971, weren't you? You must remember the 1990s, women afraid to walk the streets of their own cities, the rise in sexual and violent crime, old people self-imprisoned in their flats— some burned to death behind their bars—drunken hooligans ruining the peace of country towns, children as dangerous as their elders, no property safe if it wasn't protected with expensive burglar alarms and grilles. Everything has been tried to cure man's criminality, every type of so-called treatment, every regime in our prisons. Cruelty and severity didn't work, but neither did kindness and leniency. Now, since Omega, the people have said to us: 'Enough is enough.' The priests, the psychiatrists, the psychologists, the criminologists—none has found the answer. What we guarantee is freedom from fear, freedom from want, freedom from boredom. The other freedoms are pointless without freedom from fear."

Xan said: "The old system wasn't entirely without profit, though, was it? The police got well paid. And the middle classes did very well out of it, probation officers, social workers, magistrates, judges, court officials, quite a profitable little industry all depending on the offender. Your profession, Felicia, did particularly well, exercising their expensive legal skills in getting people convicted so that their colleagues could have the satisfaction of getting the verdicts overturned on appeal. Today the encouragement of criminals is an indulgence we cannot afford, even to provide comfortable living for middle-class liberals. But I suspect the Man Penal Colony isn't the last of your concerns."

Theo said: "There's disquiet about the treatment of Sojourners. We import them as helots and treat them as slaves. And why the quota? If they want to come, let them in. If they want to leave, let them go."

Woolvington's first two lines of cavalry were complete, prancing elegantly across the top of the paper. He looked up and said: "You're not suggesting we should have unrestricted immigration? Remember what happened in Europe in the 1990s? People became tired of invading hordes, from countries with just as many natural advantages as this, who had allowed themselves to be misgoverned for decades through their own cowardice, indolence and stupidity and who expected to take over and exploit the benefits which had been won over centuries by intelligence, industry and courage, while incidentally perverting and destroying the civilization of which they were so anxious to become part."

Theo thought: They even speak alike now. But, whoever speaks, the voice is the voice of Xan. He said: "We're not talking about history. We've no shortage of resources, no shortage of jobs, no shortage of houses. Restricting immigration in a dying and underpopulated world isn't a particularly generous policy."

Xan said: "It never was. Generosity is a virtue for individuals, not governments. When governments are generous it is with other people's money, other people's safety, other people's future."

It was then Carl Inglebach spoke for the first time. He was sitting as Theo had seen him sit dozens of times, a little forward in his seat, his two fists clenched, lying precisely side by side downwards on the table, as if concealing some treasure which it was nevertheless important to let the Council know that he possessed, or perhaps as if about to play a childish game, opening one palm and then the other to display its transferred penny. He looked—was probably tired of being told so—like a benign edition of Lenin, with his domed polished head and black bright eyes. He disliked the constriction of ties and collars and the resemblance was accentuated by the fawn linen suit he always wore, beautifully tailored, high-necked and buttoned on the left shoulder. But now he was dreadfully different. Theo had seen at first glance that he was mortally ill, perhaps even close to death. The head was a skull with a membrane of skin stretched taut over the jutting bones, the scrawny neck stuck out tortoise-like from his shirt and his mottled skin was jaundiced. Theo had seen that look before. Only the eyes were unchanged, blazing from the sockets with small pinpoints of light. But when he spoke his voice was as strong as ever. It was as if all the strength left to him was concentrated in his mind and in the voice, beautiful and resonant, which gave that mind its utterance.

"You are a historian. You know what evils have been perpetrated through the ages to ensure the survival of nations, sects, religions, even of individual families. Whatever man has done for good or ill has been done in the knowledge that he has been formed by history, that his life-span is brief, uncertain, insubstantial, but that there will be a future, for the nation, for the race, for the tribe. That hope has finally gone except in the minds of fools and fanatics. Man is diminished if he lives without knowledge of his past; without hope of a future he becomes a beast. We see in every country in the world the loss of that hope, the end of science and invention, except for discoveries which may extend life or add to its comfort and pleasure, the end of our care for the physical world and our planet. What does it matter what turds we leave behind as legacies of our brief disruptive tenancy? The mass emigrations, the great internal tumults, the religious and tribal wars of the 1990s have given way to a universal anomie which leaves crops unsown and unharvested, animals neglected, starvation, civil war, the grabbing from the weak by the strong. We see reversions to old myths, old superstitions, even to human sacrifice, sometimes on a massive scale. That this country has been largely spared this universal catastrophe is due to the five people round this table. In particular it is due to the Warden of England. We have a system extending from this Council, down to the Local Councils, which retains a vestige of democracy for those few who still care. We have a humane direction of labour which pays some regard to individual wishes and talents, and which ensures that people continue to work even though they have no posterity to inherit the rewards of their labour. Despite the inevitable desire to spend, to acquire, to satisfy immediate wants, we have sound money and low inflation. We have plans that will ensure that the last generation fortunate enough to live in the multiracial boarding house we call Britain will have stored food, necessary medicines, light, water and power. Beside these achievements, does the country greatly care that some Sojourners are discontented, that some of the aged choose to die in company, that the Man Penal Colony isn't pacified?"

Harriet said: "You distanced yourself from those decisions, didn't you? It's hardly dignified to opt out from responsibility and then complain when you don't like the result of other people's efforts. You were the one who decided to resign, remember? You historians are happier living in the past anyway, so why not stay there?"

Felicia said: "It's certainly where he's most at home. Even when he killed his child he was going backwards."

In the silence, short but intense, which greeted this comment, Theo was able to say: "I don't deny what you've achieved, but would it really prejudice good order, comfort, protection, the things you offer people, if you made some reforms? Do away with the Quietus. If people want to kill themselves—and I'll agree it's a rational way to end—then issue them with the necessary suicide pills, but do it without mass persuasion or coercion. Send a force to the Isle of Man and restore some order there. Do away with the compulsory testing of sperm and the routine examination of healthy women; they're degrading and anyway they haven't worked. Close down the State porn shops. Treat the Sojourners like human beings not slaves. You can do any of those things easily. The Warden can do them with one signature. That's all I'm asking."

Xan said: "It seems to this Council that you're asking rather a lot. Your concern would have more weight with us if you were sitting, as you could be sitting, on this side of the table. Your position is no different from the rest of Britain. You desire the end but close your eyes to the means. You want the garden to be beautiful provided the smell of manure is kept well away from your fastidious nose."

Xan got to his feet and, one by one, the rest of the Council followed. But he didn't hold out his hand. Theo was aware that the Grenadier who had shown him in had moved quietly to his side as if in obedience to some secret signal. He almost expected a hand to clamp down on his shoulder. He turned without speaking and followed him out of the Council chamber.

13

The car was waiting. On seeing him the driver got out and opened the door. But suddenly Xan was at his side. He said to Hedges, "Drive to the Mall and wait for us at the Queen Victoria statue," and, turning to Theo, he said: "We'll walk in the park. Wait while I get my coat."

He was back in less than a minute wearing the familiar tweed which he invariably wore for outdoor television shots, slightly waisted, with two capes, Regency style, which in the early 2000s had for a brief time become fashionable and expensive. The coat was old but he had kept it.

Theo could remember when he had first ordered it, their conversation: "You're mad. All that for one coat."

"It'll last for ever."

"You won't. Nor will the fashion."

"I don't care about fashions. I shall like the style better when no one else is wearing it."

And no one was wearing it now.

They crossed the road into the park. Xan said: "You were unwise to come here today. There's a limit to how far I can protect you, you or the people you've been consorting with."

"I didn't think I needed protection. I'm a free citizen consulting the democratically elected Warden of England. Why should I need protection, yours or anyone's?"

Xan didn't answer. On impulse Theo said: "Why do you do it? Why on earth do you want the job?" It was, he thought, a question that only he could, or dared to, ask.

Xan paused before replying, narrowing and focusing his eyes on the lake as if something invisible to other eyes had suddenly interested him. But surely, thought Theo, he didn't need to hesitate. It must have been a question he'd thought over often enough. Then he turned, walked on, and said: "At first because I thought I'd enjoy it. The power, I suppose. But it wasn't only that. I could never bear to watch someone doing badly what I knew I could do well. After the first five years I found I was enjoying it less, but by then it was too late. Someone has to do it and the only people who want to are the four round that table. Would you prefer Felicia? Harriet? Martin? Carl? Carl could do it, but he's dying. The other three couldn't keep the Council together, let alone the country."

"So that's why. Disinterested public duty?"

"Have you ever known anyone to give up power, real power?"

"Some people do."

"And have you seen them, the walking dead? But it's not the power, not entirely. I'll tell you the real reason. I'm not bored. Whatever else I am now, I'm never bored."

They walked on in silence, skirting the lake. Then Xan said: "The Christians believe that the Last Coming has arrived except that their God is gathering them one by one instead of descending more dramatically in the promised clouds of glory. This way heaven can control the intake. It makes it easier to process the white-robed company of the redeemed. I like to think of God concerning Himself with logistics. But they'd give up their illusion to hear the laughter of one child."

Theo didn't reply. Then Xan said quietly: "Who are these people? You'd better tell me."

"There are no people."

"All that farrago in the Council room. You didn't think that out for yourself. I don't mean that you're incapable of thinking it out. You're capable of a great deal more than that. But you haven't cared for three years, and you didn't care greatly before then. You've been got at."

"Not by anyone specifically. I live in the real world even in Oxford. I queue at cash registers, I shop, I take buses, I listen. People sometimes talk to me. Not anyone I care about, just people. What I have is communication with strangers."

"Which strangers? Your students?"

"Not students. No one in particular."

"Odd that you've become so approachable. You used to go round with an impervious membrane of privacy, your private invisible caul. When you talk to these mysterious strangers, ask them if they can do my job better than I. If so, tell them to come and say so to my face; you're not a particularly persuasive emissary. It would be a pity if we had to close down the adult education school at Oxford. There'll be no option if the place becomes a focus for sedition."

"You can't mean that."

"It's what Felicia would say."

"Since when have you taken any notice of Felicia?"

Xan smiled his inward reminiscent smile. "You're right, of course. I don't take any notice of Felicia."

Crossing the bridge which spanned the lake, they paused to gaze towards Whitehall. Here, unchanged, was one of the most exciting views which London had to offer, English and yet exotic, the elegant and splendid bastions of Empire seen across shimmering water and framed in trees. Theo recalled lingering at just this spot a week after he had joined the Council, remembered contemplating the same view, Xan wearing the same coat. And he could recall every word they had said as clearly as if it had just been spoken.

"You should give up the compulsory testing of sperm. It's degrading and it's been done now for over twenty years without success. Anyway, you only test healthy, selected males. What about the others?"

"If they can breed, good luck to them, but while there are limited facilities for the testing, let's keep it for the physically and morally fit."

"So you're planning for virtue as well as health?"

"You could say, yes. No one with a criminal record or a family record of offending ought to be allowed to breed, if we have a choice."

"So the criminal law is to be the measure of virtue?"

"How else can it be measured? The State can't look into men's hearts. All right, it's rough and ready and we'll disregard small delinquencies. But why breed from the stupid, the feckless, the violent?"

"So in your new world there will be no room for the penitent thief?"

"One can applaud his penitence without wanting to breed from him. But look, Theo, it isn't going to happen. We plan for the sake of planning, pretending that man has a future. How many people really believe that we shall find live seed now?"

"And suppose you discover somehow that an aggressive psychopath has fertile sperm. Will you use that?"

"Of course. If he's the only hope, we'll use him. We'll take what we can get. But the mothers will be carefully chosen for health, intelligence, no criminal record. We'll try to breed out the psychopathy."

"Then there are the pornography centres. Are they really necessary?"

"You don't have to use them. There has always been pornography."

"State-tolerated but not State-provided."

"There's not so great a difference. And what harm do they do to people without hope? There's nothing like keeping the body occupied and the mind quiescent."

Theo had said: "But that isn't really what they're set up for, is it?"

"Obviously not. Man has no hope of reproducing himself if he doesn't copulate. Once that goes totally out of fashion we are lost."

But now, slowly, they moved on. Breaking a

silence which was almost companionable, Theo asked: "Do you often go back to Woolcombe?"

"That living mausoleum? The place appals me. I used to make the occasional duty visit to my mother. I haven't been back for five years. No one ever dies now at Woolcombe. What the place needs is its own Quietus by way of a bomb. Odd, isn't it? Almost the whole of modern medical research is dedicated to improving health in old age and extending the human life-span and we get more senility, not less. Extending it for what? We give them drugs to improve short-term memory, drugs to raise mood, drugs to increase appetite. They don't need anything to make them sleep, that's all they seem to do. What, I wonder, goes on in those senile minds during those long periods of half-consciousness. Memories, I suppose, prayers."

Theo said: "One prayer. 'That I may see my children's children and peace upon Israel.' Did your mother recognize you before she died?"

"Unfortunately, yes."

"You told me once that your father hated her."

"I can't think why. I suppose I was trying to shock you, or impress you. You were unshockable even as a boy. And nothing I've achieved, University, soldiering, becoming Warden, has really impressed you, has it? My parents got along all right. My father was gay, of course. Didn't you realize? I used to care desperately when I was a boy, now it seems supremely unimportant. Why shouldn't he live his life as he wished? I always have. That explains the marriage, of course. He wanted respectability and he needed a son, so he chose a woman who would be so dazzled by getting Woolcombe, a baronet and a title that she wouldn't complain when she found that that was all that she was getting."

"Your father never made any approach to me."

Xan laughed. "What an egotist you are, Theo. You weren't his type and he was morbidly conventional. Never shit in your own bed. Besides, he had Scovell. Scovell was in the car with him when he crashed. I managed to hush that up pretty effectively—out of a kind of filial piety, I suppose. I didn't care who knew it, but he would have cared. I was a bad enough son. I owed him that."

Suddenly Xan said: "We shan't be the last two men on earth. That privilege will go to an Omega, God help him. But if we were, what do you think we'd do?"

"Drink. Salute the darkness and remember the light. Shout out a roll-call of names and then shoot ourselves."

"What names?"

"Michelangelo, Leonardo da Vinci, Shakespeare, Bach, Mozart, Beethoven. Jesus Christ."

"This would be a roll-call of humanity. Leave

out the gods, the prophets, the fanatics. I should like the season to be midsummer, the wine to be claret, and the place the bridge at Woolcombe."

"And since we are, after all, English, we could end with Prospero's speech from *The Tempest*."

"If we weren't too old to remember the words and, when the wine was finished, too weak to hold the guns."

They were now at the end of the lake. On the Mall, backed by Queen Victoria's statue, the car was waiting. The chauffeur stood beside it, legs parted, arms folded, staring at them from under the rim of his cap. It was the stance of a gaoler, perhaps of an executioner. Theo pictured the cap replaced by a black skull-cap, the mask, the axe at his side.

Then he heard Xan's voice, Xan's parting words: "Tell your friends, whoever they are, to be sensible. If they can't be sensible, tell them to be prudent. I'm not a tyrant, but I can't afford to be merciful. Whatever it is necessary to do, I shall do."

He looked at Theo, who thought for one extraordinary moment that he saw in Xan's eyes a plea for understanding. Then he repeated: "Tell them, Theo. I shall do what needs to be done."

14

Theo still found it difficult to get used to crossing an empty St. Giles. The memory of his first days in Oxford, the rows of tightly parked cars under the elms, of his increasing frustration waiting to cross against the almost ceaseless traffic, must have taken a firmer hold than more auspicious or significant recollections to be so easily triggered. He still found himself instinctively hesitating at the kerb, still could not see this emptiness without surprise. Crossing the wide street with a quick glance to left and right, he cut down the cobbled lane at the side of the Lamb and Flag pub and walked to the museum. The door was closed and for a moment he feared that the museum was also, and was irritated that he hadn't bothered to telephone. But it opened as he turned the handle and he saw that the inner wooden door was ajar. He moved into the great square room of glass and iron.

The air was very cold, colder, it seemed, than the street outside, and the museum was empty except for an elderly woman, so muffled that only her eyes were visible between the striped woollen scarf and her cap, who was presiding at the counter of the shop. He could see that the same postcards were on display: pictures of dinosaurs, of gems, of butterflies, of the crisply carved capitals of the pillars, photographs of the founding fathers of this secular cathedral to Victorian confidence, John Ruskin and Sir Henry Ackland sitting together in 1874, Benjamin Woodward with his sensitive melancholy face. He stood silently looking up at the massive roof supported by its series of cast-iron pillars, at the embellished spandrels between the arches branching with such elegance into leaves, fruits, flowers, trees and shrubs. But he knew that his unfamiliar tingle of excitement, more worrying than pleasant, had less to do with the building than with his meeting with Julian, and he tried to control it by concentrating on the ingenuity and quality of the wrought-iron work, the beauty of the carvings. It was, after all, his period. Here was Victorian confidence, Victorian earnestness; the respect for learning, for craftsmanship, for art; the conviction that the whole of man's life could be lived in harmony with the natural world. He hadn't been in the museum for over three years, yet nothing had changed. Nothing, indeed, had changed since he had first entered it as an undergraduate except the notice which he remembered seeing propped against a pillar, welcoming children but admonishing them—ineffectually, he recalled—not to run about or make a noise. The dinosaur with its great hooked thumb still had pride of place. Studying it, he was again in his Kingston primary school. Mrs. Ladbrook had pinned a drawing of the dinosaur on the blackboard and had explained that the great unwieldy animal with its minute head had been all body but little brain, and had accordingly failed to adapt and had perished. Even at ten years of age he had found the explanation unconvincing. The dinosaur, with its small brain, had survived for a couple of million years; it had done better than *Homo sapiens.*

He passed through the arch at the far end of the main building into the Pitt Rivers Museum, one of the world's greatest ethnological collections. The exhibits were so close together that it was difficult to know whether she was already waiting there, standing perhaps beside the forty-foot totem pole. But when he paused he heard no answering footfall. The silence was absolute, and he knew that he was alone but knew, too, that she would come.

The Pitt Rivers seemed even more densely packed than on his last visit. In the cluttered show cabinets, model ships, masks, ivory and bead-work, amulets and votive offerings seemed mutely to offer themselves for his attention. He made his path between the cases and paused at last before an old favourite, still on display but with its label now so brown and faded that the print was hardly decipherable. It was a necklace of twenty-three curved and polished teeth of the sperm whale, given by King Thakombau in 1874 to the Reverend James Calvert and presented to the museum by his great-grandson, a pilot officer who had died of wounds early in the Second World War. Theo felt again the fascination he had felt as an undergraduate with the strange concatenation of events which linked the hands of a Fijian carver with the young doomed airman. He pictured again the ceremony of presentation, the King on his throne ringed by his grass-skirted warriors, the serious-faced missionary accepting the curious tribute. The 1939–45 war had been his own grandfather's war; he, too, had been killed serving with the RAF, shot down in a Blenheim bomber on the great raid over Dresden. As an undergraduate, obsessed always with the mystery of time, he had liked to think that this gave him, also, a tenuous link with that long-dead King whose bones lay on the other side of the world.

And then he heard the footsteps. He looked round but waited until Julian moved beside him.

Her hair was uncovered but she was wearing a padded jacket and trousers. When she spoke, her breath rose in small bursts of mist.

"I'm sorry I'm late. I cycled and got a puncture. Did you see him?"

There was no greeting between them and he knew that, for her, he was just a messenger. He moved away from the showcase and she followed, looking from side to side, hoping, he supposed, to give the impression, even in this obvious emptiness, of two visitors who had casually met. It wasn't convincing and he wondered why she bothered.

He said: "I saw him. I saw the whole Council. Later I saw the Warden alone. I did no good; I may have done some harm. He knew that someone had prompted my visit. Now if you do go ahead with your plans, he's been warned."

"You explained to him about the Quietus, the treatment of the Sojourners, what's happening on the Isle of Man?"

"That's what you asked me to do and that's what I did. I didn't expect to be successful and I wasn't. I know him. Oh, he may make some changes, although he gave no promises. He'll probably shut down the remaining porn shops, but gradually, and liberalize the regulations for compulsory semen testing. It's a waste of time, anyway, and I doubt whether he's got the lab technicians to keep it going on a national scale much longer. Half of them have stopped caring. I missed two appointments last year and no one bothered to check up. I don't think he'll do anything about the Quietus except, perhaps, to ensure that in future it's better organized."

"And the Man Penal Colony?"

"Nothing. He won't waste men and resources on pacifying the island. Why should he? Setting up the Penal Colony is probably the most popular thing he's ever done."

"And the treatment of the Sojourners? Giving them full civil rights, a decent life here, the chance to stay?"

"That seems very unimportant to him compared to what is important: the good order of Britain, ensuring that the race dies with some dignity."

She said: "Dignity? How can there be dignity if we care so little for the dignity of others?"

They were close now to the great totem pole. Theo ran his hands over the wood. Not bothering to look at it, she said: "So we shall have to do what we can."

"There's nothing you can do except in the end get yourselves killed or sent to the island—that is, if the Warden and the Council are as ruthless as you apparently believe. As Miriam can tell you, death would be preferable to the island."

She said, as if considering a serious plan: "Perhaps if a few people, a group of friends, got themselves exiled to the island deliberately, they could do something to change things. Or if we offered to go there voluntarily, why should the Warden forbid us, why should he care? Even a small group could help if they arrived in love."

Theo could hear the contempt in his voice. "Holding up the Cross of Christ before the savages, as the missionaries did in South America. Like them, get yourselves butchered on the beaches? Don't you read any history? There are only two reasons for that kind of folly. One is that you have a yearning for martyrdom. There's nothing new in that, if it's the way your religion takes you. I've always seen it as an unhealthy mixture of masochism and sensuality but I can see its appeal to a certain cast of mind. What is new is that your martyrdom won't even be commemorated, won't even be noticed. In seventy-odd years it will have no possible value because there will be no one left on earth to give it value, no one even to put up a small wayside shrine to the new Oxford martyrs. The second reason is more ignoble and Xan would understand it very well. If you did succeed, what an intoxication of power! The Isle of Man pacified, the violent living in peace, crops sown and harvested, the sick cared for, Sunday services in the churches, the redeemed kissing the hands of the living saint who made it all possible. Then you'll know what the Warden of England feels every waking moment, what he enjoys, what he can't do without. Absolute power in your little kingdom. I can see the attraction of that; but it won't happen."

They stood together for a moment in silence, then he said quietly: "Let it go. Don't waste the rest of your life on a cause that is as futile as it's impossible. Things will get better. In fifteen years' time—and that's such a little space—90 per cent of the people living in Britain will be over eighty. There won't be the energy for evil any more than there will be the energy for good. Think what that England will be like. The great buildings empty and silent, the roads unrepaired, stretching between the overgrown hedges, the remnants of humanity huddling together for comfort and protection, the running-down of services of civilization and then, at the end, the failure of power and light. The hoarded candles will be lit and soon even the last candle will flicker and die. Doesn't that make what's happening on the Isle of Man seem unimportant?"

She said: "If we are dying we can die as human beings, not as devils. Goodbye, and thank you for seeing the Warden."

But he had to make one more effort. He said: "I can't think of any group less equipped to confront

the apparatus of state. You've no money, no resources, no influence, no popular backing. You
haven't even a coherent philosophy of revolt.
Miriam is doing it to avenge her brother. Gascoigne, apparently, because the Warden has ap-
propriated the word Grenadiers. Luke out of
some vague Christian idealism and a yearning for
such abstracts as compassion, justice and love.
Rolf hasn't even the justification of moral indignation. His motive is ambition; he resents the
Warden's absolute power and would like it for
himself. You're doing it because you're married to
Rolf. He's dragging you into dreadful danger to
satisfy his own ambitions. He can't compel you.
Leave him. Break free."

She said gently: "I can't not be married to him.
I can't leave him. And you're wrong, that isn't the
reason. I'm with them because this is something I
have to do."

"Yes, because Rolf wants you to."

"No, because God wants me to."

He wanted to bang his head against the totem
pole in his frustration. "If you believe He exists,
then presumably you believe that He gave you
your mind, your intelligence. Use it. I thought you
would have been too proud to make such a fool of
yourself."

But she was impervious to such facile blandish-
ments. She said: "The world is changed not by the

self-regarding, but by men and women prepared to make fools of themselves. Goodbye, Dr. Faron. And thank you for trying." She turned without touching him and he watched her leave.

She hadn't asked him not to betray them. She didn't need to, but he was glad all the same that the words hadn't been spoken. And he could have given no promise. He didn't believe that Xan would condone torture, but for him the threat of torture would have been enough, and it struck him for the first time that he had, perhaps, misjudged Xan for the most naïve of reasons; he couldn't believe that a man who was highly intelligent, who had humour and charm, a man he had called his friend, could be evil. Perhaps it was he, not Julian, who needed a lesson in history.

15

The group didn't wait long. Two weeks after his meeting with Julian he came down to breakfast and found among the scatter of post on the mat a sheet of folded paper. The printed words were headed by the precisely drawn picture of a small herring-like fish. It was like a child's drawing; trouble had been taken. Theo read the message underneath with exasperated pity.

TO THE PEOPLE OF BRITAIN
We cannot shut our eyes any longer to the evils in our society. If our race is to die, let us at least die as free men and women, as human beings, not as devils. We make the following demands to the Warden of England.

1. Call a general election and put your policies before the people.
2. Give the Sojourners full civil rights includ-

ing the right to live in their own homes, to send for their families and to remain in Britain at the end of their contract of service.

3. Abolish the Quietus.

4. Stop deporting convicted offenders to the Isle of Man Penal Colony and ensure that people already there can live in peace and decency.

5. Stop the compulsory testing of semen and the examination of healthy young women and shut down the public porn shops.

THE FIVE FISHES

The words confronted him in their simplicity, their reasonableness, their essential humanity. Why was he so certain, he wondered, that they had been written by Julian? And yet they could do no good. What were the Five Fishes proposing? That people should march in force on their Local Council or should storm the old Foreign Office building? The group had no organization, no basis of power, no money, no apparent plan of campaign. The most they could hope for would be to make people think, to provoke discontent, to encourage men not to attend their next semen testing and women to refuse their next medical examination. And what difference would that make? The examinations were becoming increasingly perfunctory as hope died.

The paper was of cheap quality, the message amateurishly printed. Presumably they had a press hidden in some church crypt or remote but accessible forest shed. But how long would it remain secret if the SSP troubled to hunt them down?

Once more he read the five demands. The first was unlikely to worry Xan. The country would hardly welcome the expense and disruption of a general election but, if he called one, his power would be confirmed by an overwhelming majority whether or not anyone had the temerity to stand against him. Theo asked himself how many of the other reforms he might have achieved had he stayed as Xan's adviser. But he knew the answer. He had been powerless then and the Five Fishes were powerless now. If there had been no Omega, these were aims which a man might be prepared to fight for, even to suffer for. But if there had been no Omega, the evils would not exist. It was reasonable to struggle, to suffer, perhaps even to die, for a more just, a more compassionate society, but not in a world with no future where, all too soon, the very words "justice," "compassion," "society," "struggle," "evil," would be unheard echoes on an empty air. Julian would say that it was worth the struggle and the suffering to save even one Sojourner from ill-treatment or prevent even one offender from being deported to the Man Penal Colony. But whatever the Five Fishes did, that wouldn't happen. It wasn't within their power. Rereading the five demands he felt a draining-away of his initial sympathy. He told himself that most men and women, human mules deprived of posterity, yet carried their burden of sorrow and regret with such fortitude as they could muster, contrived their compensating pleasures, indulged small personal vanities, behaved with decency to each other and to such Sojourners as they met. By what right did the Five Fishes seek to impose upon these stoical dispossessed the futile burden of heroic virtue? He took the paper into the lavatory and, after tearing it precisely into quarters, flushed them down the bowl. As they were sucked, swirling, out of sight he wished for a second, no more, that he could share the passion and the folly which bound together that pitiably unarmoured fellowship.

16

Saturday 6 March 2021

Today Helena rang after breakfast and invited me
to tea to see Mathilda's kittens. She had sent me
a postcard five days ago to say that they had
arrived safely but I hadn't been invited to the
birthing party. I wondered whether there had
been one, or whether they had kept the birth as a
private indulgence, a shared experience which
would belatedly celebrate and consolidate their
new life together. Even so, it seemed unlikely that
they would forgo what is generally accepted to be
an obligation, the opportunity to let your friends
witness the miracle of emerging life. A maximum
of six people are usually invited to watch, but
from a carefully judged distance so as not to fret
or disturb the mother. And afterwards, if all goes
well, there is a celebratory meal, often with cham-
pagne. The arrival of a litter is not untinged with
sadness. The regulations regarding fecund domestic animals are plain and rigorously enforced.

Mathilda will now be sterilized and Helena and Rupert will be allowed to keep one female from the litter for breeding. Alternatively, Mathilda will be permitted one more litter and all but one male kitten will be painlessly destroyed.

After Helena's call I switched on the radio to listen to the eight o'clock news. Hearing the date broadcast, I realized for the first time that it is exactly one year today since she left me for Rupert. It is, perhaps, an appropriate day for my first visit to their home. I write "home" instead of "house" because I'm sure that is how Helena would describe it, dignifying a commonplace edifice in North Oxford with the sacramental importance of shared love and shared washing-up, commitment to total honesty and to a well-balanced diet, a new hygienic kitchen and hygienic sex twice a week. I wonder about the sex, half deploring my prurience, but telling myself that my curiosity is both natural and permissible. After all, Rupert is now enjoying, or perhaps failing to enjoy, the body which I once knew almost as intimately as I know my own. A failed marriage is the most humiliating confirmation of the transitory seduction of the flesh. Lovers can explore every line, every curve and hollow, of the beloved's body, can together reach the height of inexpressible ecstasy; yet how little it matters when love or lust at last dies and we are left with disputed possessions, lawyers' bills, the sad detritus of the lumber-room, when the house chosen, furnished, possessed with enthusiasm and hope has become a prison, when faces are set in lines of peevish resentment and bodies no longer desired are observed in all their imperfections with a dispassionate and disenchanted eye. I wonder whether Helena talks to Rupert about what went on between us in bed. I imagine so, not to would require greater self-control and greater delicacy than I have ever seen in her. There is a streak of vulgarity in Helena's carefully nurtured social respectability and I can imagine what she would tell him.

"Theo thought he was a wonderful lover, but it was all technique. You'd think he'd learned it from a sex manual. And he never talked to me, not really talked. I could be any woman."

I can imagine the words because I know that they are justified. I did her more harm than she did me, even if we take out of the calculation my killing of her only child. Why did I marry her? I married her because she was the Master's daughter and that conferred prestige; because she, too, had taken a degree in history and I thought we had intellectual interests in common; and because I found her physically attractive and was thus able to convince my frugal heart that, if this wasn't love, it was still as close to it as I was ever likely to get. Being the Master's son-in-law produced more irritation than pleasure (he really was an appallingly pompous man, no wonder Helena couldn't wait to get away from him); her intellectual interests were non-existent (she had been accepted by Oxford because she was the daughter of a college head and had, by hard work and good and expensive teaching, achieved the necessary three A-levels so that Oxford was able to justify a choice they wouldn't otherwise have made). The sexual attraction? Well, that lasted longer, although subject to the law of diminishing returns, until it was finally killed when I killed Natalie. There is nothing more effective than the death of a child for exposing, without any possibility of self-deceit, the emptiness of a failing marriage.

I wonder if Helena is having better luck with Rupert. If they are enjoying their sex life, they are among the fortunate minority. Sex has become among the least important of man's sensory pleasures. One might have imagined that with the fear of pregnancy permanently removed, and the unerotic paraphernalia of pills, rubber and ovulation arithmetic no longer necessary, sex would be freed for new and imaginative delights. The opposite has happened. Even those men and women who would normally have no wish to breed apparently need the assurance that they could have a child if they wished. Sex totally divorced from procreation has become almost meaninglessly acrobatic.

Women complain increasingly of what they describe as painful orgasms: the spasm achieved but not the pleasure. Pages are devoted to this common phenomenon in the women's magazines. Women, increasingly critical and intolerant of men throughout the 1980s and 1990s, have at last an overwhelming justification for the pent-up resentment of centuries. We who can no longer give them a child cannot even give them pleasure. Sex can still be a mutual comfort; it is seldom a mutual ecstasy. The government-sponsored porn shops, the increasingly explicit literature, all the devices to stimulate desire—none has worked. Men and women still marry, although less frequently, with less ceremony and often with the same sex. People still fall in love, or say that they are in love. There is an almost desperate searching for the one person, preferably younger but at least of one's own age, with whom to face the inevitable decline and decay. We need the comfort of responsive flesh, of hand on hand, lip on lip. But we read the love poems of previous ages with a kind of wonder.

Walking down Walton Street this afternoon, I felt no particular reluctance at the prospect of meeting Helena again, and I thought of Mathilda with anticipatory pleasure. As the registered part-owner on the fecund-domestic-animal licence I could, of course, have applied to the Animal Custody Court for joint custody or an access order, but I had no wish to submit myself to that humiliation. Some of the animal custody cases are fiercely, expensively and publicly fought and I have no intention of adding to their number. I know I have lost Mathilda and she, perfidious, comfort-loving creature as are all cats, will by now have forgotten me.

When I saw her it was difficult not to deceive myself. She lay in her basket with two pulsating kittens like sleek white rats, pulling gently at her teats. She gazed at me with her blue expressionless eyes and began a loud and raucous purring which seemed to shake the basket. I put out my hand and touched her silken head.

I said: "Did everything go all right?"

"Oh, perfectly. Of course, we've had the vet here from the beginning of labour, but he said he'd seldom seen an easier birth. He took away two of the litter. We're still deciding which of these two to keep."

The house is small, architecturally undistinguished, a semi-detached, brick-built suburban villa, its main advantage being the long rear garden sloping down to the canal. Much of the furniture and all the carpets looked new, chosen, I suspected, by Helena, who had thrown out the paraphernalia of her lover's old life, the friends, the clubs, the solitary bachelor consolations, with the family furniture and pictures bequeathed to him with the house. She had taken pleasure in making a home for him—I was sure this was the phrase she had used—and he basked in the result like a child with a new nursery. Everywhere there was the smell of fresh paint. The sitting-room, as is usual with this type of Oxford house, has had the rear wall removed to make one large room with a bay window at the front and French windows leading into a glass loggia at the rear. Down one wall of the white-painted hall has been hung a row of Rupert's original drawings for book jackets, each framed in white wood. There are a dozen in all and I wondered whether this public display had been Helena's idea or his. Either way, it justified me in a moment of contemptuous disapproval. I wanted to pause and study the drawings but that would have meant commenting on them and there was nothing I wanted to say. But even my cursory glance in passing showed me that they had considerable power; Rupert isn't a negligible artist; this egotistical display of talent merely confirmed what I already knew.

We had tea in the conservatory, an over-lavish feast of pâté sandwiches, home-made scones and fruitcake brought in on a tray with a newly starched linen tray-cloth and small matching napkins. The word that came to mind was "dainty." Looking at the cloth, I recognized it as one

Helena had been embroidering shortly before she left me. So this careful, drawn thread-work had been part of her adulterous household trousseau. Was this dainty feast—and I lingered on the pejorative adjective—designed to impress me, to show how good a wife she could be to a man prepared to appreciate her talents? It was obvious to me that Rupert appreciates them. He almost basked in her maternal cosseting. Perhaps as an artist he takes this solicitude as his due. The conservatory would, I thought, be cosy in spring and autumn. Even now, with only one radiator, it was comfortably warm and I could see dimly through the glass that they had been busy working on the garden. A row of spiky rose bushes, their root-balls shrouded in sackcloth, were propped against what looked like a new boundary fence. Security, comfort, pleasure. Xan and his Council would approve.

After tea Rupert briefly disappeared into the sitting-room. He returned and handed me a pamphlet. I recognized it at once. It was identical to that which the Five Fishes had pushed through my door. Pretending it was new to me, I read it with care. Rupert seemed to be waiting for some response. When I made none he said: "They were taking a risk going from door to door."

I found myself saying what I knew must have happened, irritated that I did know, that I couldn't keep my mouth shut.

"They wouldn't do it like that. This is hardly a parish magazine, is it? It would be delivered by someone on his or her own, perhaps riding a bicycle, perhaps on foot, putting a leaflet through the occasional door when there was no one about, leaving a few of them in bus shelters, sticking one under the windscreen-wiper of a parked car."

Helena said: "It's still a risk, though, isn't it? Or will be if the SSP decide to hunt them down."

Rupert said: "I don't suppose they'll bother. No one will take this seriously."

I asked: "Did you?"

He had, after all, kept it. The question, asked more sharply than I had intended, disconcerted him. He glanced at Helena and hesitated. I wondered whether over this they had disagreed. The first quarrel, perhaps. But I was being optimistic. If they had quarrelled, the leaflet would by now have been destroyed in the first exhilaration of reconciliation.

He said: "I did wonder whether we ought to mention it to the Local Council when we called in to have the kittens registered. We decided against it. I can't see what they can do—the Local Council, I mean."

"Except tell the SSP and get you arrested for possession of seditious material."

"Well, we did wonder about that. We didn't

want officials to think we support all this."

"Has anyone else in the street had one?"

"They haven't said, and we didn't like to ask."

Helena said: "These aren't things the Council can do anything about anyway. No one wants the Man Penal Colony closed down."

Rupert was still holding the pamphlet as if uncertain what to do with it. He said: "On the other hand, one does hear rumours about what goes on in the camps for Sojourners and I suppose, since they're here, that we ought to give them a fair deal."

Helena said sharply: "They get a better deal here than they'd get back home. They're glad enough to come. Nobody forces them. And it's ridiculous to suggest closing down the Penal Colony."

That was what was worrying her, I thought. It was crime and violence that threatened the little house, the embroidered tray-cloth, the cosy sitting-room, the conservatory with its vulnerable glass walls, its view of the dark garden in which she could now be confident that nothing malignant lurked.

I said: "They aren't suggesting that it should be closed. But you can argue that it ought to be properly policed and the convicts given a reasonable life."

"But that's not what these Five Fishes are suggesting. The paper says that the deportations should stop. They want it closed. And policed by whom? I wouldn't let Rupert volunteer for the job. And the convicts can have a reasonable life. It's up to them. The island is large enough and they have food and shelter. Surely the Council wouldn't evacuate the island. There would be an outcry—all those murderers and rapists loose again. And aren't the Broadmoor inmates there too? They're mad, mad and bad."

I noticed that she used the word "inmate," not "patient." I said: "The worst of them must be getting too old to present much danger."

She cried: "But some are only in their late forties and they're sending new people there every year. Over two thousand last year, wasn't it?" She turned to Rupert. "Darling, I think we ought to tear it up. There's no point in keeping it. We can't do anything. Whoever they are they have no right to print stuff like that. It only worries people."

He said: "I'll flush it down the lavatory."

When he'd gone out she turned to me. "You don't believe any of that, do you, Theo?"

"I can believe that life is peculiarly unpleasant on the Isle of Man."

She reiterated obstinately: "Well, that's up to the convicts themselves, isn't it?"

We didn't mention the leaflet again and ten

minutes later, after a final visit to Mathilda which Helena obviously expected of me and Mathilda tolerated, I left them. I'm not sorry I made the visit. It wasn't only the need to see Mathilda; our brief reunion had been pain rather than joy. Something left unfinished can now be put behind me. Helena is happy. She even looks younger, more handsome. The fair, willowy prettiness which I used to elevate into beauty has matured into an assured elegance. I can't honestly say I'm glad for her. It is difficult to be generous-minded to those we have greatly harmed. But at least I'm no longer responsible for her happiness or unhappiness. I have no particular wish to see either of them again, but I can think of them without bitterness or guilt.

There was only one moment shortly before I left when I felt more than a cynical, detached interest in their self-sufficient domesticity. I had left them to go to the lavatory, clean embroidered hand-towel, new soap, the bowl a frothy, disinfectant blue, a small bowl of potpourri; I noted and despised it all. On my quiet return I saw that, sitting a little apart, they had stretched out their hands across the gap to each other, then, hearing my step, had quickly, almost guiltily, drawn apart. That moment of delicacy, tact, perhaps even of pity, produced a second of conflicting emotions, experienced so faintly that they passed almost as soon as I recognized their nature. But I knew that what I had felt was envy and regret, not for something lost but for something never achieved.

17

Monday 15 March 2021

Today I had a visit from two members of the State Security Police. The fact that I am able to write this shows that I wasn't arrested and that they didn't find the diary. Admittedly they didn't search for it; they didn't search for anything. God knows the diary is incriminating enough to anyone interested in moral deficiencies and personal inadequacy, but their minds were on more tangible malefactions. As I said, there were two of them, a young man, obviously an Omega—extraordinary how one can always tell—and a senior officer, a little younger than I, who was carrying a raincoat and a black leather attaché case. He introduced himself as Chief Inspector George Rawlings and his companion as Sergeant Oliver Cathcart. Cathcart was saturnine, elegant, expressionless, a typical Omega. Rawlings, thickset, a little clumsy in his movements, had a disciplined thatch of thick grey-white hair, which

looked as if it had been expensively cut to emphasize the crimped waves at the side and back. His
face was strong-featured with narrow eyes, so
deep-set that the irises were invisible, and a long
mouth with the upper lip arrow-shaped, sharp as
a beak. Both were in civilian clothes, their suits
extremely well cut. In other circumstances, I
might have been tempted to inquire whether they
went to the same tailor.

It was eleven o'clock when they arrived. I
showed them into the ground-floor sitting-room
and asked whether they would like coffee. They
refused. Offered seats, Rawlings settled himself
comfortably in a chair by the fireplace while Cathcart, after a moment's hesitation, sat opposite
him, sitting stiffly upright. I took the swivel chair
at the desk and swung round to face them.

Rawlings said: "A niece of mine, my sister's
youngest, she just missed Omega by one year,
attended your little talks on Victorian Life and
Times. She's not a very intelligent woman, you
probably won't remember her. But, then, of
course, you might. Marion Hopcroft. It was a
small class, she said, and got smaller by the week.
People have no persistence. They take up en-
thusiasms but quickly tire, particularly if their
interest isn't continually stimulated."

In a few sentences he had reduced the lectures
to boring talks for a dwindling number of the

unintelligent. The ploy had not been subtle but, then, I doubt whether he dealt in subtlety. I said: "The name is familiar but I can't recall her."

"Victorian Life and Times. I thought the word 'times' was redundant. Why not just Victorian Life? Or you could have advertised Life in Victorian England."

"I didn't choose the title of the course."

"Didn't you? That's odd. I should have thought that you did. I think you should insist on choosing the title for your own talks."

I made no reply. I had little doubt that he knew perfectly well that I had taken the course for Colin Seabrook, but if he didn't I had no intention of enlightening him.

After a moment's silence which neither he nor Cathcart seemed to find embarrassing, he went on: "I thought I might take one of these adult courses myself. In history, not literature. But I wouldn't choose Victorian England. I'd go further back, the Tudors. I've always been fascinated by the Tudors, Elizabeth I particularly."

I said: "What attracts you about the period? The violence and the splendour, the glory of their achievements, the admixture of poetry and cruelty, those shrewd clever faces above the ruffs, that magnificent court underpinned by the thumbscrew and the rack?"

He seemed to consider the question for a moment, then said: "I wouldn't say the Tudor age was uniquely cruel, Dr. Faron. They died young in those days and I dare say most died in pain. Every age has its cruelties. And if we consider pain, dying of cancer without drugs which has been the lot of man through most of his history was a more horrible torment than anything the Tudors could devise. Particularly for the children, wouldn't you say? It's difficult to see the purpose of that, isn't it? The torment of children."

I said: "We should not, perhaps, assume that nature has a purpose."

He went on as if I hadn't spoken. "My grandfather, he was one of those hellfire preachers—thought that everything had a purpose, particularly pain. Born out of time, he would have been happier in your nineteenth century. I remember when I was nine I had a very bad toothache, an abscess. I said nothing, fearing the dentist, but then woke up one night in agony. My mother said we'd go along to the surgery as soon as it was open, but I lay until morning writhing with pain. My grandfather came in to see me. He said, 'We can do something about the small pains of this world but not about the everlasting pains of the world to come. Remember that, boy.' He certainly chose his moment well. Eternal toothache. It was a terrifying thought for a nine-year-old."

I said: "Or for an adult."

"Well, we've abandoned that belief, except for Roaring Roger. He still seems to have his following." He paused for a minute as if to ruminate on the fulminations of Roaring Roger, then went on without any change of tone: "The Council are worried, 'concerned' is perhaps a more appropriate word, about the activities of certain people."

He waited, perhaps for me to ask: "What activities? What people?" I said: "I have to leave in a little over half an hour. If your colleague wants to search the house perhaps he could do it now, while we're talking. There are one or two small things I value, the caddy-spoons in the Georgian display cabinet, the Staffordshire Victorian commemorative pieces in the drawing-room, one or two of the first editions. Normally I would expect to be present during a search but I have every confidence in the probity of the SSP."

With these last words I looked straight into Cathcart's eyes. They didn't even flicker.

Rawlings permitted in his voice a small note of reproach: "There's no question of a search, Dr. Faron. Why would you suppose, now, that we want to search? Search for what? You're not a subversive, sir. No, this is just a talk, a consultation if you like. As I said, there are things happening which cause some concern to the Council. I am speaking now, of course, in confidence. These matters have not been made public by newspapers, radio or TV."

I said: "That was wise of the Council. Troublemakers, assuming you've got them, feed on publicity. Why give it to them?"

"Exactly. It's taken governments a long time to realize that you don't need to manipulate unwelcome news. Just don't show it."

"And what aren't you showing?"

"Small incidents, unimportant in themselves, but possibly evidence of a conspiracy. The last two Quietus were interrupted. The ramps were blown up on the morning of the ceremony, just half an hour before the sacrificial victims—or perhaps 'victims' is hardly the appropriate word, let's say the sacrificial martyrs—were due to arrive."

He paused, then added: "But 'martyrs' is perhaps redundant. Let's say before the potential suicides were due to arrive. It caused them considerable distress. The terrorist, he or she, was cutting it rather fine. Thirty minutes later and the old people would have died rather more spectacularly than was planned. There was a telephone warning—a young male voice—but it came too late to do more than keep the crowds away from the scene."

I said: "An irritating inconvenience. I went to see a Quietus about a month ago. The ramp from which the boat embarked could, I should have thought, have been constructed fairly quickly. I don't suppose that particular act of criminal damage held up the Quietus for more than a day."

"As you implied, Dr. Faron, a minor inconvenience, but not, perhaps, without significance. There have been too many minor inconveniences recently. And then there are the pamphlets. Some of them are directed to the treatment of the Sojourners. The last batch of Sojourners, the sixty-year-olds and some who had fallen sick, had to be forcibly repatriated. There were unfortunate scenes at the quay. I don't say there's a connection between that débâcle and the dissemination of the pamphlets but it could be more than a coincidence. The distribution of political material among Sojourners is illegal but we know that the subversive pamphlets have been circulated in the camps. Other leaflets have been delivered house to house, complaining about the treatment of Sojourners generally, conditions on the Isle of Man, compulsory semen testing and what the dissidents apparently see as a defect in the democratic process. A recent one incorporated all these dissatisfactions in a list of demands. You may perhaps have seen it?"

He reached down to the black leather attaché case, lifted it on to his lap and clicked it open. He was playing the part of an avuncular casual caller, not very confident about the purpose of this visit, and I half-expected him to pretend to rummage ineffectively among his papers before finding the one he wanted. However, he surprised me by laying his hand on it immediately.

He passed it to me and said: "Have you seen one of these before, sir?"

I glanced at it and said: "Yes, I've seen it. One was pushed through my door a few weeks ago." There was little point in a denial. Almost certainly the SSP know that the leaflets have been distributed in St. John Street and why should my house have been neglected? After rereading it I handed it back.

"Has anyone else you know received one?"

"Not to my knowledge. But I imagine they must have been fairly widely disseminated. I wasn't interested enough to inquire."

Rawlings studied it as if it were new to him. He said: "The Five Fishes. Ingenious but not very clever. I suppose we look for a little group of five. Five friends, five family members, five fellow-workers, five fellow-conspirators. Perhaps they got the idea from the Council of England. It's a useful number, wouldn't you say, sir? In any discussion it ensures that there can always be a majority." I didn't reply. He went on: "The Five Fishes. I imagine they each have a code name probably based on forenames; that way it's easy for everyone to remember. *A* would be difficult, though. I can't offhand think of a fish with a name beginning with *A*. Perhaps none of them has *A* as an initial. They could have bream for *B,* I suppose, and *C* wouldn't be difficult: cod, codling. Dogfish would do for *D. E* might present a difficulty. Although I may, of course, be wrong, I reckon they wouldn't have chosen to call themselves the Five Fishes if they couldn't find an appropriate fish for each member of the gang. What do you think of that, sir? As a process of reasoning, I mean."

I said: "Ingenious. It's interesting to see the thought processes of the SSP in action. Few citizens can have had that opportunity, at least few citizens actually at liberty."

I might just as well not have spoken. He continued to study the pamphlet. Then he said: "A fish. Quite nicely drawn. Not, I think, by a professional artist, but by someone with a feeling for design. The fish is a Christian symbol. Could this be a Christian group, I wonder?" He looked up at me. "You admit that you had one of these pamphlets in your possession, sir, but you did nothing about it? You didn't feel that it was your duty to report?"

"I treated it as I treat all unimportant, unsolicited mail." Then, deciding it was time I went on the offensive, I said: "Forgive me, Chief Inspector, but I don't see what precisely is worrying the Council. There are malcontents in any society. This particular group have apparently done little harm apart from blowing up a couple of flimsy, temporary ramps and distributing some ill-thought-out criticisms of the government."

"Some might describe the pamphlets as seditious literature, sir."

"You can use what words you like, but you can hardly elevate this into a great conspiracy. You're surely not mobilizing the battalions of state security because a few bored malcontents prefer to amuse themselves by playing a more dangerous game than golf. What precisely is worrying the Council? If there is a group of dissidents they will be fairly young, or at least middle-aged. But time will pass for them, time is passing for all of us. Have you forgotten the figures? The Council of England reminds us of them often enough. A population of fifty-eight million in 1996, fallen to thirty-six million this year, 20 per cent of them over seventy. We're a doomed race, Chief Inspector. With maturity, with old age, all enthusiasm fades, even for the seductive thrill of conspiracy. There's no real opposition to the Warden of England. There never has been since he took power."

"It is our business, sir, to see that there isn't."

"You will, of course, do what you think is necessary. But I would only take this seriously if I thought that it was, in fact, serious: opposition, perhaps within the Council itself, to the authority of the Warden."

The words had been a calculated risk, perhaps even a dangerous one, and I saw that I had worried him. I had intended to.

After a moment's pause, which was involuntary, not calculated, he said: "If there were any question of that, the matter wouldn't be in my hands, sir. It would be dealt with at an altogether higher level."

I got to my feet. I said: "The Warden of England is my cousin and my friend. He was kind to me in childhood, when kindness is particularly important. I am no longer his adviser on the Council but that doesn't mean that I am no longer his cousin and his friend. If I have evidence of a conspiracy against him, I shall tell him. I shan't tell you, Chief Inspector, nor shall I get in touch with the SSP. I shall tell the person most concerned, the Warden of England."

This was play-acting, of course, and we knew it. We didn't shake hands or speak as I showed them out but this wasn't because I had made an enemy. Rawlings didn't permit himself the indulgence of personal antipathy any more than he would have allowed himself to feel sympathy, liking or the stirrings of pity for the victims he visited and interrogated. I thought I understood his kind: the petty bureaucrats of tyranny, men who relish the carefully measured meed of power permitted to them, who need to walk in the aura of manufactured fear, to know that the fear precedes them as they enter a room and will linger like a smell after they have left, but who have neither the sadism nor the courage for the ultimate cruelty. But they need their part of the action. It isn't sufficient for them, as it is for most of us, to stand a little way off to watch the crosses on the hill.

18

Theo closed the diary and put it in the top drawer of his desk, turning the key and slipping it into his pocket. The desk was well made, the drawers strong, but it would hardly resist an expert or determined assault. But then, one was hardly likely to be made and, if it were, he had taken care that his account of Rawlings's visit should be innocuous. That he felt this need to self-censor was, he knew, evidence of unease. He was irritated that the precaution was necessary. He had begun the diary less as a record of his life (for whom and why? What life?) than as a regular and a self-indulgent exploration, a means of making sense of the past years, part catharsis, part comforting affirmation. The diary, which had become a routine part of his life, was pointless if he had to censor, to leave out, if he had to deceive not illumine.

He thought back over the visit of Rawlings and Cathcart. He had been surprised at the time how unfrightening he had found them. After they had left he had felt a certain satisfaction in this lack of fear, in the competence with which he had handled the encounter. Now he wondered whether his confidence was justified. He had almost perfect recall of what had been said; verbal recall had always been one of his talents. But the exercise of writing down their elliptical conversation raised anxieties that he hadn't felt at the time. He told himself that he had nothing to fear. He had only lied directly once, when he had denied knowing anyone else who had received one of the Five Fishes pamphlets. It was a lie he could justify if challenged. Why, he would argue, should he name his ex-wife and expose her to the inconvenience and anxiety of a visit from the SSP? There was no particular relevance in the fact that she or anyone else had received a pamphlet; the sheets must have been pushed through practically every door on the street. One lie wasn't evidence of guilt. He was unlikely to be arrested because of one small lie. There was, after all, still law in England, at least for Britons.

He moved down to the drawing-room and walked restlessly about the wide room, mysteriously aware of the unlit and empty storeys above and beneath him as if each of those silent rooms held a menace. He paused at a window overlooking the street and looked out over the wrought-iron balcony. A thin rain was falling. He could see silver shafts falling against the street lights and, far below, the dark tackiness of the pavement. The curtains opposite had been drawn and the flat stone façade showed no sign of life, not even a chink where the curtains met. Depression settled on him like a familiar heavy blanket. Weighted with guilt and memory and anxiety, he could almost smell the accumulated rubbish of the dead years. His confidence drained away and fear strengthened. He told himself that during the encounter he had thought only of himself, his safety, his cleverness, his self-respect. But they weren't primarily interested in him, they were seeking Julian and the Five Fishes. He had given nothing away, he need feel no guilt about that, but still they had come to him, which meant they suspected he knew something. Of course they did. The Council had never really believed that his visit was entirely of his own volition. The SSP would come again; the next time the veneer of politeness would be thinner, the questions more searching, the outcome possibly more painful.

How much more did they know than Rawlings had revealed? Suddenly it seemed to him that they hadn't already pulled in the group for questioning. But perhaps they had. Was that the reason for the call today? Were they already holding Julian and the group and testing how far he was involved? And surely they could get on to Miriam quickly enough. He remembered his question to the Council about conditions on the Isle of Man, and the reply: "We know; the question is, how do you?" They were looking for someone who had knowledge of conditions on the island; and with visitors forbidden and no letters to or from the island permitted, no publicity, how could that knowledge have been gained? The escape of Miriam's brother would be on record. It was remarkable that once the Five Fishes began acting they hadn't taken her in for questioning. But perhaps they had. Perhaps even now she and Julian were in their hands.

His thoughts had come full circle and he felt for the first time an extraordinary loneliness. It wasn't an emotion with which he was familiar. He both distrusted and resented it. Looking down over the empty street, he wished for the first time that there was someone, a friend he could trust, in whom he could confide. Before she had left him, Helena had said: "We live in the same house, but we're like lodgers or guests in the same hotel. We never really talk." Irritated by such a banal, predictable complaint, the commonplace lament of discontented wives, he had answered: "Talk about what? Here I am. If you want to talk now, I'm listening."

It seemed to him that it would be a comfort

even to talk to her, to hear her reluctant and unhelpful response to his dilemma. And mixed with the fear, the guilt, the loneliness, there was a renewed irritation—with Julian, with the group, with himself that he had ever become involved. At least he'd done what they'd asked. He'd seen the Warden of England and then he'd warned Julian. It wasn't his fault that the group hadn't taken the warning. No doubt they would argue that he had an obligation to get a message to them, to let them know they were in danger. But they must know that they were in danger. And how could he warn them? He knew none of their addresses, where any of them worked or at what. The only thing he could do if Julian was taken would be to intercede with Xan on her behalf. But would he even know when she was arrested? It should be possible, if he searched, to find one of the gang, but how could he safely inquire without making the search obvious? From now on the SSP might even be keeping him under secret surveillance. There was nothing he could do but wait.

19

Friday 26 March 2021

I saw her today for the first time since our meeting in the Pitt Rivers Museum. I was buying cheese in the covered market and had turned from the counter with my small, carefully wrapped packets of Roquefort, Danish blue, Camembert, when I saw her only a few yards from me. She was choosing fruit, not shopping as I was for the increasingly finicky taste of one, but pointing out her choice without hesitation, holding out an open canvas bag with liberality to receive fragile brown bags almost bursting with the golden, pitted globes of oranges, the gleaming curves of bananas, the russet of Cox's Orange Pippins. I saw her in a glow of effulgent colour, skin and hair seeming to absorb radiance from the fruit, as if she were lit not by the hard glaring lights of the store, but by a warm southern sun. I watched while she handed over a note, then counted out coins to give the storekeeper the exact money, smiling as she handed it over, watched still as she hoisted the wide strap of the canvas bag over her shoulder, sagging a little with the weight. Shoppers shuffled between us but I stood rooted, unwilling, perhaps unable to move, my mind a tumult of extraordinary and unwelcome sensations. I was seized with a ludicrous urge to dash to the flower-stall, press notes into the florist's hands, seize from their tubs the bundles of daffodils, tulips, hot-house roses and lilies, pile them into her arms and take the bag from her encumbered shoulder. It was a romantic impulse, childish and ridiculous, which I hadn't felt since I was a boy. I had distrusted and resented it then. Now it appalled me by its strength, its irrationality, its destructive potential.

She turned, still not seeing me, and made her way towards the exit into the High Street. I followed, weaving my way through the Friday morning shoppers with their baskets on wheels, impatient when my path was momentarily blocked. I told myself that I was behaving like a fool, that I should let her pass out of sight, that she was a woman I had met only four times and on none of them had she shown any interest in me except an obstinate determination that I should do what she wanted, that I knew nothing about her except that she was married, that this overwhelming need to hear her voice, to touch her, was no more than the first symptom of the morbid

emotional instability of solitary middle age. I tried
not to hurry, a demeaning acknowledgement of
need. Even so, I managed to catch her up as she
turned into the High Street.

I touched her shoulder and said: "Good
morning."

Any greeting would have seemed banal. This at
least was innocuous. She turned towards me and
for a second I was able to deceive myself that her
smile was one of joyous recognition. But it was
the same smile she had given to the greengrocer.

I laid my hand on the bag and said: "May I
carry this for you?" I felt like an importunate
schoolboy.

She shook her head and said: "Thank you, but
the van is parked very close."

What van? I wondered. For whom was the fruit
intended? Surely not just for the two of them, Rolf
and herself. Did she work in some kind of institution? But I didn't ask, knowing that she wouldn't
have told me.

I said: "Are you all right?"

Again she smiled. "Yes, as you see. And you?"

"As you see."

She turned away. The action was gentle—she
had no wish to hurt me—but it was deliberate and
she meant it to be final.

I said in a low voice: "I have to speak to you.

It's important. It won't take long. Isn't there somewhere we can go?"

"It's safer in the market than here."

She turned back, and I walked at her side casually, not looking at her, two shoppers in the crowd forced into temporary proximity by the press of shuffling bodies. Once in the market she paused to look into a window where an elderly man and his assistant were selling flans and tarts fresh from the oven. I stood beside her, pretending an interest in the bubbling cheese, the seeping gravy. The smell came to me, savoury and strong, a remembered smell. They had been baking pies here since I was an undergraduate.

I stood watching as if considering what was on offer, then said very quietly into her ear: "The SSP have been to see me—they may be very close. They're looking for a group of five."

She turned from the window and walked on. I kept to her side.

She said: "Of course. They know there are five of us. There's no secret about that."

Standing at her shoulder, I said: "I don't know what else they've found out or guessed. Stop now. You're doing no good. There may not be much time. If the others won't stop then get out yourself."

It was then that she turned and looked at me.

Our eyes met for only a second but now, away from the flaming lights and the richness of the gleaming fruit, I saw what I hadn't noticed before: that her face looked tired, older, drained.

She said: "Please go. It's better that we don't see each other again."

She held out her hand, and in defiance of risk I took it. I said: "I don't know your surname. I don't know where you live or where to find you. But you know where to find me. If you ever need me send for me at St. John Street and I'll come."

Then I turned and walked away so that I need not watch her walking away from me.

I am writing this after dinner, looking out from the small back window towards the distant slope of Wytham Wood. I am fifty years old and I have never known what it is to love. I can write those words, know them to be true, but feel only the regret that a tone-deaf man must feel because he can't appreciate music, a regret less keen because it is for something never known, not for something lost. But emotions have their own time and place. Fifty is not an age to invite the turbulence of love, particularly not on this doomed and joyless planet when man goes to his last rest and all desire fades. So I shall plan my escape. It isn't easy for anyone under sixty-five to get an exit permit; since Omega only the aged can travel as they will. But I don't expect any difficulty. There are still some advantages in being the Warden's cousin, even if I never mention the relationship. As soon as I'm in touch with officialdom it is known. My passport is already stamped with the necessary travel permit. I shall get someone to take my summer course, relieved to be spared that shared boredom. I have no new knowledge, no enthusiasm to communicate. I shall take the ferry and drive, revisit the great cities, the cathedrals and temples of Europe while there are still roads that are passable, hotels with sufficient staff to provide at least an acceptable standard of comfort, where I can be reasonably sure of buying petrol, at least in the cities. I shall put behind me the memory of what I saw at Southwold, Xan and the Council, and this grey city, where even the stones bear witness to the transience of youth, of learning, of love. I shall tear this page from my journal. Writing these words was an indulgence; to let them stand would be folly. And I shall try to forget this morning's promise. It was made in a moment of madness. I don't suppose she will take it up. If she does, she will find this house empty.

Book Two

ALPHA

October 2021

20

He returned to Oxford on the last day of September, arriving in mid-afternoon. No one had tried to prevent him from going and no one welcomed him home. The house smelt unclean, the basement dining-room damp and musty, the upper rooms unaired. He had instructed Mrs. Kavanagh to open the windows from time to time but the air, with its disagreeable sourness, smelt as if they had been tightly closed for years. The narrow hall was littered with post; some of it looked as if the flimsy envelopes were adhering to the carpet. In the drawing-room, its long curtains drawn against the afternoon sun as if in the house of the dead, small chunks of rubble and gouts of soot had fallen from the chimney, and were ground into the rug under his unwary feet. He breathed in sootiness and decay. The house itself seemed to be disintegrating before his eyes.

The small top room, with its view of the cam-

panile of St. Barnabas Church and the trees of
Wytham Wood tinged with the first hues of autumn, struck him as very cold but unchanged.
Here he sat and listlessly turned over the pages of
his diary where he had recorded each day of his
travels, joylessly, meticulously, mentally ticking
off each of the cities and sights he had planned to
revisit as if he were a schoolboy fulfilling some
holiday task. The Auvergne, Fontainebleau, Car-
cassonne, Florence, Venice, Perugia, the cathedral at Orvieto, the mosaics in San Vitale,
Ravenna, the Temple of Hera at Paestum. He had
set out in no mood of excited anticipation, had
invited no adventures, sought no unfamiliar primitive places where novelty and discovery could
more than compensate for monotonous food or
hard beds. He had moved in organized and expensive comfort from capital to capital: Paris, Ma-
drid, Berlin, Rome. He hadn't even been
consciously saying farewell to the beauty and
splendours he had first known in youth. He could
hope to come again; this needn't be a final visit.
This was a journey of escape, not a pilgrimage in
search of forgotten sensations. But he knew now
that the part of him from which he most needed
to escape had remained in Oxford.

By August Italy had become too hot. Fleeing
from the heat, the dust, the grey company of the
old who seemed to shuffle through Europe like a

moving fog, he took the twisting road to Ravello, strung like an eyrie between the deep blue of the Mediterranean and the sky. Here he found a small family-run hotel, expensive and half-empty. He stayed for the rest of the month. It couldn't give him peace, but it did give him comfort and solitude.

His keenest memory was of Rome, standing before the Michelangelo *Pietà* in St. Peter's, of the rows of spluttering candles, the kneeling women, rich and poor, young and old, fixing their eyes on the Virgin's face with an intensity of longing almost too painful to witness. He remembered their outstretched arms, their palms pressed against the glass protective shield, the low continual mutter of their prayers as if this ceaseless anguished moan came from a single throat and carried to that unregarding marble the hopeless longing of all the world.

He returned to an Oxford which lay bleached and exhausted after a hot summer, to an atmosphere which impressed itself upon him as anxious, fretful, almost intimidating. He walked through the empty quads, their stones gold in the mellow autumn sun, the last gauds of high summer still flaming against their walls, and met no face he knew. It seemed to his depressed and distorted imagination that the previous inhabitants had been mysteriously evicted and that strangers walked the grey streets and sat like returning ghosts under the trees of the college gardens. The talk in the Senior Common Room was forced, desultory. His colleagues seemed unwilling to meet his eyes. Those few who realized that he had been away inquired about the success of the trip, but without curiosity, a mere sop to politeness. He felt as if he had brought back with him some foreign and disreputable contagion. He had returned to his own city, his own familiar place, yet was revisited by that peculiar and unfamiliar unease which he supposed could only be called loneliness.

After the first week he telephoned Helena, surprised that he should wish not only to hear her voice, but to hope for an invitation. Helena gave none. She made no attempt to hide her disappointment at hearing his voice. Mathilda was listless and off her food. The vet had done some tests and she was expecting him to telephone.

He said: "I've been out of Oxford for the whole summer. Has anything been happening?"

"What do you mean, has anything been happening? What sort of things? Nothing's been happening."

"I suppose not. One returns after six months expecting to find things changed."

"Things don't change in Oxford. Why should anything change?"

"I wasn't thinking of Oxford. The country as a whole. I didn't get much news when I was away."

"Well, there isn't any. And why ask me? There's been trouble about some dissidents, that's all. It's mostly rumour. Apparently they've been blowing up piers, trying to stop the Quietus. And there was something on the television news about a month ago. The announcer said that a group of them are planning to free all the convicts on the Isle of Man, that they might even organize an invasion from the island and try to depose the Warden."

Theo said: "That's ridiculous."

"That's what Rupert says. But they shouldn't publicize things like that if they aren't true. It only upsets people. Everything used to be so peaceful."

"Do they know who these dissidents are?"

"I don't think so. I don't think they know. Theo, I've got to get off the line now. I'm expecting the vet to call."

Without waiting for his goodbye, she put down the receiver.

In the early hours of the tenth day after his return the nightmare returned. But this time it wasn't his father who stood at the foot of his bed pointing his bleeding stump, but Luke, and he wasn't in bed but sitting up in his car, not outside the Lathbury Road house but actually in the nave of Binsey Church. The windows of the car were closed. He could hear a woman screaming as Helena had screamed. Rolf was there, scarlet-faced, pounding his fists against the car and shouting: "You've killed Julian, you've killed Julian!" At the front of the car stood Luke, mutely pointing his bleeding stump. He was unable to move, locked in a rigor like the rigor of death. He heard their angry voices, "Get out! Get out!," but he couldn't move. He sat there staring with blank eyes through the windscreen at Luke's accusing figure, waiting for the door to be wrenched open, for hands to drag him out and confront him with the horror of what he, and he alone, had done.

The nightmare left its legacy of unease, which deepened day by day. He tried to throw it off but nothing in his uneventful, solitary, routine-dominated life was powerful enough to engage more than a part of his mind. He told himself that he must act normally, appear unconcerned, that he was under some kind of surveillance. But there was no sign of it. He heard nothing from Xan, nothing from the Council, received no communications, was not aware that he was being followed. He dreaded hearing from Jasper, with a renewal of his suggestion that they should join forces. But Jasper hadn't been in touch since the Quietus and no call came. He took his usual exercise and two weeks after his return set off for an

early-morning run across Port Meadow to Binsey
Church. He knew that it would be unwise to visit
and question the old priest and he found it difficult to explain to himself why revisiting Binsey
was so important, or what he hoped to gain. Running with his long regular strides across Port
Meadow he was for a moment worried in case he
should lead the State Security Police to one of the
group's normal meeting places. But when he
reached Binsey he saw that the hamlet was completely deserted and told himself that they would
hardly continue to meet in any of their old haunts.
Wherever they were, he knew them to be in terrible danger. He ran now, as he had every day, in a
tumult of conflicting and familiar emotions: irritation that he had become involved, regret that he
hadn't handled the interview with the Council
better, terror that Julian might even now be in the
hands of the Security Police, frustration that there
was no way in which he could get in touch with
her, no person to whom he could safely talk.

The lane to St. Margaret's Church was even
more dishevelled, even more overgrown than
when he had last walked it, the interlocking
boughs overhead making it dark and sinister as a
tunnel. When he reached the churchyard he saw
that there was a mortuary van outside the house
and that two men were carrying a simple pine
coffin down the path.

He said: "Is the old parson dead?"

The man who replied barely gazed at him. "He'd better be. He's in the box." He slid the coffin expertly into the back of the van, slammed the door and the two of them drove away.

The door to the church was open and he moved into its dim secular emptiness. Already there were signs of its impending decay. Leaves had blown in through the open door and the floor of the chancel was muddy and stained with what looked like blood. The pews were thick with dust and it was apparent from the smell that animals, probably dogs, had been loose. Before the altar, curious signs had been painted on the floor, some of which were vaguely familiar. He was sorry he had come to this desecrated hovel. He left it, closing the heavy door behind him with a sense of relief. But he had learned nothing, done no good. His pointless small pilgrimage had only deepened his sense of impotence, of impending disaster.

21

It was at half past eight that night that he heard the knock. He was in the kitchen dressing a salad for his dinner, carefully mixing the olive oil and the wine vinegar in the right proportions. He was to eat, as he usually did at night, from a tray in his study and the tray with its clean cloth and table napkin was already set and waiting on the kitchen table. The lamb chop was in the grilling pan. The claret had been uncorked an hour earlier and he had poured the first glass to drink while he was cooking. He went through the familiar motions without enthusiasm, almost without interest. He supposed he needed to eat. It was his habit to take trouble with the salad dressing. Even as his hands were at the familiar business of preparation his mind told him that it was all supremely unimportant.

He had drawn the curtains across the french doors leading to the patio and the steps up to the garden, less to preserve privacy—that was hardly necessary—than because it was his habit to shut out the night. Apart from the small noises of his own making he was surrounded by total silence, the empty floors of the house piled above him like a physical weight. And it was at the moment when he raised the glass to his lips that he heard a knock. It was low but urgent, a single tap on the glass quickly followed by three others, as definite as a signal. He drew back the curtains and could just make out the outlines of a face almost pressed to the glass. A dark face. He knew instinctively rather than could see that it was Miriam. He drew back the two bolts and unlocked the door and immediately she slipped in.

She wasted no time on greeting but said: "You're alone?"

"Yes. What is it? What's happened?"

"They've got Gascoigne. We're on the run. Julian needs you. It wasn't easy for her to come herself so she sent me."

He was surprised that he could match her excitement, the half-suppressed terror, with such calmness. But, then, this visit, although unforeseen, seemed but the natural culmination of the week's mounting anxiety. He had known that something traumatic would happen, that some extraordinary demand would be made on him. Now the summons had come.

When he didn't reply, she said: "You told Julian you'd come if she wanted you. She wants you now."

"Where are they?"

She paused for a second as if even now wondering if it was safe to tell him, then said: "They're in a chapel at Widford outside Swinbrook. We've got Rolf's car but the SSP will know the number. We need your car and we need you. We've got to get away before Gascoigne breaks and gives them the names."

Neither of them doubted that Gascoigne would break. Nothing as crude as physical torture would be necessary. The State Security Police would have the necessary drugs and the knowledge and ruthlessness to use them.

He asked: "How did you get here?"

She said impatiently: "Bicycle. I've left it outside your back gate. It was locked but luckily your neighbour had put out his dustbin. I climbed over. Look, there isn't time to eat. You'd better grab what food you've got handy. We've got some bread, cheese, a few tinned goods. Where's your car?"

"In a garage off Pusey Lane. I'll get my coat. There's a bag hanging behind that cupboard door. The larder's through there. See what food you can get together. And you'd better recork and put in the wine."

He went upstairs to fetch his heavy coat, and, mounting one more staircase to the small back room, slipped his diary into the large inner pocket. The action was instinctive; if asked, he would have had difficulty in explaining it even to himself. The diary wasn't particularly incriminating; he had taken care over that. He had no premonition that he was leaving for more than a few hours the life which the diary chronicled and this echoing house enclosed. And even if the journey were the beginning of an odyssey, there were more useful, more valued, more relevant talismans which he could have slipped into his pocket.

Miriam's last call to him to hurry had been unnecessary. Time, he knew, was very short. If he were to get to the group to discuss with them how best he could use his influence with Xan, above all if he were to see Julian before her arrest, he must get on the road without a second's unnecessary delay. Once the SSP knew that the group had flown they would turn their attention to him. His car registration was on record. The abandoned dinner, even if he could spare the time to throw it into the waste bin, would be evidence enough that he had left in a hurry. In his anxiety to get to Julian he felt no more than a slight concern for his own safety. He was still ex-adviser to the Council. There was one man in Britain who had absolute power, absolute authority, absolute control, and he was that man's cousin. Even the State Security Police couldn't in the end prevent him from seeing Xan. But they could prevent him from getting to Julian; that at least was within their power.

Miriam, holding a bulging tote-bag, was waiting for him beside the front door. He opened it but she motioned him back, put her head against the doorpost and glanced quickly each way. She said: "It looks clear."

It must have rained. The air was fresh but the night dark, the street lamps cast their dim light over the grey stones, the rain-mottled roofs of the parked cars. On each side of the street curtains were drawn, except in one high window where a square of light shone out and he could see dark heads passing, hear the faint sound of music. Then someone in the room turned up the volume and suddenly there poured out over the grey street, piercingly sweet, mingled tenor, bass, soprano voices singing a quartet, surely Mozart, though he couldn't recognize the opera. For one vivid moment of nostalgia and regret the sound took him back to the street he had first known as an undergraduate thirty years ago, to friends who had lodged here and were gone, to the memory of windows open to the summer night, young voices calling, music and laughter.

There was no sign of prying eyes, no sign of life except for that one surge of glorious sound, but he and Miriam walked swiftly and quietly the thirty yards down Pusey Street, heads bent and in silence as if even a whisper or a heavy footfall could wake the street into clamorous life. They turned into Pusey Lane and she waited, still silently, while he unlocked the garage, started up the Rover and opened the door for her to slide quickly in. He drove fast down Woodstock Road but carefully and well within the speed limit. They were on the outskirts of the city before he spoke.

"When did they take Gascoigne?"

"About two hours ago. He was placing explosives to blow up a landing stage at Shoreham. There was to be another Quietus. The Security Police were waiting for him."

"Not surprisingly. You've been destroying the embarkation stages. Obviously they kept watch. So they've had him for two hours. I'm surprised they haven't picked you up yet."

"They probably waited to question him until they got him back to London. And I don't suppose they're in much of a hurry, we're not that important. But they will come."

"Of course. How do you know they've got Gascoigne?"

"He rang to say what he was going to do. It was a private initiative, Rolf hadn't authorized it. We always ring back when the job's completed; he didn't. Luke went round to his lodgings in Cowley. The State Security Police had been to search—at least, the landlady said someone had been to search. Obviously it was the State Security Police."

"That wasn't sensible of Luke, to go to the house. They could have been waiting for him."

"Nothing we've done has been sensible, only necessary."

He said: "I don't know what you're expecting from me, but if you want me to help you'd better tell me something about yourselves. I know nothing except your forenames. Where do you live? What do you do? How did you meet?"

"I'll tell you, but I don't see why it matters or why you need to know. Gascoigne is—was—a long-distance lorry-driver. That's why Rolf recruited him. I think they met in a pub. He could distribute our leaflets over the whole of England."

"A long-distance driver who's an explosives expert. I can see his usefulness."

"His granddad taught him about explosives. He was in the army and the two of them were close. He didn't need to be an expert. There's nothing very complicated about blowing up landing stages or anything else. Rolf is an engineer. He works in the electricity-supply industry."

"And what did Rolf contribute to the enterprise apart from not particularly effective leadership?"

Miriam ignored the taunt. She went on: "You know about Luke. He used to be a priest. I suppose he still is. According to him, once a priest, always a priest. He hasn't got a parish, because there aren't many churches left that want his brand of Christianity."

"What brand is that?"

"The sort the Church got rid of in the 1990s. The old Bible, the old prayer book. He takes the occasional service if people ask him. He's employed at the botanical gardens and he's learning animal husbandry."

"And why did Rolf recruit him? Hardly to provide spiritual consolation to the group?"

"Julian wanted him."

"And you?"

"You know about me. I was a midwife. That's all I've ever wanted to be. After Omega I took a job at a supermarket check-out in Headington. Now I manage the store."

"And what do you do for the Five Fishes? Slip the pamphlets into packets of breakfast cereal?"

She said: "Look, I said we weren't sensible. I didn't say we were daft. If we hadn't been careful, if we were as incompetent as you make out, we wouldn't have lasted this long."

He said: "You've lasted this long because the Warden wanted you to last. He could have had you picked up months ago. He didn't because you're more useful to him at large than imprisoned. He doesn't want martyrs. What he does want is the pretence of an internal threat to good public order. It helps buttress his authority. All tyrants have needed that from time to time. All he has to do is tell the people that there's a secret society operating whose published manifesto may be beguilingly liberal but whose real aim is to close down the Isle of Man Colony, let loose ten thousand criminal psychopaths on an ageing society, send home all the Sojourners so that the rubbish isn't collected and the streets are unswept, and ultimately overthrow the Council and the Warden himself."

"Why should people believe that?"

"Why not? Between the five of you you'd probably like to do all those things. Rolf certainly would like to do the last. Under an undemocratic government there can be no acceptable dissent any more than there can be moderate sedition. I know you call yourselves the Five Fishes. You may as well tell me your code names."

"Rolf is Rudd, Luke is Loach, Gascoigne is Gurdon, I'm Minnow."

"And Julian?"

"We had difficulty there. There's only one fish we could find which begins with *J*, a John Dory."

He had to stop himself from laughing aloud. He said: "What on earth was the point of it?

You've advertised to the whole country that you call yourselves the Five Fishes? I suppose that when Rolf telephones you he says this is Rudd calling Minnow, in the hope that if the SSP are listening they'll tear their hair and bite the carpet with frustration."

She said: "All right, you've made your point. We didn't actually use the names, not often anyway. It was just an idea of Rolf's."

"I thought it might be."

"Look, cut out all this supercilious chat, will you? We know you're clever and sarcasm is your way of showing us just how clever, but I can't cope with it for the moment. And don't antagonize Rolf. If you care at all about Julian, calm it, OK?"

For the next few minutes they drove in silence. Glancing at her he saw that she was gazing at the road ahead with an almost passionate intensity as if expecting to find that it was mined. Her hands clutching the bag were taut, the knuckles white, and it seemed to him that there flowed from her a surge of excitement which was almost palpable. She had answered his questions, but as if her mind were elsewhere.

Then she spoke, and when she used his name he felt a small shock at the unexpected intimacy. "Theo, there's something I have to tell you. Julian said not to tell you until we were on our way. It wasn't a test of your good faith. She knew you'd come if she sent for you. But if you didn't, if there was something important to prevent you, if you couldn't come, then I wasn't to tell. There'd be no point in it anyway."

"Tell me what?" He gave her a long glance. She was still staring ahead, lips moving silently as if she were searching for words. "Tell me what, Miriam?"

Still she didn't look at him. She said: "You won't believe me. I don't expect you to believe me. Your disbelief isn't important, because in little more than thirty minutes you'll see the truth for yourself. Only don't argue about it. I don't want to cope right now with protestations, arguments. I'm not going to try to convince you, Julian will do that."

"Just tell me. I'll decide whether to believe you."

And now she turned her head and looked at him. She said, her voice clear above the noise of the engine: "Julian is pregnant. That's why she needs you. She's going to have a child."

In the silence that followed he was aware firstly of a plunging disappointment followed by irritation and then disgust. It was repugnant to believe that Julian was capable of such self-deceiving nonsense or that Miriam should be fool enough to connive in it. At their first and only meeting at

Binsey, brief though it had been, he had liked
her, had thought her sensible and intelligent. He
didn't like having his judgement of a person so
confounded.

After a moment he said: "I won't argue, but I
don't believe you. I'm not saying you're deliberately lying, I believe you think it's true. But it
isn't."

It used, after all, to be a common delusion. In
the first years after Omega women all over the
world believed themselves to be pregnant, displayed the symptoms of pregnancy, walked
proud-bellied—he had seen them walking down
the High Street in Oxford. They had made plans
for the birth, had even gone into spurious labour,
groaning and straining and bringing forth nothing but wind and anguish.

After five minutes he said: "How long have you
believed this story?"

"I said I didn't want to talk about it. I said you
were to wait."

"You said I wasn't to argue. I'm not arguing.
I'm only asking one question."

"Since the baby quickened. Julian didn't know
until then. How could she? Then she spoke to me
and I confirmed the pregnancy. I'm a midwife,
remember? We'd thought it wise not to be together more than necessary during the last four
months. If I'd seen her more often I should have

known earlier. Even after twenty-five years, I should have known."

He said: "If you believe it—the unbelievable—then you're taking it very calmly."

"I've had time to get used to the glory of it. Now I'm more concerned with the practicalities."

There was a silence. Then she said, as if reminiscing with all the time in the world: "I was twenty-seven at Omega and working in the maternity department of the John Radcliffe. I was doing a stint in the ante-natal clinic at the time. I remember booking a patient for her next appointment and suddenly noticing that the page seven months ahead was blank. Not a single name. Women usually booked in by the time they'd missed their second period, some as soon as they'd missed one. Not a single name. I thought, what's happening to the men in this city? Then I rang a friend who was working at Queen Charlotte's. She said the same. She said she'd telephone someone she knew at the Rosie Maternity Hospital in Cambridge. She rang me back twenty minutes later. It was the same there. It was then I knew, I must have been one of the first to know. I was there at the end. Now I shall be there at the beginning."

They were coming into Swinbrook now and he drove more slowly, dimming the headlights, as if these precautions could somehow make them invisible. But the village was deserted. The waxy moon, half full, swayed against a sky of blue-grey trembling silk, pierced by a few high stars. The night was less dark than he had expected, the air still and sweet, with a grassy smell. In the pale moonlight the mellow stones gave out a faint glow which seemed to suffuse the air and he could clearly make out the shape of the houses, the high sloping roofs and the flower-hung garden walls. There were no lights in any of the windows and the village lay silent and empty as a deserted film set, outwardly solid and permanent but ephemeral, the painted walls backed only by wooden supports and concealing the rotting debris of the departed crew. He had a momentary delusion that he would only have to lean against one of the walls and it would collapse in a crumble of plaster and snapping batons. And it was familiar. Even in this unreal light he could recognize the landmarks: the small green beside the pond with its huge overhanging tree and surrounding seat, the entrance to the narrow lane leading up to the church.

He had been here before, with Xan, in their first year. It had been a hot day in late June when Oxford had become a place to escape from, her hot pavements blocked with tourists, her air stinking with car fumes and loud with the clatter of alien tongues, her peaceful quads invaded. They had been driving down the Woodstock

Road with no clear idea of their destination when Theo had remembered his wish to see St. Oswald's Chapel at Widford. It was as good a destination as any. Glad that the expedition had a purpose, they had taken the road to Swinbrook. The day, in memory, was an icon which he could conjure up to represent the perfect English summer: an azure almost cloudless sky, the haze of cow parsley, the smell of mown grass, the rushing air tearing at their hair. It could conjure up other things too, more transitory, which, unlike the summer, had been lost for ever: youth, confidence, joy, the hope of love. They had been in no hurry. Outside Swinbrook there had been a village cricket match and they had parked the car and sat on the grass bank behind the dry-stone wall to watch, criticize, applaud. They had parked again where he parked now, beside the pond, had taken the same walk which he and Miriam would take, past the old post office, up the narrow cobbled lane bordered by the high, ivy-clad wall, to the village church. There had been a christening. A small procession of villagers was straggling up the path towards the porch, the parents at the head, the mother carrying the baby in its white flounced christening robe, the women in flowered hats, the men, a little self-conscious, perspiring in close-fitting blue and grey suits. He remembered thinking that the scene was timeless and had amused himself for a moment

imagining earlier christenings, the clothes different but the country faces, with their mixture of
serious purpose and anticipated pleasure, unchanged. He thought then, as he thought now, of
time passing, inexorable, unforgiving, unstoppable time. But the thought then had been an intellectual exercise devoid of pain or nostalgia, since
time still stretched ahead and for a nineteen-year-
old seemed an eternity.

Now, turning to lock the car, he said: "If the
meeting place is St. Oswald's Chapel the Warden
knows it."

Her reply was calm: "But he doesn't know that
we do."

"He will when Gascoigne talks."

"Gascoigne doesn't know either. This is a fall-
back meeting place which Rolf kept to himself in
case one of us was taken."

"Where has he left his car?"

"Concealed somewhere off the road. They
planned to do the last mile or so on foot."

Theo said: "Across rough fields, and in the
dark. Not exactly an easy place for a quick
getaway."

"No, but it's remote, unused, and the chapel is
always open. We don't have to worry about a
quick getaway if no one knows where to find us."

But there must be a more suitable place,
thought Theo, and felt again a doubt of Rolf's

competence to plan and lead. Comforted by disdain, he told himself: He's got looks and a certain crude force but not much intelligence, an ambitious barbarian. How on earth did she come to marry him?

The lane came to an end and they turned left down a narrow path of earth and stone between the ivy-covered walls, across a cattle-grid and into the field. Down the hill to the left was a low farmhouse which he hadn't remembered seeing before.

Miriam said: "It's empty. All the village is deserted now. I don't know why that's happened with one place more than another. I suppose one or two key families leave and the rest panic and follow."

The field was rough and tussocky and they walked with care, their eyes on the ground. From time to time one of them would stumble and the other put out a quick supporting hand, while Miriam shone her torch, searching in the pool of light for a non-existent path. It seemed to Theo that they must look like a very old couple, the last inhabitants of a deserted village making their way through the final darkness to St. Oswald's Chapel out of some perverse or atavistic need to die on consecrated ground. To his left the fields stretched down to a high hedge behind which, he knew, ran the Windrush. Here, after visiting the chapel, he and Xan had lain on the grass watching the slow-flowing stream for the dart and rise of the fish, then, turning on their backs, had stared upwards through the silvered leaves to the blue of the sky. They had brought wine with them and strawberries purchased on the road. He found that he could recall every word of their talk.

Xan, dropping a strawberry into his mouth, then twisting over to reach for wine: "How too Brideshead, dear boy. I feel the need of a teddy bear." And then, with no change of tone: "I'm thinking of joining the army."

"Xan, whatever for?"

"No particular reason. At least it won't be boring."

"It will be unutterably boring, except for people who like travel and sport, and you've never particularly cared for either, except cricket, and that's hardly an army game. They play rough, those boys. Anyway, they probably won't have you. Now they've got so small I'm told they've become very choosy."

"Oh, they'll have me. And then later I might try politics."

"Even more boring. You've never shown the slightest interest in politics. You've no political convictions."

"I can acquire them. And it won't be as boring as what you've got planned for yourself. You'll get your First, of course; then Jasper will find a research job for his favourite pupil. Then there'll be the usual provincial appointment, serving your time with red-brick nonentities, publishing your papers, writing the occasional well-researched book which will be respectfully received. Then back to Oxford with a fellowship. All Souls, if you're lucky and haven't already got it, and a job for life teaching undergraduates who see history as a soft option. Oh, I forgot. A suitable wife, intelligent enough to make acceptable dinner-table talk but not so intelligent that she'll compete with you, a mortgaged house in North Oxford and two intelligent, boring children who will re-peat the pattern."

Well, he got most of it right, all of it right except the intelligent wife and the two children. And what he had spoken in that seemingly casual con-versation, had it even then been part of a plan? He was right, the army did take him. He became the youngest colonel for 150 years. He still had no political allegiance, no convictions beyond his conviction that what he wanted he should have and that when he set his hand to something he would succeed. After Omega, with the country sunk in apathy, no one wanting to work, services almost at a stop, crime uncontrollable, all hope and ambition lost for ever, England had been a ripe plum for his picking. The metaphor was trite but none was more accurate. It had hung there,

overripe, rotten; and Xan had only to put out his
hand. Theo tried to thrust the past out of memory, but the voices of that last summer echoed in
his mind, and even on this chill autumnal night he
could feel its sun on his back.

And now the chapel was plain before them, the
chancel and nave under one roof, the central bell-
turret. It looked just as it had when he first saw it,
incredibly small, a chapel built by some over-
indulgent deist as a child's plaything. As they
approached the door he was seized with a sudden
reluctance which momentarily froze his footsteps,
wondering for the first time with an upsurge of
curiosity and anxiety what exactly he would find.
He couldn't believe that Julian had conceived,
that wasn't why he was here. Miriam might be a
midwife but she hadn't practised for twenty-five
years and there were numerous medical conditions which could simulate pregnancy. Some of
them were dangerous; was this a malignant tu-
mour left untreated because Miriam and Julian
had been deceived by hope? It had been a common enough tragedy in the first years after
Omega, almost as common as the phantom preg-
nancies. He hated the thought that Julian was a
deluded fool, but hated more the fear that she
might be mortally ill. He half-resented his concern, what seemed his obsession with her. But

what else had brought him to this rough unencumbered place?

Miriam swept the torchlight over the door, then switched it off. The door opened easily under her hand. The chapel was dark but the group had lit eight night lights and had set them in a line in front of the altar. He wondered whether Rolf had secreted them here in advance of need or whether they had been left by other, less transient visitors. The wicks flickered briefly in the breeze from the open door, throwing shadows on the stone floor and on the pale, unpolished wood before settling into a gentle milky glow. At first he thought that the chapel was empty, and then he saw their three dark heads rising from one of the box pews. They moved out into the narrow aisle and stood regarding him. They were dressed as for a journey, Rolf in a Breton cap and large, grubby sheepskin jacket, Luke in a shabby black coat and muffler, Julian in a long cloak almost to the ground. In the dim light of the candles their faces were soft blurs. No one spoke. Then Luke turned, picked up one of the candles and held it high. Julian moved towards Theo and looked up into his face, smiling.

She said: "It's true, Theo, feel."

Under the cloak she was wearing a smock over baggy trousers. She took his right hand and guided it under the cotton of the smock, pulling the elastic of the trousers taut. The swollen belly felt tight and his first thought was of wonder that this huge convexity was so little visible beneath her clothes. At first her skin, stretched but silken smooth, felt cool under his resting hand, but imperceptibly the warmth passed from his skin to hers so that he could no longer feel any difference and it seemed to him that their flesh had become one. And then, with a sudden convulsive spasm, his hand was almost kicked away. She laughed, and the joyous peal rang out and filled the chapel.

"Listen," she said, "listen to her heartbeat."

It was easier for him to kneel, so he knelt, unselfconsciously, not thinking of it as a gesture of homage but knowing that it was right that he should be on his knees. He placed his right arm round her waist and pressed his ear against her stomach. He couldn't hear the beating heart, but he could hear and feel the movements of the child, feel its life. He was swept by a tide of emotion which rose, buffeted and engulfed him in a turbulent surge of awe, excitement and terror, then receded, leaving him spent and weak. For a moment he knelt there, unable to move, half-supported by Julian's body, letting the smell of her, the warmth of her, the very essence of her seep into him. Then he straightened himself and got to his feet, aware of their watching eyes. But still no one spoke. He wished that they would go away so that he could lead Julian into the darkness and silence of the night and with her be part of that darkness and stand together in that greater silence. He needed to rest his mind in peace, to feel and not speak. But he knew that he had to speak and that he would need all his persuasive power. And words might not be enough. He would need to match will with will, passion with passion. All he had on offer was reason, argument, intelligence, and he had put his faith in them all his life. Now he felt vulnerable and inadequate where once he had felt most confident and sure.

He drew apart from Julian and said to Miriam: "Give me the torch."

She handed it to him without a word and he switched it on and swept the beam over their faces. They gazed back at him: Miriam's eyes quizzical and smiling, Rolf's resentful but triumphant, Luke's full of a desperate appeal.

It was Luke who spoke first: "You see, Theo, that we had to get away, that we must keep Julian safe."

Theo said: "You won't keep her safe by running. This changes everything, changes it not only for you but for the whole world. Nothing matters now except the safety of Julian and the child. She ought to be in hospital. Telephone the Warden, or let me. Once this is known no one is going to worry about seditious pamphlets or dissent. There isn't anyone on the Council, anyone in the country, anyone of importance in the world for that matter, who won't be concerned only for one thing; the safe birth of this child."

Julian put her deformed hand over his own. She said: "Please don't make me. I don't want him to be there when my baby is born."

"He needn't actually be present. He'll do what you want. Everyone will do what you want."

"He will be there. You know he will be. He'll be there at the birth and he'll be there always. He killed Miriam's brother; he's killing Gascoigne now. If I fall into his hands I'll never be free of him. My baby will never be free."

How, Theo wondered, would she and her baby keep out of Xan's hands? Did she propose to keep the child a secret for ever? He said: "You must think first of your baby. Suppose there are complications, a haemorrhage?"

"There won't be. Miriam will look after me."

Theo turned to her. "Speak to her, Miriam. You're the professional. You know she ought to be in hospital. Or are you thinking of yourself? Is that all any of you are thinking of, yourselves? Your own glory? It would be quite a thing, wouldn't it? Midwife to the first of a new race, if that is what this child is destined to be. You don't want to share the glory; you're afraid you might not be allowed even a share. You want to be the only one to see this miracle child into the world."

Miriam said calmly: "I've delivered two hundred and eighty babies. They all seemed like miracles, at least at the time of birth. All I want is for the mother and child to be safe and well. I wouldn't hand over a pregnant bitch to the mercies of the Warden of England. Yes, I'd prefer to deliver the child in hospital, but Julian has a right to her choice."

Theo turned to Rolf. "What does the father think?"

Rolf was impatient. "If we stand here talking about it much longer we won't have a choice. Julian's right. Once she's in the Warden's hands he'll take over. He'll be there at the birth. He'll announce it to the world. He'll be the one on television showing my child to the nation. That's for me to do, not him."

Theo thought: He thinks he's supporting his wife. But all he really cares about is getting the child safely born before Xan and the Council find out about the pregnancy.

Anger and frustration made his voice harsh: "This is crazy. You aren't children with a new toy which you can keep to yourselves, play with by yourselves, prevent the other children from sharing. This birth is the concern of the whole world, not just England. The child belongs to mankind."

Luke said: "The child belongs to God."

Theo turned on him. "Christ! Can't we discuss this at least on the basis of reason?"

It was Miriam who spoke. She said: "The child belongs to herself, but her mother is Julian. Until she's born and for a time after the birth, the baby and her mother are one. Julian has the right to say where she will give birth."

"Even if it means risking the baby."

Julian said: "If I have my baby with the Warden present we shall both die."

"That's ridiculous."

Miriam said calmly: "Do you want to take the risk?" He didn't reply. She waited, then reiterated: "Are you prepared to take that responsibility?"

"So what are your plans?"

It was Rolf who replied. "To find somewhere safe, or as safe as possible. An empty house, a cottage, any kind of shelter where we can shack up for four weeks. It needs to be in remote country, perhaps a forest. We need provisions and water and we need a car. The only car we've got is mine and they'll know the number of that!"

Theo said: "We can't use mine, either, not for long. The SSP are probably at St. John Street now. The whole enterprise is futile. Once Gascoigne talks—and he will talk, they don't need torture, they've got drugs—once the Council know about the pregnancy they'll come after you with all they've got. How far do you think you'll get before they find you?"

Luke's voice sounded calm and patient. He could have been explaining the reading of the situation to a not very intelligent child. "We know they'll come. They've been looking for us and they want us destroyed. But they may not come quickly, may not bother too much at first. You see, they don't know about the baby. We never told Gascoigne."

"But he was part of you, part of the group. Didn't he guess? He had eyes, couldn't he see?"

Julian said: "He was thirty-one and I doubt whether he ever saw a pregnant woman. No one has given birth for twenty-five years. It wasn't a possibility his mind was open to. And the Sojourners I worked with in the camp, their minds weren't open to it either. No one knows but we five."

Miriam said: "And Julian is wide-hipped, carrying high. It wouldn't have been obvious to you if you hadn't felt the foetus move."

Theo thought, so they hadn't trusted Gascoigne, at least not with the most valuable secret of all. Gascoigne hadn't been thought worthy of it, that sturdy, simple, decent man who had seemed to Theo at their first meeting the stolid, dependable anchor of the group. And if they had trusted him, he would have obeyed orders. There would have been no attempted sabotage, no capture.

As if reading his thoughts, Rolf said: "It was for his own protection, and ours. The fewer people who knew, the better. I had to tell Miriam, of course. We needed her skills. Then I told Luke, because Julian wanted him to know. It was something to do with his being a priest, some superstition or other. He's supposed to bring us good luck. It was against my advice, but I told him."

Julian said: "I was the one who told Luke."

Theo thought that it was probably also against Rolf's advice that he had been sent for. Julian had wanted him, and what she wanted they were trying to give. But the secret, once revealed, could never be unlearned. He might still try to escape commitment but he couldn't now escape knowledge.

For the first time there was a note of urgency in Luke's voice. "Let's get away before they come. We can use your car. We can go on talking while we travel. You'll have the time and chance to persuade Julian to change her mind."

Julian said: "Please come with us, Theo. Please help us."

Rolf said impatiently: "He has no choice. He knows too much. We can't let him go free now."

Theo looked at Julian. He wanted to ask: "Is

this the man you and your God between you have chosen to repopulate the world?"

He said coldly: "For God's sake, don't start threatening. You can reduce everything, even this, to the level of a cheap feature film. If I come with you it will be because I choose to."

22

One by one they blew out the candles. The little chapel returned to its ageless calm. Rolf closed the door and they began their careful trudge across the field, Rolf leading. He had taken the torch and its small moon of light moved like a will-o'-the-wisp over the matted tussocks of brown grass, briefly illuminating as if with a miniature searchlight a single trembling flower and patches of daisies, bright as buttons. Behind Rolf the two women walked together, Julian with her arm in Miriam's. Luke and Theo brought up the rear. They didn't speak but Theo was aware that Luke was glad of his company. He was interested that he himself could be possessed by such strong feelings, by surges of wonder, excitement and awe, and yet be able to observe and analyse the effect of feelings on action and thought. He was interested, too, that amid the tumult he could have room for irritation. It seemed so petty and irrelevant a response to the overwhelming importance of his dilemma. But the whole situation was one of paradox. Could ever aims and means have been so mismatched? Had there ever been an enterprise of such immense importance embarked upon by such frail and pathetically inadequate adventurers? But he didn't need to be one of them. Unarmed they couldn't permanently hold him by force, and he had his car keys. He could get away, telephone Xan, put an end to it. But if he did, Julian would die. At least she thought she would, and the conviction might be powerful enough to kill both her and her child. He had been responsible for the death of one child. That was enough.

When they at last reached the pond and the green where he had parked the Rover, he half-expected to see it surrounded by the SSP, black immobile figures, stony-eyed, guns at the ready. But the village was as deserted as when they had arrived. As they came up to the car he decided to make one more attempt.

It was to Julian he turned. He said: "Whatever you feel about the Warden, whatever you fear, let me ring him now. Let me speak to him. He's not the devil you think."

It was Rolf's impatient voice that answered. "Don't you ever give up? She doesn't want your patronage. She doesn't trust your promises. We'll do what we've planned, get as far from here as we can and find shelter. We'll steal what food we need until the child's born."

Miriam said: "Theo, we've no choice. Somewhere there must be a place for us, perhaps a deserted cottage in deep woodland."

Theo turned on her. "Quite an idyll, isn't it? I can picture you all. A snug little cottage in some remote forest glade, smoke from your wood fire rising from the chimney, a well of clean water, rabbits and birds sitting around ready to be caught, the rear garden stocked with vegetables. Perhaps you'll even find a few chickens and a goat to provide milk. And no doubt the previous owners will have obligingly left a pram in the garden shed."

Miriam said again, calmly but firmly, her eyes fixed on his: "Theo, we have no choice."

And nor had he. That moment when he had knelt at Julian's feet, had felt her child move under his hand, had bound him to them irrevocably. And they needed him. Rolf might resent him but he was still needed. If the worst came to the worst he could intercede with Xan. If they were to fall into the hands of the State Security Police, his was a voice they might listen to.

He took the car keys from his pocket. Rolf put out his hand for them. Theo said: "I'll drive. You can choose the route. I take it you can read a map."

The cheap jibe had been unwise. Rolf's voice was dangerously calm: "You despise us, don't you?"

"No, why should I?"

"You don't need a reason. You despise the whole world except people of your own sort, people who have had your education, your advantages, your choices. Gascoigne was twice the man you are. What have you ever produced in your life? What have you ever done except talk about the past? No wonder you chose museums as meeting places. That's where you feel at home. Gascoigne could destroy a landing stage and put a stop to a Quietus single-handed. Could you?"

"Use explosives? No, I admit that that isn't among my accomplishments."

Rolf mimicked his voice: " 'I admit that that isn't among my accomplishments'! You should hear yourself. You're not one of us, you never have been. You haven't got the guts. And don't think we really want you. Don't think we like you. You're here because you're the Warden's cousin. That might be useful."

He had used the plural, but both of them knew of whom he was speaking. Theo said: "If you admired Gascoigne so much why didn't you confide in him? If you'd told him about the baby he wouldn't have disobeyed orders. I might not be one of you, but he was. He had a right to know.

You're responsible for his capture and, if he's dead, you're responsible for his death. Don't blame me if you're feeling guilty."

He felt Miriam's hand on his arm. She said with quiet authority: "Cool it, Theo. If we quarrel, we're dead. Let's get away from here, OK?"

When they were in the car, Theo and Rolf in the front seats, Theo asked: "Which way?"

"North-west and into Wales. We'll be safer over the border. The Warden's diktat runs there, but he's more resented than loved. We'll move by night, sleep by day. And we'll keep to the minor roads. It's more important not to be detected than to cover the miles. And they'll be looking for this car. If we get a chance we'll change it."

It was then that inspiration came to Theo. Jasper. Jasper so conveniently close, so well provisioned. Jasper who desperately needed to join him in St. John Street.

He said: "I have a friend who lives outside Asthall, practically the next village. He's got a store of food and I think I could persuade him to lend us his car."

Rolf asked: "What makes you think he's going to agree?"

"There's something he wants badly which I can give him."

Rolf said: "We haven't got time to waste. How long will this persuasion take?"

Theo controlled his irritation. He said: "Getting a different car and stocking it with what we need is hardly a waste of time. I'd have said it was essential. But if you've a better suggestion, let's hear it."

Rolf said: "All right, let's go."

Theo slipped in the clutch and drove carefully through the darkness. When they reached the outskirts of Asthall, he said: "We'll borrow his car and leave mine in his garage. With any luck it will be a long time before they get on to him. And I think I can promise he won't talk."

Julian leaned forward and said: "Wouldn't that mean putting your friend in danger? We mustn't do that."

Rolf was impatient. "He'll have to take his chance."

Theo spoke to Julian: "If we're caught, all they'll have to connect him with us is the car. He can argue that it was taken in the night, that we stole it, or that we forced him to co-operate."

Rolf said: "Suppose he won't co-operate? I'd better come in with you and see that he does."

"By force? Don't be a fool. How long would he remain silent after that? He'll co-operate, but not if you start threatening him. I'll need one person with me. I'll take Miriam."

"Why Miriam?"

"She knows what she wants for the birth."

Rolf didn't argue further. Theo wondered if he'd handled Rolf with enough tact, then felt resentment at the arrogance which made that tact necessary. But somehow he must avoid an open quarrel. Compared with Julian's safety, the appalling importance of their enterprise, his increasing irritation with Rolf seemed a trivial but dangerous indulgence. He was with them by choice but there had, in fact, been no choice. It was to Julian and her unborn child, and to them only, that he owed allegiance.

When he lifted his hand to press the doorbell at the huge gate in the wall he saw to his surprise that the gate was open. He beckoned Miriam and they went in together. He closed the gate behind him. The house was in darkness except for the sitting-room. The curtains were drawn but with an inch of light shining through. He saw that the garage, too, was unlocked, the door up and the dark bulk of the Renault parked inside. He was not surprised now to find the side door unlocked. He switched on the light of the hall, calling softly, but there was no reply. With Miriam at his shoulder, he walked down the passage to the sitting-room.

As soon as he pushed open the door he knew what he would find. The smell choked him, strong and evil as a contagion: blood, faeces, the stink of death. Jasper had made himself comfortable for the final act of his life. He was seated in the armchair before the empty fire, hands hanging loosely over the arms. The method he had chosen had been certain and catastrophic. He had put the muzzle of a revolver in his mouth and blown off the top of his head. What remained of it was slumped forward on his chest, where there was a stiffened bib of brown blood which looked like dried vomit. He had been left-handed and the gun lay on the floor by the chair, under a small round table which held his house and car keys, an empty glass, an empty claret bottle and a handwritten note, the first part in Latin, the last in English.

Quid te exempta iuvat spinis de pluribus una?
Vivere si recte nescis, decede peritis.
Lusisti satis, edisti satis atque bibisti:
Tempus abire tibi est.

Miriam moved up to him and touched the cold fingers in an instinctive and futile gesture of compassion. She said: "Poor man. Oh, poor man."

"Rolf would say he's done us a service. No time wasted now in persuasion."

"Why did he do it? What does the note say?"

"It's a quotation from Horace. It says that there's no pleasure in getting rid of one thorn among so many. If you can't live well, get out. He probably found the Latin in the *Oxford Dictionary of Quotations.*"

The English underneath was shorter and plainer. "I apologize for the mess. There is one bullet left in the gun." Was that, Theo wondered, a warning or an invitation? And what had led Jasper to this act? Remorse, regret, loneliness, despair, or the realization that the thorn had been drawn but the pain and the hurt remained and were past healing? He said: "You'll probably find the linen and blankets upstairs. I'll get the stores."

He was glad that he was wearing his long country coat. The inner pocket in the lining would easily take the revolver. He checked that there was one bullet in the chamber, removed it, and placed both gun and bullet in his pocket.

The kitchen, its working surfaces bare, a row of mugs hanging with their handles aligned, was grubby but tidy, with no sign that it had ever been used except for a tea-towel, crumpled and obviously recently washed, which had been laid across the empty draining rack to dry. The only discordant note in the ordered neatness was two rush mats rolled up and propped against the wall. Had Jasper perhaps intended to kill himself here and been concerned that the blood should be easily swabbed from the stone floor? Or had he intended once more to wash the stones and then realized the futility of this last obsessional concern for appearance?

The door of the store-room was unlocked. After twenty-five years of anxious husbandry, having no further need of his treasure store, he had left it open, as he had left open his life, to casual despoilers. Here too all was neatness and order. The wooden racks held large tin boxes, the edges sealed with tape. Each was labelled in Jasper's elegant script: *Meat, Tinned Fruit, Milk Powder, Sugar, Coffee, Rice, Tea, Flour.* The sight of the labels, the letters so meticulously written, provoked in Theo a small spasm of compassion, painful and unwelcome, a surge of pity and regret, which the sight of Jasper's splattered brains and bloody chest had been powerless to touch. He let it flow briefly over him, then concentrated on the job in hand. His immediate thought was to empty the tins over the floor and make a selection of the things they were most likely to need, at least for the first week, but he told himself there wasn't time. Even to strip away the tape would hold him up. Better to take a selection unopened: meat, milk powder, dried fruit, coffee, sugar, tinned vegetables. The smaller tins labelled *Drugs and Syringes, Water Purifying Tablets* and *Matches* were obvious choices, as was a compass. Two paraffin stoves presented a more difficult decision. One was an old-fashioned single-burner, the other a more modern, cumbersome, triple-burner stove which he rejected as taking up too much room. He was relieved to find a tin of oil and a two-gallon tin of petrol. He hoped that the tank in the car wasn't empty.

He could hear Miriam moving rapidly but quietly above, and as he came back from carrying out the second lot of tins to the car he met her coming down the stairs, her chin resting on four pillows.

She said: "May as well be comfortable."

"They'll take up quite a bit of room. Have you got all you need for the birth?"

"Plenty of towels and single sheets. We can sit on the pillows. And there's a medicine chest in the bedroom. I've cleared that out, shoved everything in a pillowcase. The disinfectant will be useful but it's mainly simple remedies—aspirin, bicarb, cough mixture. This place has got everything. Pity we can't stay here."

It was not, he knew, a serious suggestion, but he countered it. "Once they find I'm missing, this will be one of the very first places they'll call. All the people I know will be visited and questioned."

They worked together silently, methodically. The boot at last full, he closed it quietly then said: "We'll put my car in the garage and lock it. I'll lock the outer gate, too. It won't keep out the SSP but it may prevent premature discovery."

As he was locking the door of the cottage, Miriam laid a hand on his arm and said quickly: "The gun. Better not let Rolf know you've got it."

There was an insistence, almost an authority in her voice which echoed his own instinctive anxiety. He said: "I've no intention of letting Rolf know."

"Better not tell Julian either. Rolf would try to take it from you and Julian would want you to throw it away."

He said curtly: "I shan't tell either of them. And if Julian wants protection for herself and her child she'll have to stomach the means. Does she aspire to be more virtuous than her God?"

Carefully he edged the Renault out of the gate and parked it behind the Rover. Rolf, pacing beside the car, was indignant.

"You've been a hell of a time. Did you have trouble?"

"No. Jasper's dead. Suicide. We've collected as much as the car will hold. Drive the Rover into the garage and I'll lock it and the gate. I've already locked the house."

There was nothing worth transferring from the Rover to the Renault except his road maps and a paperback edition of *Emma,* which he found in the glove box. He slipped the book into his inner coat pocket, which held the revolver and his diary. Two minutes later they were together in the Renault. Theo took the driver's seat. Rolf, after a moment's hesitation, got in beside him. Julian sat in the back between Miriam and Luke. Theo locked the gate and tossed the key over. Nothing could be seen of the darkened house except the high black slope of the roof.

23

In the first hour they had to stop twice so that
Miriam and Julian could disappear into the darkness. Rolf strained his eyes after them, uneasy
once they were out of his sight. In reply to his
obvious impatience, Miriam said: "You'll have to
get used to it. It happens in late pregnancy. Pres-
sure on the bladder."

At the third stop they all got out to stretch their
legs and Luke too, with a muttered excuse, made
off towards the hedgerow. With the car lights off
and the engine still, the silence seemed absolute.
The air was warm and sweet as if it were still
summer; the stars were bright but high. Theo
thought he could smell a distant bean field, but
that was surely illusory; the flowers would have
dropped by now, the beans would be in full pod.

Rolf moved up to stand beside him. "You and
I have got to talk."

"Then talk."

"We can't have two leaders of this expedition."

"Expedition, is that what it is? Five ill-equipped fugitives with no clear idea where we're going or what we're going to do when we get there. It hardly requires a hierarchy of command. But if you get any satisfaction from calling yourself the leader, it doesn't worry me as long as you don't expect unquestioning obedience."

"You were never part of us, never part of the group. You had your chance to join and turned it down. You're only here because I sent for you."

"I'm here because Julian sent for me. We're stuck with each other. I can put up with you since I have no choice. I suggest that you exercise a similar tolerance."

"I want to drive." Then, as if he hadn't made his meaning clear: "I want to take over the driving from now on."

Theo laughed, his mirth spontaneous and genuine. "Julian's child will be hailed as a miracle. You will be hailed as the father of that miracle. The new Adam, begetter of the new race, the saviour of mankind. That's enough potential power for any man—more power, I suspect, than you'll be able to cope with. And you're worried that you're not getting your share of the driving!"

Rolf paused before replying. "All right, we'll make a pact. I may even be able to use you. The Warden thought you had something to offer. I shall want an adviser too."

"I seem to be the universal confidant. You'll probably find me as unsatisfactory as he did." He was silent for a moment, then asked: "So you're thinking of taking over?"

"Why not? If they want my sperm they'll have to take me. They can't have one without the other. I could do the job as well as he does."

"I thought that your group were arguing that he does it badly, that he's a merciless tyrant. So you're proposing to replace one dictatorship with another. Benevolent this time, I suppose. Most tyrants begin that way."

Rolf didn't reply. Theo thought: We're alone. It may be the only chance I have to talk to him without the others being present. He said: "Look, I still feel that we should telephone the Warden, get Julian the care she needs. You know it's the only sensible course."

"And you know she can't cope with that. She'll be all right. Childbirth is a natural process, isn't it? She's got a midwife."

"Who hasn't delivered a baby for twenty-five years. And there's always the chance of complications."

"There won't be any complications. Miriam isn't worried. Anyway, she'll be in greater danger from complications, physical or mental, if she's forced into hospital. She's terrified of the Warden, she thinks he's evil. He killed Miriam's brother and he's probably killing Gascoigne now. She's terrified that he'll harm her baby."

"That's ridiculous! Neither of you can believe that. It's the last thing he'll want to do. Once he gets possession of the child his power will be immensely increased, not just in Britain, all over the world."

"Not his power, mine. I'm not worried about her safety. The Council won't harm her, or the baby. But it will be me, not Xan Lyppiatt, who presents my child to the world, and then we'll see who's Warden of England."

"So what are your plans?"

"How do you mean?" Rolf's voice was suspicious.

"Well, you must have some idea what you plan to do if you manage to wrest power away from the Warden."

"It won't be a question of wresting it away. The people will give it to me. They'll have to if they want Britain repopulated."

"Oh, I see. The people will give it to you. Well, you're probably right. What then?"

"I shall appoint my own Council but without Xan Lyppiatt as a member. Lyppiatt's had his share of power."

"Presumably you'll do something about pacifying the Isle of Man."

"That's hardly a high priority. The country won't exactly thank me for releasing a gang of criminal psychopaths on them. I'll wait until they reduce themselves by natural wastage. That problem will solve itself."

Theo said: "I imagine that's Lyppiatt's idea, too. It won't please Miriam."

"I don't have to please Miriam. She has her job to do and when that's done she'll be appropriately rewarded."

"And the Sojourners? Are you planning better treatment for them or will you put a stop to all immigration of young foreigners? After all, their own countries need them."

"I'll control it and see that the ones we do let in get fair and firm treatment."

"I imagine that's what the Warden thinks he's doing. What about the Quietus?"

"I shan't interfere with people's liberty to kill themselves in the way they find most convenient."

"The Warden of England would agree."

Rolf said: "What I can do and he can't is to father the new race. We've already got details of all healthy females in the thirty-to-fifty age group on the computer. There'll be tremendous competition for fertile sperm. Obviously there's a danger in interbreeding. That's why we have got to select very carefully for superb physical health and high intelligence."

"The Warden of England would approve. That was his plan."

"But he hasn't got the sperm, I have."

Theo said: "There's one thing you haven't apparently considered. It will depend on what she gives birth to, won't it? The child will have to be normal and healthy. Suppose she's carrying a monster?"

"Why should he be a monster? Why shouldn't he be normal, my child and hers?"

The moment of vulnerability, of shared confidence, the secret fear at last acknowledged and given voice, provoked in Theo a second of sympathy. It wasn't enough to make him like his companion; it was enough to prevent him speaking what was in his mind: "It may be luckier for you if the child is abnormal, deformed, an idiot, a monster. If he's healthy you'll be a breeding, experimental animal for the rest of your life. You don't imagine the Warden will give up his power, even to the father of the new race? They may need your sperm, but they can get possession of enough of that to populate England and half the world, and then decide that you're expendable. Once the Warden sees you as a threat that's probably what will happen."

But he didn't speak.

Three figures appeared out of the darkness,

Luke first, behind him Miriam and Julian, holding hands, walking carefully over the humpy verge. Rolf got in behind the wheel.

"All right," he said, "let's get moving. From now on, I'm doing the driving."

24

As soon as the car jolted forward Theo knew that Rolf would drive too fast. He glanced at him, wondering if he dared risk a warning, hoping that the surface would improve and make it unnecessary. In the bleaching beam of the headlights the pustulous road looked as eerie and alien as a moon landscape, at once close yet mysteriously remote and perpetual. Rolf was gazing through the windscreen with the fierce intensity of a rally driver, wrenching the wheel as each fresh obstruction sprang up from the darkness. The road, with its pot-holes, its ruts and ridges, would have been hazardous for a careful driver. Now, under Rolf's brutal handling, the car jumped and lurched, swaying the three tightly wedged back passengers from side to side.

Miriam struggled free to lean forward, and said: "Take it easy, Rolf. Slow down. This isn't good for Julian. D'you want a premature labour?"

Her voice was calm, but her authority was absolute, its effect immediate. Rolf at once eased his foot on the accelerator. But it was too late. The car juddered and leapt, swerved violently and for three seconds spun out of control. Rolf slammed his foot on the brake and they jerked to a stop.

He said, almost under his breath: "Bloody hell! A front puncture."

There was no point in recriminations. Theo undid his seat belt. "There's a spare wheel in the boot. Let's get the car off the road."

They clambered out and stood in the dark shadow of the hedge while Rolf steered the car on to the grass verge. Theo saw that they were in open rolling country, probably, he thought, about ten miles from Stratford. On either side ran an unkempt hedge of high, tangled bushes broken by torn gaps through which they could see the scarred ridges of the ploughed field. Julian, wrapped in her cloak, stood calmly and silently, like a docile child taken on a picnic and waiting patiently for some minor mishap to be remedied by the adults.

Miriam's voice was calm, but she could not disguise the underlying note of anxiety. "How long will it take?"

Rolf was looking round. He said: "About twenty minutes, less if we're lucky. But we'll be safer off the road, where we can't be seen."

Without an explanation he walked briskly ahead. They waited, their eyes staring after him. Within less than a minute he was back. "About a hundred yards to the right there's a gate and a rough track. It looks as if it leads to a clump of trees. We'll be safer there. God knows this road's practically impassable, but if we can drive down it so can others. We can't risk some fool stopping and offering to help."

Miriam objected: "How far is it? We don't want to go further than we need and it will be tough on the wheel rim."

Rolf said: "We've got to get under cover. I can't be sure how long the job will take. We have to get well out of sight of the road."

Silently Theo agreed with him. It was more important to remain undetected than to cover the miles. The SSP would have no idea in which direction they were travelling and, unless they had already discovered Jasper's body, no name or number for the car. He got into the driver's seat and Rolf made no objection.

Rolf said: "With all those supplies in the boot we'd better lighten the load. Julian can ride, the rest of us will walk."

The gate and the path were closer than Theo

had expected. The rough track ran gently uphill along the edge of an unploughed field, obviously long ago left to seed. The track had been rutted and chevroned by the heavy tyres of tractors; the central ridge was crowned with tall grasses which shook like frail antennae in the headlights. Theo drove slowly and with great care, Julian in the seat beside him, the three silent figures moving like dark shadows alongside. When they came to the clump of trees he saw that the wood offered denser cover than he had expected. But there was a final obstacle. Between it and the track was a deep gully over six feet wide.

Rolf banged on the car window. He said: "Wait here a moment," and again dashed ahead. He came back and said: "There is a way across about thirty yards on. It looks as if it leads into a kind of clearing."

The entrance to the wood was a narrow bridge compounded of sliced logs and earth now covered with grass and weeds. Theo saw with relief that it was wide enough to take the car, but waited while Rolf took the torch and inspected the logs to make sure they hadn't rotted. He gave a wave and Theo manoeuvred the car across with little difficulty. The car bumped gently forward and was enclosed by a grove of beech trees, their high boughs arched into a canopy of bronzed leaves, intricate as a carved roof. Getting out, Theo saw that they had come to a stop in a mush of dead and crackling leaves and split beech nuts.

It was Rolf and Theo who together tackled the front wheel, with Miriam holding the torch. Luke and Julian stood together and watched silently while Rolf lugged out the spare wheel, the jack and the wheel brace. But removing the wheel proved more difficult than Theo had expected. The bolts had been screwed very tightly and neither he nor Rolf could get them to move.

The torchlight moved erratically as Miriam squatted to a more comfortable position. Rolf said impatiently: "For God's sake, hold it steady. I can't see what I'm doing. And it's very dim."

A second later the light went out.

Miriam didn't wait for Rolf's question. She said: "There isn't a spare battery. Sorry. We'll have to stick here until morning."

Theo waited for Rolf's explosion of irritation. It didn't come. Instead he got up and said calmly: "Then we may as well have something to eat and make ourselves comfortable for the rest of the night."

25

Theo and Rolf elected to sleep on the ground; the other three chose the car, Luke in the front seat and the two women curled up in the back. Theo scooped up armfuls of beech leaves, spread out Jasper's raincoat and covered himself with a blanket and his own coat. His last consciousness was of distant voices as the women settled themselves for sleep, of the crackle of twigs as he wriggled deeper into the bed of leaves. Before he slept the wind began to rise, not strong enough to agitate the low boughs of the beech above his head, but making a far-off, distant sound as if the wood was stirring into life.

Next morning he opened his eyes to the pattern of bronze-and-russet beech leaves broken by thin shafts of pale milky light. He was aware of the hardness of the earth, of the smell of loam and leaves, pungent and obscurely comforting. He struggled from under the weight of blanket and coat and stretched, aware of an ache in his shoulders and the small of his back. He was surprised that he had slept so soundly on a bed which, initially wonderfully soft, had compacted under his weight and now felt like a board.

It looked as if he was the last to wake. The doors of the car were open, the seats empty. Someone had already brewed the morning tea. On the flattened ridge of a log were five mugs, all from Jasper's collection of coronation mugs, and a metal teapot. The coloured mugs looked curiously festive.

Rolf said: "Help yourself."

Miriam had a pillow in each hand and was shaking them vigorously. She carried them back to the car, where Rolf had already started work on the wheel. Theo drank his tea, then went over to help him, and they worked together, efficiently and companionably. Rolf's large, square-fingered hands were remarkably dextrous. Perhaps because they were both rested, less anxious, no longer dependent on a single beam of torchlight, the previously intractable nuts yielded to their joint effort.

Gathering up a fistful of leaves to wipe his hands, Theo asked: "Where are Julian and Luke?"

It was Rolf who replied. "Saying their prayers. They do every day. When they come back we'll have breakfast. I've put Luke in charge of the rations. It's good for him to have something more useful to do than saying his prayers with my wife."

"Couldn't they pray here? We ought to keep together."

"They aren't far off. They like to be private. Anyway, I can't stop them. Julian likes it and Miriam tells me I'm to keep her calm and happy. Apparently praying keeps her calm and happy. It's some kind of ritual for them. It doesn't do any harm. Why don't you go and join them if you're worried?"

Theo said: "I don't think they'd want me."

"I don't know, they might. They might try to convert you. Are you a Christian?"

"No, I'm not a Christian."

"What do you believe, then?"

"Believe about what?"

"The things that religious people think are important. Whether there is a God. How do you explain evil? What happens when we die? Why are we here? How ought we to live our lives?"

Theo said: "The last is the most important, the only question that really matters. You don't have to be religious to believe that. And you don't have to be a Christian to find an answer."

Rolf turned to him and asked, as if he really wanted to know: "But what do you believe? I don't just mean religion. What are you sure of?"

"That once I was not and that now I am. That one day I shall no longer be."

Rolf gave a short laugh, harsh as a shout. "That's safe enough. No one can argue with that. What does he believe, the Warden of England?"

"I don't know. We never discussed it."

Miriam came over and, sitting with her back against a trunk, stretched out her legs wide, closed her eyes and lifted her face, gently smiling, to the sky, listening but not speaking.

Rolf said: "I used to believe in God and the Devil and then one morning, when I was twelve, I lost my faith. I woke up and found that I didn't believe in any of the things the Christian Brothers had taught me. I thought if that ever happened I'd be too frightened to go on living, but it didn't make any difference. One night I went to bed believing and the next morning I woke up un-believing. I couldn't even tell God I was sorry, because He wasn't there any more. And yet it didn't really matter. It hasn't mattered ever since."

Miriam said without opening her eyes: "What did you put in His empty place?"

"There wasn't any empty place. That's what I'm telling you."

"What about the Devil?"

"I believe in the Warden of England. He exists.

He's Devil enough for me to be going on with."

Theo walked away from them and made his way down the narrow path between the trees. He was still uneasy about Julian's absence, uneasy and angry. She ought to know that they must keep together, ought to realize that someone, a rambler, a woodman, an estate worker, might come along the lane and see them. It wasn't only the State Security Police or the Grenadiers they needed to fear. He knew that he was feeding irritation with irrational anxieties. Who in this deserted place and at this hour was likely to surprise them? Anger welled up in him, disturbing in its vehemence.

And then he saw them. They were only fifty yards away from the clearing and the car, kneeling in a small green patch of moss. They were totally absorbed. Luke had set up his altar—one of the tin boxes upturned and spread with a tea-towel. On it was a single candle stuck in a saucer. Beside it was another saucer with two crumbs of bread and, beside that, a small mug. He was wearing a cream stole. Theo wondered if he had been carrying it rolled in his pocket. They were unaware of his presence and they reminded him of two children totally absorbed in some primitive game; their faces grave and dappled by the shadow of the leaves. He watched as Luke lifted the saucer with the two crumbs in his left hand, placing his right palm above it. Julian bent her head lower so that she seemed to crouch into the ground.

The words, half-remembered from his distant childhood, were spoken very quietly but came to Theo clearly. "Hear us, O merciful Father, we most humbly beseech thee; and grant that we receiving these thy creatures of bread and wine, according to thy Son our Saviour Jesus Christ's holy institution, in remembrance of his death and passion, may be partakers of his most blessed Body and Blood: who, in the same night that he was betrayed, took Bread; and, when he had given thanks, he brake it, and gave it to his disciples, saying, Take, eat; this is my Body which is given for you; Do this in remembrance of me."

He stood back in the shelter of the trees and watched. In memory he was back in that dull little church in Surrey in his Sunday dark-blue suit, Mr. Greenstreet, his self-importance carefully controlled, ushering the congregation pew by pew to the communion rail. He remembered his mother's bent head. He had felt excluded then and he felt excluded now.

Slipping away from the trees he went back to the clearing. He said: "They've nearly finished. They won't be long now."

Rolf said: "They never are long. We may as well wait breakfast for them. I suppose we should be grateful Luke doesn't feel the need to preach her a sermon."

His voice and smile were indulgent. Theo wondered abut his relationship with Luke, whom he seemed to tolerate as he might a well-meaning child who couldn't be expected to make a full adult contribution but who was doing his best to be useful and was no trouble. Was Rolf merely indulging what he saw as the whim of a pregnant woman? If Julian wanted the services of a personal chaplain, then he was prepared to include Luke in the Five Fishes even though he had no practical skills to offer. Or had Rolf in that single and complete rejection of his childhood religion retained an unacknowledged vestige of superstition? Did he with part of his mind see Luke as the miracle-worker who could turn dry crumbs into flesh, the bringer of luck, the possessor of mystic powers and ancient charms, whose very presence among them could propitiate the dangerous gods of the forest and the night?

26

Friday 15 October 2021

I am writing this entry sitting in the glade of a beechwood, my back against a tree. It is late afternoon and the shadows are beginning to lengthen but, within the grove, the warmth of day still lingers. I have a conviction that this is the last diary entry I shall make, but even if neither I nor these words survive, I need to record this day. It has been one of extraordinary happiness and I have spent it with four strangers. In the years before Omega, at the beginning of each academic year, I used to write an assessment of the applicants I had selected for admission to college. This record, with a photograph from their application form, I kept in a private file. At the end of their three years it used to interest me to see how often my preliminary pen-portrait was accurate, how little they had changed, how powerless I was to alter their essential natures. I was seldom wrong about them. The exercise reinforced my natural confi-

dence in my judgement; perhaps that was its purpose. I believed that I could know them and did
know them. I can't feel that about my fellow-
fugitives. I still know practically nothing about
them: their parents, their families, their education,
their loves, their hopes and desires. Yet I have
never felt so much at ease with other human beings as I have been today with these four strangers
to whom I am now, still half-reluctantly, commit-
ted and one of whom I am learning to love.

It has been a perfect autumn day, the sky a clear
azure blue, the sunlight mellow and gentle but
strong as high June, the air sweet-scented, carrying the illusion of wood smoke, mown hay, the
gathered sweets of summer. Perhaps because the
beech grove is so remote, so enclosed, we have
shared a sense of absolute safety. We have occupied our time in dozing, talking, working, playing
childish games with stones and twigs and pages
torn from my diary. Rolf has checked and cleaned
the car. Watching his meticulous attention to
every inch, his energetic rubbing and polishing, I
found it impossible to believe this innocently employed natural mechanic with his simple pleasure
in the job was the same Rolf who yesterday had
displayed such arrogance, such naked ambition.

Luke busied himself with the stores. Rolf
showed some natural leadership in giving him this
responsibility. Luke decided that we should eat

the fresh food first and then the tins in their date-stamped order, discovering in this obviously sensible priority an unwonted confidence in his own administrative ability. He has sorted out the tins, made lists, devised menus. After we had eaten he would sit quietly with his prayer book or come to join Miriam and Julian while I read to them from *Emma*. Lying back on the beech leaves and gazing up at the glimpses of the strengthening blue sky, I felt as innocently joyous as if we were having a picnic. We were having a picnic. We didn't discuss plans for the future or the dangers to come. Now that seems extraordinary to me, but I think it was less a conscious decision not to plan or argue or discuss than a wish to keep this day inviolate. And I haven't spent time rereading the early entries in this diary. In my present euphoria I have no wish to encounter that self-regarding, sardonic and solitary man. The diary has lasted less than ten months and, after today, I shall no longer have need of it.

The light is failing now and I can hardly see the page. In another hour we shall begin the journey. The car, shining under Rolf's ministrations, is packed and ready. Just as I feel confident that this will be the last entry in my diary, so I know that we shall face dangers and horrors at present unimaginable to me. I have never been superstitious, but this belief cannot be argued or reasoned away.

Believing it, I am still at peace. And I am glad we have had this respite, these happy innocent hours stolen, it seems, out of inexorable time. During the afternoon, while rummaging in the back of the car, Miriam found a second torch, little larger than a pencil, wedged down the side of a seat. It would hardly have been adequate to replace the one which failed, but I am grateful we didn't know it was there. We needed this day.

27

The dashboard clock showed five minutes to three, later than Theo had expected. The road, narrow and deserted, opened palely before them, then slid under the wheels like a strip of torn and soiled linen. The surface was deteriorating and from time to time the car jolted violently as they struck a pot-hole. It was impossible to drive fast on such a road; he dared not risk a second puncture. The night was dark but not totally black; the half-moon reeled between the scudding clouds, the stars were high pin-pricks of half-formed constellations, the Milky Way was a smudge of light. The car, handling easily, seemed to be a moving refuge, warmed by their breath, smelling faintly of familiar, unfrightening things which in his bemused state he tried to identify: petrol, human bodies, Jasper's old dog, long since dead, even the faint aroma of peppermint. Rolf was beside him, silent but tense, staring ahead. In the back seat

Julian sat squashed between Miriam and Luke. It was the least comfortable seat but the one she had wanted; perhaps being buttressed by the two bodies gave her an illusion of added safety. Her eyes were closed, her head rested on Miriam's shoulder. Then, as he watched in the mirror, it jerked, slipped and lolled forward. Gently Miriam raised it to a more comfortable position. Luke, too, looked asleep, his head thrown back, his mouth a little open.

The road curved and twisted but its surface became smoother. Theo was lulled into confidence by the hours of trouble-free motoring. Perhaps, after all, the journey need not be disastrous. Gascoigne would have talked, but he hadn't known about the child. In Xan's eyes the Five Fishes were surely a small and contemptible band of amateurs. He might not even bother to have them hunted down. For the first time since the journey began there rose in him a spring of hope.

He saw the fallen trunk only just in time and braked violently a moment before the car bonnet scraped its jutting branches. Rolf jerked awake and swore. Theo switched off the engine. There was a moment of silence in which two thoughts, following so quickly they were almost instantaneous, shook him into full consciousness. The first was relief; the trunk didn't look heavy despite its bush of autumn leaves. He and the other two men could probably drag it clear without much trouble. The second realization was horror. It couldn't have fallen so inconveniently; there had been no recent strong winds. This was a deliberate obstruction.

And in that second the Omegas were upon them. Horribly, they came at first unheard, in total silence. At each car window the painted faces stared in, lit by the flames of torches. Miriam gave a short involuntary scream. Rolf yelled "Back! Reverse!" and tried to seize the wheel and gearstick. Their hands locked. Theo thrust him aside and slammed the gears into reverse. The engine roared into life, the car shot back. They crashed to a stop with a violence which threw him forward. The Omegas must have moved quickly and silently, imprisoning them with a second obstruction. And now the faces were at the windows again. He stared into two expressionless eyes, gleaming, white-rimmed, in a mask of blue, red and yellow swirls. Above the painted forehead the hair was dragged back into a top-knot. In one hand the Omega held a flaming torch, in the other a club, like a policeman's truncheon, decorated with thin pigtails of hair. Theo remembered with horror being told that when the Painted Faces killed they cut off the hair of the victim and braided it into a trophy, a rumour he had only half believed, part of the folklore of terror. Now he gazed in fascinated horror at the dangling plait and wondered whether it had come from the head of a man or a woman.

No one in the car spoke. The silence, which had seemed to last for minutes, could have been held for seconds only. And then the ritual dance began. With a great whoop the figures slowly pranced round the car, beating their truncheons on the sides and the roof, a rhythmic drumbeat to the high chanting voices. They were wearing shorts only but their bodies were unpainted. The naked chests looked white as milk in the flame of the torches, the rib-cages delicately vulnerable. The jerking legs, the ornate heads, the patterned faces slit by wide, yodelling mouths, made it possible to see them as a gang of overgrown children playing their disruptive but essentially innocent games.

Was it possible, Theo wondered, to talk to them, to reason with them, establish at least a recognition of common humanity? He wasted no time on the thought. He remembered once meeting one of their victims and a snatch of their conversation came into his mind. "They're said to kill the single sacrificial victim, but on this occasion, thank God, they were satisfied with the car." He had added: "Just don't meddle with them. Abandon your vehicle and get away." For him, escape hadn't been easy; for them, encumbered with a pregnant woman, it seemed impossible. But there was one fact which might divert them from murder, if they were capable of rational thought and believed it: Julian's pregnancy. The evidence was now sufficient even for an Omega. But he had no need to ask himself what Julian's reaction to that would be; they hadn't fled from Xan and the Council to fall into the power of the Painted Faces. He looked back at Julian. She was sitting with her head bowed. Presumably she was praying. He wished her good luck with her god. Miriam's eyes were wide and terrified. It was impossible to see Luke's face, but from his seat Rolf poured out a stream of obscenities.

The dance continued, the whirling bodies moving ever faster, the chanting louder. It was difficult to see how many there were but he judged there couldn't be fewer than a dozen. They were making no move to open the car doors but the locks, he knew, provided no real safety. There were enough of them to overturn the car. There were torches to set it alight. It was only a matter of time before they were forced out.

Theo's thoughts were racing. What chance was there of a successful flight, at least for Julian and Rolf? Through the kaleidoscope of prancing bodies he studied the terrain. To the left was a low crumbling stone wall, in parts, he judged, no more than three feet high. Beyond it he could see a dark fringe of trees. He had the gun, the single bullet, but he knew that even to show the gun could be fatal. He could kill only one; the rest would fall on them in a fury of retaliation. It would be a massacre. It was useless to think of physical force, outnumbered as they were. The darkness was their only hope. If Julian and Rolf could reach the fringe of trees there was at least a chance of concealment. To keep running, crashing dangerously and noisily through the undergrowth of an unfamiliar wood, would only invite pursuit, but it might be possible to hide. Success would depend on whether the Omegas bothered to pursue. There was a chance, if only a small one, that they would content themselves with the car and their remaining three victims.

He thought: They mustn't see that we're talking, mustn't know that we're scheming to get away. There was no fear that their words would be overheard; the whoops and cries which made the night hideous almost drowned his voice. It was necessary to speak loudly and clearly if Luke, Miriam and Julian in the back were to hear, but he was careful not to turn his head.

He said: "They'll make us get out in the end. We'll have to plan exactly what we're going to do. It's up to you, Rolf. When they pull us out, get

Julian over that wall, then run for the trees and hide. Choose your moment. The rest of us will try to cover for you."

Rolf said: "How? How do you mean cover? How can you cover for us?"

"By talking. By taking their attention." Then inspiration came to him. "By joining the dance."

Rolf's voice was high, close to hysteria. "Dance with those fuckers? What sort of a gig d'you think this is? They don't talk. These fuckers don't talk and they don't dance with their victims. They burn, they kill."

"Never more than one victim. We have to see that it isn't Julian or you."

"They'll come after us. Julian can't run."

"I doubt whether they'll bother with three other possible victims and the car to burn. We've got to choose the right moment. Get Julian over that wall if you have to drag her. Then make for the trees. Understand?"

"It's crazy."

"If you can think of another plan, let's have it."

After a moment's thought, Rolf said: "We could show Julian to them. Tell them she's pregnant, let them see for themselves. Tell them I'm the father. We could make a pact with them. At least that would keep us alive. We'll talk to them now, before they try to drag us from the car."

From the back seat Julian spoke for the first

time. She said clearly: "No."

After that single word no one spoke for a moment. Then Theo said again: "They'll make us get out in the end. Either that, or they'll fire the car. That's why we have to plan now exactly what we're going to do. If we join the dance—if they don't kill us then—we may distract their attention for long enough to give you and Julian a chance."

Rolf's voice was close to hysteria. "I'm not moving. They'll have to drag me out."

"That's what they will do."

Luke spoke for the first time. He said: "If we don't provoke them perhaps they'll get tired and go away."

Theo said: "They won't go away. They always burn the car. It's a choice for us of being outside or in when they do."

There was a crash. The windscreen shivered into a maze of cracks but didn't break. Then one of the Omegas swung his club at the front window. The glass smashed, falling over Rolf's lap. The night air rushed into the car with the chill of death. Rolf gasped and jerked back as the Omega thrust in his lighted torch and held it blazing against his face.

The Omega laughed, then said in a voice that was ingratiating, educated, almost enticing: "Come out, come out, come out, whoever you are."

There were two more crashes and the rear windows went. Miriam gave a cry as a torch scorched her face. There was a smell of singeing hair. Theo had only time to say, "Remember. The dance. Then make for the wall," before the five of them tumbled from the car and were seized and dragged clear.

They were at once surrounded. The Omegas, holding their torches high in their left hands, their clubs in their right, stood for a second regarding them, and then began again their ritual dance with their captives in the centre. But this time their movements were at first slower, more ceremonial, the chanting deeper, no longer a celebration but a dirge. At once Theo joined in, raising his arms, twisting his body, mixing his voice with theirs. One by one the other four slipped into place in the ring. They were separated. That was bad. He wanted Rolf and Julian close so that he could give them the signal to move. But the first part of the plan and the most dangerous had worked. He had feared that, with his first move, they would have struck him down, had braced himself for the one annihilating blow that would have put an end to responsibility, an end to life. It hadn't come.

And now, as if in obedience to secret orders, the Omegas began to stamp in unison, faster and faster, then broke out again into their whirling dance. The Omega in front of him twisted, then began to prance backwards with light delicate steps, like a cat, whirling his club above his head. He grinned into Theo's face, their noses almost touching. Theo could smell him, a musty smell which was not unpleasant, could see the intricate whirls and curves of the paint, blue, red and black, outlining cheekbones, sweeping above the line of the brow, covering every inch of the face in a pattern which was at once barbaric and sophisticated. For a second he had a memory of the painted South Sea Islanders with their top-knots in the Pitt Rivers Museum, of Julian and himself standing together in that quiet emptiness.

The Omega's eyes, black pools among the blaze of colour, held his. He dared not shift his glance to look for Julian or Rolf. Round and round they danced, faster and faster. When would Rolf and Julian make their move? Even as he gazed into the Omega's eyes his mind was willing them to make a dash for it, now, before their captors tired of this spurious comradeship. And then the Omega twisted away from him to dance forward and he was able to turn his head. Rolf, with Julian beside him, was at the far side of the ring, Rolf jigging in a clumsy parody of a dance, holding his arms stiffly aloft, Julian clasping her cloak with her left hand, her right hand free, her cloaked body swaying in time to the clamour of the dancers.

And then there was a moment of horror. The Omega prancing behind her put out his left hand and caught her plaited hair. He gave it a tug and the plait came apart. She paused for a second, then began dancing again, the hair swirling about her face. They were coming up now to the grass verge and to the lowest part of the wall. He could see it clearly in the torchlight, the fallen stones on the grass, the black shape of the trees beyond. He wanted to cry aloud: "Now. Make it now. Go! Go!" And at that moment Rolf acted. He grabbed Julian's hand and together they dashed for the wall. Rolf jumped it first, then half-swung, half-dragged Julian across. Some of the dancers, absorbed, ecstatic, went on with their high wailing, but the Omega closest to them was swift. He dropped his torch and, with a wild cry, dashed after them and seized the end of Julian's cloak as it brushed across the wall.

And then Luke sprang forward. Seizing the Omega he tried ineffectually to drag him back, crying out: "No, no. Take me! Take me!"

The Omega let go of the cloak and, with a cry of fury, turned on Luke. For a second Theo saw Julian hesitate, stretching out an arm, but Rolf jerked her away and the two fleeing figures were lost among the shadows of the trees. It was over in seconds, leaving Theo with a confused picture of Julian's outstretched arm and beseeching eyes, of Rolf hauling her away, of the Omega's torch flaming among the grasses.

And now the Omegas had their self-selected victim. A terrible silence fell as they closed around him, ignoring Theo and Miriam. At the first crack of wood on bone, Theo heard a single scream but he couldn't tell whether it came from Miriam or Luke. And then Luke was down, and his murderers fell upon him like beasts round their prey, jostling for a place, raining their blows in a frenzy. The dance was over, the ceremony of death ended, the killing had begun. They killed in silence, a terrible silence in which it seemed to Theo that he could hear the crack and splinter of every single bone, could feel his ears bursting with the gushing of Luke's blood. He seized Miriam and dragged her to the wall.

She gasped: "No. We can't, we can't! We can't leave him."

"We must. We can't help him now. Julian needs you."

The Omegas made no move to follow. When Theo and Miriam gained the outskirts of the wood they paused and looked back. And now the killing looked less like a frenzy of blood-lust than a calculated murder. Five or six of the Omegas were holding their torches aloft in a circle within which, silently now, the dark shapes of the half-naked bodies, arms wielding their clubs, rose and fell in a ritual ballet of death. Even from this distance it seemed to Theo that the air was splintered with the smashing of Luke's bones. But he knew that he could hear nothing, nothing but the rasp of Miriam's breathing and the thudding of his own heart. He was aware that Rolf and Julian had come up quietly behind them. Together they watched in silence as the Omegas, their work completed, broke again into a whoop of triumph and rushed to the captured car. In the torchlight Theo could make out the shape of a wide gate to the field bordering the road. Two of the Omegas held it open and the car lurched over the grass verge and through the gate, driven by one of the gang, the rest pushing it from behind. They must, Theo knew, have their own vehicle, probably a small van, although he couldn't remember seeing it. But he had a moment's ridiculous hope that they might temporarily abandon it in the excitement of firing the car, that there might be a chance, however small, that he could get to it, might even find that they had left the keys in the ignition. The thought, he knew, had never been rational. Even as it entered his mind he saw that a small black van was being driven up the road and through the gate into the field.

They didn't go far, Theo judged no more than fifty yards. Then the whooping and the wild dancing began again. There was an explosion as the

Renault burst into flames. And with it went Miriam's medical supplies, their food, their water, their blankets. With it went all their hope.

He heard Julian's voice: "We can get Luke now. Now, while they're occupied."

Rolf said: "Better leave it. If they find he's gone it will only remind them that we're still here. We'll get him later."

Julian tugged gently at Theo's sleeve. "Please get him. There may be a chance that he's still alive."

Miriam spoke out of the darkness: "He won't be alive, but I'm not leaving him there. Dead or alive, we're together."

She was already moving forward when Theo caught her by her sleeve. He said quietly: "Stay with Julian. Rolf and I will manage."

Without looking at Rolf, he made for the road. At first he thought he was alone, but in a few moments Rolf had moved alongside him.

When they reached the dark shape huddled on its side as if asleep, Theo said: "You're the stronger. You take the head."

Together they turned the body over. Luke's face had gone. Even in the distant ruddy light cast by the flaming car they could see that the whole head had been battered into a mess of blood, skin and cracked bones. The arms lay askew, the legs seemed to buckle as Theo braced himself to lift him. It was like trying to take hold of a broken marionette.

He was lighter than Theo had expected, although he could hear his and Rolf's rasping breath as they crossed the shallow ditch between the road and the wall and eased the body over. When they joined the others Julian and Miriam turned without a word and walked ahead, as if part of a pre-arranged funeral procession. Miriam switched on the torch and they followed the tiny pool of light. The journey seemed endless but Theo judged that they could only have been walking for a minute when they came across a fallen tree.

He said: "We'll lay him down here."

Miriam had been careful not to shine the torch on Luke. Now she said to Julian: "Don't look at him. You don't need to look at him."

Julian's voice was calm. "I have to see. If I don't see it will be worse. Give me the torch."

Without another protest Miriam handed it over. Julian shone it slowly over Luke's body then, kneeling at his head, tried to wipe the blood from his face with her skirt.

Miriam said gently: "It's no use. There's nothing there any more."

Julian said: "He died to save me."

"He died to save all of us."

Theo was suddenly aware of a great weariness.

He thought: We've got to bury him. We have to get him underground before we move on. But move on where and how? Somehow they must get hold of another car, food, water, blankets. But the greatest need now was water. He craved water, thirst driving out hunger. Julian was kneeling by Luke's body, cradling his shattered head in her lap, her dark hair falling over his face. She made no sound.

Then Rolf bent down and took the torch from Julian's hand. He shone it full on Miriam's face. She blinked in the thin but intense beam, instinctively putting up her hand. His voice was low and harsh, and so distorted that it might have been forced through a diseased larynx. He said: "Whose child is she carrying?"

Miriam put down her hand and looked at him steadily but didn't speak.

He repeated: "I asked you, whose child is she carrying?"

His voice was clearer now, but Theo could see that his whole body was shaking. Instinctively he moved closer to Julian.

Rolf turned on him. "Keep out of this! This is nothing to do with you. I'm asking Miriam." Then he repeated more violently. "Nothing to do with you! Nothing!"

Julian's voice came out of the darkness: "Why not ask me?"

For the first time since Luke had died he turned to her. The torchlight moved steadily and slowly from Miriam's face to hers.

She said: "Luke's. The child is Luke's."

Rolf's voice was very quiet: "Are you sure?"

"Yes, I'm sure."

He shone the torch down on Luke's body and scrutinized it with the cold professional interest of an executioner checking that the condemned is dead, that there is no need for the final *coup de grâce*. Then, with a violent motion he turned away from them, stumbled between the trees and flung himself against one of the beeches, encircling it with his arms.

Miriam said: "My God, what a time to ask! And what a time to be told."

Theo said: "Go to him, Miriam."

"My skills aren't any use to him. He'll have to cope with this by himself."

Julian still knelt by Luke's head. Theo and Miriam, standing together, stared fixedly at that dark shadow as if afraid that, unmarked, it would disappear among the darker shadows of the wood. They could hear no sound but it seemed to Theo that Rolf was rubbing his face against the bark like a tormented animal trying to rid itself of stinging flies. And now he was thrusting his whole body against the tree as if venting his anger and agony on the unyielding wood. Watching those

jerking limbs in their obscene parody of lust reinforced for Theo the indecency of witnessing so
much pain.

He turned away and said quietly to Miriam:
"Did you know that Luke was the father?"

"I knew."

"She told you?"

"I guessed."

"But you said nothing."

"What did you expect me to say? It was never
my practice to inquire who fathered the babies I
delivered. A baby is a baby."

"This one is different."

"Not to a midwife."

"Did she love him?"

"Ah, that's what men always want to know.
You'd better ask her."

Theo said: "Miriam, please talk to me about
this."

"I think she was sorry for him. I don't think she
loved either of them, neither Rolf nor Luke. She's
beginning to love you, whatever that means, but
I think you know that. If you hadn't known it, or
hoped for it, you wouldn't be here."

"Wasn't Luke ever tested? Or did both he and
Rolf give up going for their sperm test?"

"Rolf has, at least during the last few months.
He thought that the technicians had been careless
or that they're just not bothering to test half the

specimens they take. Luke was exempt from testing. He had mild epilepsy as a child. Like Julian,
Luke was a reject."

They had moved a little apart from Julian.
Now, looking back at her dark kneeling shape,
Theo said: "She's so calm. Anyone would think
she's having this child under the best possible
circumstances."

"What are the best possible circumstances?
Women have given birth in war, revolutions, fam-
ine, concentration camps, on the march. She's got
the essentials, you and a midwife she trusts."

"She trusts in her God."

"Perhaps you should try doing the same. It
might give you some of her calm. Later, when the
baby comes, I shall need your help. I certainly
don't need your anxiety."

"Do you?" he asked.

She smiled, understanding the question. "Be-
lieve in God? No, it's too late for me. I believe in
Julian's strength and courage and in my own skill.
But if He gets us through this maybe I'll change
my mind, see if I can't get something going with
Him."

"I don't think He bargains."

"Oh yes He does. I may not be religious but I
know my Bible. My mother saw to that. He bargains all right. But He's supposed to be just. If He
wants belief He'd better provide some evidence."

"That He exists?"

"That He cares."

And still they stood, eyes watching that dark figure, hardly discernible against the darker trunk of which he seemed to be part, but quiet now, unmoving, resting against the tree as if in an extremity of exhaustion.

Theo said to Miriam, knowing the futility of the question even as he asked it: "Will he be all right?"

"I don't know. How can I know?"

She moved from his side and walked towards Rolf, then stopped and stood quietly waiting, knowing that if he needed the comfort of a human touch, there was no one else to whom he could turn.

Julian got up from Luke's body. Theo felt her cloak brush his arm but he did not turn to look at her. He was aware of a mixture of emotions, anger which he knew he had no right to feel, and relief, so strong that it was close to joy, that Rolf wasn't the father of the child. But the anger was for the moment the stronger. He wanted to lash out at her, to say: "Is that what you were, then? Camp-follower to the group? What about Gascoigne? How do you know the child isn't his?" But those words would be unforgivable and, worse, unforgettable. He knew that he had no right to question her but he couldn't bite back the stark accusatory words nor hide the pain behind them.

"Did you love them, either of them? Do you love your husband?"

She said quietly: "Did you love your wife?"

It was, he saw, a serious question, not a retaliation, and he gave it a serious and truthful answer. "I convinced myself I did when I married. I willed myself into the appropriate feelings without knowing what the appropriate feelings were. I endowed her with qualities she didn't have and then despised her for not having them. Afterwards I might have learned to love her if I had thought more of her needs and less of my own."

He thought: Portrait of a marriage. Perhaps most marriages, good and bad, could be summed up in four sentences.

She looked at him steadily for a moment, then said: "That's the answer to your question."

"And Luke?"

"No, I didn't love him, but I liked having him in love with me. I envied him because he could love so much, could feel so much. No one has wanted me with that intensity of emotion. So I gave him what he wanted. If I had loved him it would have been . . ." She paused for a moment, then said: "It would have been less sinful."

"Isn't that a strong word for a simple act of generosity?"

"But it wasn't a simple act of generosity. It was

an act of self-indulgence."

It wasn't, he knew, the time for such a conversation, but when would there be a time? He had to
know, had to understand. He said: "But it would
have been all right, 'less sinful' are the words
you used, if you'd loved him. So you agree with
Rosie McClure, love justifies everything, excuses
everything?"

"No, but it's natural, it's human. What I did
was to use Luke out of curiosity, boredom, perhaps to get back a little at Rolf for caring more for
the group than he did for me, punishing Rolf
because I'd stopped loving him. Can you understand that, the need to hurt someone because you
can no longer love?"

"Yes, I understand that."

She added: "It was all very commonplace, predictable, ignoble."

Theo said: "And tawdry."

"No. Not that. Nothing to do with Luke was
tawdry. But it harmed him more than it gave him
joy. But then you didn't think I was a saint."

"No, but I thought you were good."

She said quietly: "Now you know that I'm
not."

Staring into the half-darkness, Theo saw that
Rolf had detached himself from the tree and was
walking back to join them. Miriam moved forward to meet him. The three pairs of eyes gazed at

Rolf's face, watching, waiting for his first words. When he got close, Theo saw that the left cheek and forehead were an open wound, the skin had been rubbed raw.

Rolf's voice was perfectly calm but oddly pitched, so that, for one ridiculous moment, Theo thought a stranger had crept up on them in the darkness: "Before we move we must get him buried. That means waiting until it's light. We'd better get his coat off before he stiffens too much. We need all the warm clothes we have."

Miriam said: "Burying him won't be easy without some kind of spade. The ground's soft but we need to scrape a hole somehow. We can't just cover him with leaves."

Rolf said: "It can wait till morning. We'll get the coat off now. It's no use to him."

Having made the suggestion, he took no action to carry it out and it was Miriam and Theo who between them rolled over the body and eased the coat from both arms. The sleeves were heavily bloodstained. Theo could feel them wet under his hands. They composed the body again on its back, the arms straight at the side.

Rolf said: "Tomorrow I'll get hold of another car. In the meantime we'll get what rest we can."

They wedged themselves together in the wide fork of a fallen beech. A jutting branch, still thickly hung with the brittle bronze pennants of autumn, provided an illusion of security, and they huddled beneath it like children conscious of grave delinquencies, hiding ineffectively from the searching adults. Rolf took the outside place, with Miriam next to him, then Julian between Miriam and Theo. Their rigid bodies seemed to infect the air around them with anxiety. The wood itself was distraught; its ceaseless small noises hissed and whispered on the agitated air. Theo couldn't sleep, and knew from the uneven breathing, suppressed coughs, and small grunts and sighs that the others shared his vigil. There would be a time for sleep. It would come with the greater warmth of the day, with the burial of that dark, stiffening shape which, out of sight on the other side of the fallen tree, was a living presence in all their minds. He was aware of the warmth of Julian's body pressed against his and knew that she must feel from him a similar comfort. Miriam had tucked Luke's coat around Julian and it seemed to Theo that he could smell the drying blood. He felt suspended in a limbo of time, aware of the cold, of thirst, of the innumerable small sounds of the wood, but not of the passing hours. Like his companions, he endured and waited for the dawn.

28

Daylight, tentative and bleak, stole like a chill breath into the wood, wrapping itself round barks and broken boughs, touching the boles of the trees and the low denuded branches, giving darkness and mystery form and substance. Opening his eyes, Theo couldn't believe that he had actually dozed, although he must have momentarily lost consciousness since he had no recollection of Rolf getting up and leaving them.

Now he saw him striding back through the trees. Rolf said: "I've been exploring. This isn't a proper wood, more a copse. It's only about eighty yards wide. We can't hide here for long. There's a kind of ditch between the end of the wood and the field. That should do for him."

Again Rolf made no move to touch Luke's body. It was Miriam and Theo who managed between them to raise it. Miriam held Luke's legs, parted, resting against her thighs. Theo took the weight of the head and shoulders, sensing that he could already detect the onset of rigor. The body sagged between them as they followed Rolf through the trees. Julian walked beside them, her cloak clutched tightly round her, her face calm but very pale, Luke's bloodstained coat and his cream stole folded over her arm. She carried them like trophies of battle.

It was only about fifty yards to the edge of the copse and they found themselves looking out over a gently rolling countryside. The harvest was over and bales of straw lay like pale bolsters haphazard on the distant uplands. The sun, a ball of harsh white light, was already beginning to dispel the thin mist which lay over fields and far hills, absorbing the autumn colours and merging them to a soft olive green in which the individual trees stood out like black cut-outs. It was going to be another mellow autumn day. With a lifting of the heart, Theo saw that there was a hedge of laden blackberry bushes edging the wood. It took all his self-control not to drop Luke's body and fall on them.

The ditch was shallow, no more than a narrow gully between the copse and the field. But it would have been difficult to find a more convenient burial place. The field had recently been ploughed and the ridged earth looked relatively soft. Bending, Theo and Miriam let the body roll from their grasp and tumble into the shallow depression. Theo wished that they could have done it more reverently, less as if dumping an unwanted animal. Luke had come to rest face-downwards. Sensing that this wasn't what Julian wanted, he jumped into the ditch and tried to turn the body over. The task was more difficult than he had expected, better not attempted. In the end Miriam had to help and they struggled together in the earth and leaves before what remained of Luke's battered and mud-caked face was turned upwards to the sky.

Miriam said: "We can cover him first with leaves, and then with the earth."

Still Rolf made no move to help, but the other three went back into the wood and came with armfuls of dried and mouldering leaves, the brown lightened by the bright bronze of the newly fallen beech leaves. Before they began the burial Julian rolled up Luke's stole and dropped it into the grave. For a second Theo was tempted to protest. They had so little: their clothes, a small torch, the gun with the bullet. The stole could have been useful. But for what? Why grudge Luke what was his? The three of them covered the body with leaves, then began with their hands shifting the soil from the edge of the field on top of the grave. It would have been quicker and easier for Theo to kick the sliced clots of earth over the body and stamp them down but in Julian's presence he felt unable to act with such brutal efficiency.

Throughout the burial Julian had been silent but perfectly calm. Suddenly she said: "He should lie in consecrated ground." For the first time she sounded distressed, uncertain, plaintive as a worried child.

Theo felt a spurt of irritation. What, he nearly asked, did she expect them to do? Wait until dark then dig up the body, lug it to the nearest cemetery and reopen one of the graves?

It was Miriam who replied. Looking at Julian, she said gently: "Every place where a good man lies is consecrated ground."

Julian turned to Theo. "Luke would want us to say the Burial Service. His prayer book is in his pocket. Please do it for him."

She shook out the bloodstained coat and took from an inside breast pocket the small black leather prayer book, then handed it to Theo. It took only a little time to find the place. He knew that the service wasn't long, but even so decided to truncate it. He couldn't refuse her, but it wasn't a task he welcomed. He began speaking the words, Julian standing on his left and Miriam on his right. Rolf stood at the foot of the grave, straddling it with his legs, his arms folded, gazing ahead. His ravaged face was so white, the body so

rigid, that, looking up, Theo almost feared that he
would crash forward over the soft earth. But he
felt an increased respect for him. It was impossible
to imagine the enormity of his disappointment or
the bitterness of his betrayal. But at least he was
still on his feet. He wondered if he would have
been capable of such control. He kept his eyes on
the prayer book but he was aware of Rolf's dark
eyes staring at him across the grave.

At first his voice sounded strange to his own
ears, but by the time he got to the psalm the words
had taken over and he spoke quietly, with confidence, seeming to know them by heart. " 'Lord,
thou hast been our refuge: from one generation to
another. Before the mountains were brought
forth, or ever the earth and the world were made:
thou art God from everlasting, and world without
end. Thou turnest man to destruction: again thou
sayest, Come again, ye children of men. For a
thousand years in thy sight are but as yesterday:
seeing that is past as a watch in the night.' "

He came to the words of the committal. As he
spoke the sentence "Earth to earth, ashes to ashes,
dust to dust; in sure and certain hope of the Resur-
rection to eternal life, through our Lord Jesus
Christ," Julian squatted down and threw a handful
of earth over the grave. After a second's hesitation
Miriam did the same. With her graceless swollen
body, it was difficult for Julian to squat, and Mir-

iam put out a supporting hand. There came into Theo's mind, unsought and unwelcome, the image of a defecating animal. Despising himself, he thrust it aside. When he spoke the words of the grace, Julian's voice joined his. Then he closed the prayer book. Still Rolf neither moved nor spoke.

Suddenly, in one violent movement, he turned on his heel and said: "Tonight we'll have to get hold of another car. Now I'm going to sleep. You'd better do the same."

But first they made their way along the hedge, stuffing their mouths with the blackberries, hands and lips purple-stained. The bushes, unplundered, were heavy with the ripe berries, small plump grenades of sweetness. Theo marvelled that Rolf could resist them. Or had he already that morning eaten his fill? The berries, breaking against his tongue, restored hope and strength in beads of unbelievably delicious juice.

Then, with hunger and thirst partly assuaged, they returned to the copse, to the same fallen trunk which seemed to offer at least the psychological reassurance of a hiding place. The two women lay down closely together, Luke's stiffening coat wrapped round them. Theo stretched himself at their feet. Rolf had already found his bed on the other side of the trunk. The earth was soft with the mulch of decades of fallen leaves but even had it been hard as iron Theo would still have slept.

29

It was early evening when he awoke. Julian was standing over him. She said: "Rolf's gone."

He was instantly wide awake. "Are you sure?"

"Yes, I'm sure."

He believed her, yet even then he had to speak the spurious words of hope: "He could have gone for a walk, needed to be alone, wanted to think."

"He has thought; now he's gone."

Still obstinately trying to convince her, if not himself, he said: "He's angry and confused. He no longer wants to be with you when the child is born, but I can't believe he'll betray you."

"Why not? I betrayed him. We'd better wake Miriam."

But there was no need. Their voices had reached Miriam's wakening consciousness. She sat up abruptly and looked across to where Rolf had lain. Struggling to her feet, she said: "So he's gone. We ought to have known he would. Anyway we couldn't have prevented him."

Theo said: "I might have kept him with us. I've got the gun."

It was Miriam who answered the question in Julian's eyes. "We've got a gun. Don't worry, it could be a useful thing to have." She turned from Julian to Theo. "Kept him with us maybe, but for how long? And how? One of us holding the gun to his head night and day, taking it in turns to sleep, to guard him?"

"You think he's gone to the Council?"

"Not to the Council, to the Warden. He's changed his allegiance. He's always been fascinated by power. Now he's joined forces with the source of power. But I don't think he'll telephone London. This news is too important to be leaked. He'll want to give it in person to the Warden alone. That gives us a few hours, maybe more— say five if we're lucky. It depends when he left, how far he's got."

Theo thought: Five hours or fifty, what difference does it make? A weight of despair dragged at mind and limbs, leaving him physically weakened so that the instinct to sink to the earth almost overpowered him. There was a second—hardly more—in which even thought was numbed; but it passed. Intelligence reasserted itself and with thought came a renewal of hope. What would he do if he were Rolf? Make his way to the road, hail the first car, find the nearest telephone? But was it that simple? Rolf was a hunted man without money, transport or food. Miriam was right. The secret he carried was of such importance that it must be kept inviolate until it could be told to the one man to whom it would mean most and who would pay most for it: Xan.

Rolf had to reach Xan, and to reach him safely. He couldn't risk capture, the casual bullet from some trigger-happy member of the State Security Police. Even arrest by the Grenadiers would be hardly less disastrous; the prison cell in which he would be at their mercy, his demands to see the Warden of England immediately meeting with laughter and contempt. No, he would try to make his way to London, travelling, as they were, under cover of night, living off the land. Once in the capital, he would show himself at the old Foreign Office, demand to see the Warden, secure in the knowledge that he had reached the place where that demand would be taken seriously, where power was absolute and would be exercised. And, if persuasion failed and access was denied, he would have that final card to play. "I have to see him. Tell him from me that the woman is pregnant." Xan would see him then.

But once the news was given and believed, they would come quickly. Even if Xan thought that Rolf was lying or mad they would still come. Even if they thought that this was the final phantom pregnancy, the signs, the symptoms, the bulging womb, all destined to end in farce, they would still come. This was too important to chance a mistake. They would come by helicopter with doctors and midwives and, once the truth was established, with television cameras. Julian would be tenderly lifted away to that public hospital bed, to the medical technology of childbirth which had not been used for twenty-five years. Xan himself would preside and would give the news to an incredulous world. There would be no simple shepherds at this cradle.

He said: "I reckon we're about fifteen miles south-west of Leominster. The original plan still holds. We find a refuge, a cottage or house, as deep in woodland as possible. Obviously Wales is out. We could strike south-east to the Forest of Dean. We need transport, water and food. As soon as it's dark I'll walk into the nearest village and steal a car. We're only a few miles from one. I saw its lights in the distance just before the Omegas got us."

He almost expected Miriam to ask how. Instead she said: "It's worth a try. Don't take more risks than you need."

Julian said: "Please, Theo, don't take the gun."

He turned on her, biting back anger. "I shall take what I need to take and do what I have to do.

How much longer can you go on without water? We can't live on blackberries. We need food, drink, blankets, things for the birth. We need a car. If we can get into hiding before Rolf gets to the Council there's still a hope. Or perhaps you've changed your mind. Perhaps you want to follow his example and give yourself up."

She shook her head but didn't speak. He saw that there were tears in her eyes. He wanted to take her in his arms. Instead he stood distanced, and, putting his hand in his inner pocket, felt for the cold weight of the gun.

30

He set off immediately darkness fell, impatient to be gone, resenting every wasted moment. Their safety depended on the speed with which he could get hold of a car. Julian and Miriam came to the edge of the wood and watched him out of sight. Turning to take a final glance he had to fight down a momentary conviction that this might be the last time he saw them. He remembered that the lights of a village or small town had lain to the west of the road. The most direct way might be to cross the fields, but he had left the torch with the women and to attempt a cross-country route with no light and in unknown country could invite disaster. He broke into a run and then, half-walking, half-running, followed the route they had travelled. After half an hour he reached a cross-roads and, after a little thought, took the left fork.

It took him another hour's brisk walking to get to the outskirts of the town. The country road, unlit, was bordered on one side by tall straggling hedges and on the other by a thin copse. He walked on that side and, when he heard a car approaching, stepped into the shadow of the trees, partly from an instinctive wish for conceal-ment, partly from the fear, not wholly irrational, that a solitary man walking briskly through the darkness might arouse interest. But now hedge-row and copse were giving way to isolated houses, detached, set back from the road in large gardens. These would certainly have a car in their garage, probably more than one. But houses and garages would be well protected. This ostentatious pros-perity was hardly vulnerable to a casual and inex-perienced thief. He was looking for victims more easily intimidated.

And now he had reached the town. He walked more slowly. He could feel his heartbeat quicken-ing, the strong rhythmic thump against the rib-cage. He didn't want to penetrate too far into the centre. It was important to find what he needed as soon as possible and make a getaway. And then he saw, in a small close to the right of him, a row of semi-detached, pebble-dashed villas. Each pair was identical, with a bay window beside the door and a garage built on to the end wall. He moved up almost on tiptoe to inspect the first pair. The house on the left was empty, the windows boarded up and a sale board wired to the front gate. It had obviously been empty for some time. The grass was long and straggly and the single round flowerbed in the middle was a mass of overgrown rose bushes, spiky stems entwined, the last overblown flowers drooping and dying.

The house on the right was occupied and looked very different. There was a light in the front room behind the drawn curtains, the front garden had a neatly cut lawn with a bed of chrysanthemums and dahlias edging the path. A new fence had been nailed against the boundary, perhaps to conceal the desolation next door, or to keep the weeds at bay. It seemed ideal for his purpose. With no neighbours, there would be no one secretly to watch or hear, and with easy access to the road he could hope to make a relatively quick getaway. But was there a car in the garage? Walking to the gate, he looked intently at the gravel path and could make out the mark of tyres, a small stain of oil. The stain of oil was worrying, but the little house was so well kept, the garden so immaculate, that he couldn't believe the car, however small and old, wouldn't be in running order. But if not? Then he would have to start again and a second attempt would be twice as dangerous. As he paused beside the gate, glancing left and right to see that this loitering wasn't observed, his mind explored the possibilities. He could prevent the people in this house giving the alarm; it would only be necessary to cut off the telephone and tie them up. But suppose he was equally unsuccessful in finding a car at the next house he tried, and then the next? The prospect of tying up a succession of victims was as risible as it was dangerous. At best he would have only two chances. If he were unsuccessful here the best plan might be to stop a car on the road and force the driver and passengers out. That way he would at least be certain that he had a vehicle that was running.

With one final quick glance round, he unlatched the gate quietly and walked swiftly, almost on tiptoe, to the front door. He breathed a small sigh of relief. The curtains had been only partially drawn over the side pane of the bow window and there was a gap of about three inches between the curtain edge and the frame of the window through which he could clearly observe what was happening in the room.

There was no fireplace and the room was dominated by a very large television set. In front of it were two armchairs and he could see the grey heads of an elderly couple, probably man and wife. The room was sparsely furnished with a table and two chairs set in front of a side window, and a small oak bureau. He could see no pictures, no books, no ornaments, no flowers, but on one wall hung a large coloured photograph of a young girl and beneath it was a child's high-chair with a teddy bear wearing an immense spotted necktie.

Even through the glass he could hear the television clearly. The old people must be deaf. He recognized the programme: *Neighbours,* a low-budget television series from the late 1980s and early 1990s, made in Australia, and preceded by a jingle of unparalleled banality. The programme had apparently had a huge following when first shown on the old-type television sets and now, adapted for the modern high-definition sets, was enjoying a revival, becoming indeed something of a cult. The reason was obvious. The stories, set in a remote, sun-warmed suburb, evoked a nostalgic longing for a make-believe world of innocence and hope. But, above all, they were about the young. The insubstantial but glowing images of young faces, young limbs, the sound of young voices, created the illusion that somewhere under an antipodean sky this comforting, youthful world still existed and could be entered at will. In the same spirit and from the same need, people bought videos of childbirth, or nursery rhymes and old television programmes for the young, *The Flower-Pot Men, Blue Peter.*

He rang the doorbell and waited. After dark he guessed they would answer the ring together. Through the insubstantial wood he could hear the shuffle of feet and then the grating of the bolts. The door opened on the chain and through the inch gap he could see that the couple were older than he had expected. A pair of rheumy eyes, more suspicious than anxious, looked into his.

The man's voice was unexpectedly sharp. "What do you want?"

Theo guessed that his quiet, educated voice would be reassuring. He said: "I'm from the Local Council. We're doing a survey into people's hobbies and interests. I have a form for you to fill in. It won't take a moment. It has to be done now."

The man hesitated, then took off the chain. With one swift shove Theo was inside, his back against the door, the revolver in his hand. Before they could speak or scream he said: "It's all right. You're in no danger. I'm not going to hurt you. Keep quiet, do what I say, and you'll be safe."

The woman had started a violent trembling, clutching at her husband's arm. She was very frail, small-boned, her fawn cardigan drooping from shoulders which looked too brittle to bear the weight.

Theo looked into her eyes, holding her gaze of bewildered terror, and said, with all the persuasion he could command: "I'm not a criminal. I need help. I need the use of your car, food and drink. You have a car?"

The man nodded.

Theo went on: "What make?"

"A Citizen." The people's car, cheap to buy

and economical to run. They were all ten years old now, but they had been well built, and were reliable. It could have been worse.

"Is there petrol in the tank?"

The man nodded again.

Theo said: "Roadworthy?"

"Oh yes, I'm particular about the car."

"Right. Now I want you upstairs."

The order terrified them. What did they suppose, that he planned to butcher them in their own bedroom?

The man pleaded: "Don't kill me. I'm all she's got. She's ill. Heart. If I go it will be the Quietus for her."

"No one's going to harm you. There will be no Quietus." He repeated violently: "No Quietus!"

They climbed slowly, step by step, the woman still clutching her husband.

Upstairs a quick glance showed that the plan of the house was simple. At the front was the main bedroom and, opposite it, the bathroom, with a separate lavatory next door. To the rear were two smaller bedrooms. With the gun he motioned them into the bigger of the two back bedrooms. There was a single bed and, stripping back the counterpane, he saw that it was made up.

He said to the man: "Tear the sheets into strips."

The man took them in his gnarled hands and

made an ineffectual attempt to rip the cotton. But the top hem was too strong for him.

Theo said impatiently: "We need scissors. Where are they?"

It was the woman who spoke: "In the front room. On my dressing table."

"Please fetch them."

She tottered stiffly out and was back in a few seconds with a pair of nail scissors. They were small but adequate. But it would waste precious minutes if he left the task to the old man's trembling hands.

He said harshly: "Stand back, both of you, side by side, against the wall."

They obeyed, and he faced them with the bed between them, the gun placed close to his right hand. Then he began tearing up the sheets. The noise seemed unusually loud. He seemed to be ripping apart the air, the very fabric of the house. When he had finished he said to the woman: "Come and lie on the bed."

She glanced at her husband as if asking for his permission and he gave a quick nod.

"Do what he says, dear."

She had some difficulty in getting on to the bed and Theo had to lift her. Her body was extraordinarily light and his hand under her thigh swung her upwards so quickly that she was in danger of being propelled over the bed on to the floor. After taking off her shoes, he bound her ankles strongly together, then tied her hands behind her back.

He said: "Are you all right?"

She gave a little nod. The bed was narrow and he wondered if there would be room for the man beside her, but the husband, sensing what was in his mind, said quickly: "Don't part us. Don't make me go next door. Don't shoot me."

Theo said impatiently: "I'm not going to shoot you. The gun isn't even loaded." The lie was safe enough now. The gun had served its purpose.

He said curtly: "Lie down beside her."

There was room, but only just. He tied the man's hands behind his back, then bound his ankles and, with a final strip of the cotton, bound their legs together. They lay both on their right sides, fitted closely together. He couldn't believe that their arms were comfortable, wrenched as they were behind their backs, but had not dared to tie them in front of the body in case the man used his teeth to break free.

He said: "Where are the keys to the garage and the car?"

The man whispered: "In the bureau in the sitting-room. The top drawer, on the right."

He left them. The keys were easily found. Then he went back to the bedroom. "I'll need a large suitcase. Have you one?"

It was the woman who answered: "Under the bed."

He dragged it out. It was large but light, made only of cardboard reinforced at the corners. He wondered whether the remnants of torn sheet were worth taking. While he was hesitating, holding them in his hand, the man said: "Please don't gag us. We won't call out, I promise. Please don't gag us. My wife won't be able to breathe."

Theo said: "I'll have to notify someone that you're tied up here. I can't do that for at least twelve hours, but I will do it. Are you expecting anyone?"

The man, not looking at him, said: "Mrs. Collins, our home help, will be here at half past seven tomorrow. She comes early because she has another morning job after us."

"Has she a key?"

"Yes, she always has a key."

"No one else is expected? No member of the family, for example?"

"We have no family. We had a daughter but she died."

"But you're sure Mrs. Collins will be here at half past seven?"

"Yes, she's very reliable. She'll be here."

He parted the curtains of light flowered cotton and looked out into the darkness. All he could see was a stretch of garden and behind it the black outline of a hill. They could call out all night but it was unlikely that their frail voices would be heard. All the same, he would leave the television on as loudly as possible.

He said: "I won't gag you. I'll leave the television on loudly so that no one will hear you. Don't waste energy trying to shout. But you'll be released when Mrs. Collins comes tomorrow. Try to rest, to sleep. I'm sorry I have to do this. You'll get your car back eventually."

Even as he spoke it seemed a ridiculous and dishonest promise to make. He said: "Is there anything you want?"

The woman said feebly: "Water."

The single word reminded him of his own thirst. It seemed extraordinary that, after the long hours of craving water, he could have forgotten his need even for a moment. He went into the bathroom, and taking a tooth mug, not even bothering to rinse it, gulped down cold water until his stomach could hold no more. Then he refilled the mug and went back to the bedroom. He raised the woman's head on his arm and put the mug to her lips. She drank thirstily. The water spilled down the side of her face and on to the thin cardigan. The purple veins at the side of her forehead throbbed as if they would burst and the sinews of the thin neck were taut as cords. After she had finished he took a piece of linen and wiped her mouth. Then he refilled the glass and helped the husband to drink. He felt a strange reluctance to leave them. An unwelcome and malignant guest, he could find no appropriate words of farewell.

At the door he turned and said: "I'm sorry I had to do this. Try to get some sleep. Mrs. Collins will be here in the morning."

He wondered whether he was reassuring them or himself. At least, he thought, they are together.

He added: "Are you reasonably comfortable?"

The silliness of the question struck him even as he asked it. Comfortable? How could they be comfortable, trussed up like animals on a bed so narrow that any movement might cause them to fall off. The woman whispered something which his ears couldn't catch but which her husband seemed to understand. Stiffly he raised his head and looked straight at Theo who saw in the faded eyes a plea for understanding, for pity.

He said: "She wants to go to the toilet."

Theo almost laughed aloud. He was an eight-year-old again hearing his mother's impatient voice. "You should have thought of that before we started out." What did they expect him to say? "You should have thought of that before I tied you up"? One of them should have thought of it. It was too late now. He had wasted too much time on them already. He thought of Julian and Miriam waiting in desperate anxiety in the shadow of the trees, ears strained for the approach of every car, pictured their disappointment as each one swept past. And there was so much still to be done: the car to be checked, the stores collected. It would take him minutes to untie these tight multiple knots and he hadn't minutes to spare. She would have to lie there in her own mess until Mrs. Collins arrived in the morning.

But he knew he couldn't do it. Trussed and helpless as she was, stinking with fear, lying in rigid embarrassment, unable to meet his eyes, there was one indignity which he couldn't inflict on her. His fingers began scrabbling at the taut cotton. It was even more difficult than he had expected and in the end he took the nail scissors and cut her loose, freeing her ankles and hands, trying not to notice the weals on her wrists. Getting her off the bed wasn't easy; her brittle body, which had seemed as light as a bird, was now set in the rigor of terror. It was nearly a minute before she could begin her slow shuffle to the lavatory with his arm around her waist supporting her.

He said, shame and impatience making his voice gruff: "Don't lock the door. Leave it ajar."

He waited outside, resisting the temptation to pace the landing, his heartbeats thudding out the seconds which lengthened into minutes before he heard the flush of the cistern and slowly she emerged. She whispered: "Thank you."

Back in the bedroom, he helped her on to the bed, then ripped more lengths from the remainder of the sheet and bound her again, but this time less tightly. He said to her husband: "You'd better go too. You can hop there if I give you a hand. I've only time to free your hands."

But this was no easier. Even with his hands free and one arm resting across Theo's shoulders the old man lacked the strength and balance to give even the smallest jump, and Theo had almost to drag him physically to the lavatory.

At last he got the old man back on the bed. And now he must hurry. He had wasted too much time already. Suitcase in hand, he made his way quickly to the back of the house. There was a small kitchen, meticulously clean and tidy, an over-large refrigerator, and a small pantry leading from the kitchen. But the spoils were disappointing. The refrigerator, despite its size, held only a one-pint carton of milk, a packet containing four eggs, half a pound of butter on a saucer covered with foil, a slab of wrapped cheddar cheese and an opened packet of biscuits. In the freezer compartment above he discovered nothing but one small packet of peas and a slab of cod, frozen hard. The pantry was equally disappointing, yielding only a small quantity of sugar, coffee and tea. It was ridiculous that a house should be so underprovisioned. He felt a rush of anger against the old couple, as if his disappointment were their deliberate fault. Presumably they shopped once a week and he had been unlucky with the day. He grabbed everything, stuffing the provisions into a plastic bag. There were four mugs hanging on a stand. He took two and found three plates from a cupboard above the sink. From a drawer he took a sharp paring knife, a carving knife, three sets of table knives, forks and spoons; he put a box of matches in his pocket. Then he ran upstairs, this time to the front bedroom, where he lugged sheets, blankets and pillows from the bed. Miriam would need clean towels for the birth. He ran into the bathroom and found half a dozen towels folded in the airing cupboard. They should be enough. He stuffed all the linen into the suitcase. He had put the nail scissors in his pocket, remembering that Miriam had asked for scissors. In the bathroom cupboard he found a bottle of disinfectant and added that to his spoils.

He could spend no further time in the house, but one problem remained: water. He had the pint carton of milk; that was hardly enough to satisfy even Julian's thirst. He searched for a suitable container. Nowhere was there an empty bottle. He found himself almost cursing the old couple as he hunted feverishly for any kind of receptacle that would hold water. All he could find was a small thermos flask. At least he could take Julian and Miriam some hot coffee. He needn't wait for the kettle to boil. Better to make it with hot tap-water, however odd the taste. They would be frantic to drink it immediately. That done, he filled the kettle and the only two saucepans he could find which had close-fitting lids. They would have to be carried separately to the car, wasting more time. Last of all he again drank his fill from the tap, swilling the water over his face.

On the wall just inside the front door was a row of coat-hooks. They held an old jacket, a long woollen scarf and two raincoats, both obviously new. He hesitated for only a second before taking them down and slinging them over his shoulder. Julian would need them if she were not to lie on damp ground. But they were the only new things in the house and stealing them seemed the meanest act of his petty depredations.

He unlocked the garage door. The Citizen had only a small boot but he wedged the kettle and one of the saucepans carefully between the suitcase and the bedclothes and raincoats. The other saucepan, and the plastic bag containing the food and the mugs and cutlery he placed on the back seat. When he started the engine he found to his relief that it ran smoothly. The car had obviously been well maintained. But he saw that the tank

was less than half full and that there were no maps
in the pocket. Probably the old people only used
the car for short journeys and for shopping. As
he backed carefully into the drive, then closed the
garage door behind him, he remembered that he
had forgotten to turn up the volume on the television set. He told himself that the precaution was
unimportant. With the house next door empty
and the long garden stretching at the rear, the
couple's feeble cries were unlikely to be heard.

As he drove he pondered the next move. To go
on or to double back? Xan would know from Rolf
that they planned to cross the border into Wales
and find wooded country. He would expect the
plan to be changed. They might be anywhere in
the West Country. The search would take time
even if Xan sent out a large party of the SSP or the
Grenadiers. But he wouldn't. This quarry was
unique. If Rolf succeeded in reaching him without
revealing his news until that vital, final encounter,
then Xan too would keep it secret until its truth
was verified. He wouldn't risk Julian falling into
the hands of an ambitious or unscrupulous SSP or
Grenadier officer. And Xan wouldn't know how
little time he had if he were to be there for the
birth. Rolf couldn't tell him what he didn't know.
How far, too, did he really trust the other members of the Council? No, Xan would come himself, probably with a small and carefully selected

band. They would succeed in the end; that was inevitable. But it would take time. The very importance and delicacy of the task, the need for secrecy, the size of the search party, all would militate against speed.

So where and in what direction? For a moment he wondered whether it would be an effective ploy to double back to Oxford, hide in Wytham Wood, above the city, surely the last place which Xan would think of searching. Too dangerous a journey? But any road was dangerous and would be doubly so when the old people were discovered at seven-thirty and told their story. Why did it seem more hazardous to go back than to go on? Perhaps because Xan was in London. And yet for an ordinary fugitive London itself was the obvious place of concealment. London, despite its depleted population, was still a collection of villages, of secret alleyways, of vast, half-empty tower blocks. But London was full of eyes and there was no one there to whom he could safely turn, no house to which he had entry. His instinct—and he guessed it would be Julian's—was to put as many miles as possible between them and London and to keep to the original plan to hide in deep and remote country. Every mile from London seemed a mile towards safety.

As he drove along the mercifully deserted road, carefully, getting the feel of the car, he indulged a fantasy which he tried to convince himself was a rational, attainable aim. He pictured a wood-man's cottage, sweet-smelling, the resinous walls still holding the warmth of the summer sun, rooted as naturally as a tree in deep woodland under the sheltering canopy of strong, leaf-laden boughs, deserted years ago and now decaying, but with linen, matches, tinned food enough to provide for the three of them. There would be a spring of fresh water, wood they could gather for the fires when autumn gave way to winter. They could live there for months if necessary, perhaps even for years. It was the idyll which, standing beside the car at Swinbrook, he had mocked and despised, but now he took comfort in it, even while knowing that the dream was a fantasy.

Somewhere in the world other children would be born; he made himself share Julian's confidence. This child would no longer be unique, no longer in special danger. Xan and the Council would have no need to take him from his mother even if he were known to be the first-born of a new age. But all that was in the future and could be faced and dealt with when the time came. For the next few weeks the three of them could live in safety until the child was born. He could see no further and he told himself that he need see no further.

31

His mind and all his physical energies had for the last two hours been so fiercely concentrated on the task in hand that it hadn't occurred to him that he might have difficulty in recognizing the fringes of the wood. Turning right from the lane on to the road, he tried to remember how far he had travelled before the taking the turning to the town. But the walk had in memory become a turbulence of fear, anxiety and resolution, of agonizing thirst, of panting breath and an aching side, with no clear recollection of distance or time. A small copse came into view on the left, seeming at once familiar, raising his spirits. But almost immediately the trees ended, giving way to a low hedge and open ground. And then there were more trees and the beginning of a stone wall. He drove slowly, his eyes on the road. Then he saw what he had both feared and hoped to see: Luke's blood spattered on the tarmac, no longer red, a black splurge in the headlights, and to his left the broken stones of the wall.

When they didn't at once come forward out of the trees to meet him, he felt a moment of appalled anxiety that they weren't there, that they had been taken. He drove the Citizen close against the wall, vaulted over and passed into the wood. At the sound of his footsteps they came forward and he heard Miriam's muttered "Thank God, we were beginning to get worried. Have you got a car?"

"A Citizen. That's about all I have got. There wasn't much to take in the house. Here's a thermos of hot coffee."

Miriam almost snatched it from him. She unscrewed the top and poured the coffee carefully, every drop precious, then handed it to Julian.

She said, her voice deliberately calm: "Things have changed, Theo. We haven't much time now. The baby has started."

Theo said: "How long?"

"You can't always tell with a first labour. It might be only a few hours. It could be twenty-four. Julian's in the very early stages but we have to find somewhere quickly."

And then, suddenly, all his previous indecision was swept away by a cleansing wind of certainty and hope. A single name came into his mind, so clearly that it was as if a voice, not his own, had spoken it aloud. Wychwood Forest. He pictured a solitary summer walk, a shadowed path beside a broken stone wall leading deep into the forest, then opening out into a mossy glade with a lake and, further up the path to the right, a wood-shed. Wychwood wouldn't have been his first or an obvious choice: too small, too easily searched, less than twenty miles from Oxford. But now that closeness was an advantage. Xan would expect them to press on. Instead they would double back to a place he remembered, a place he knew, a place where they could be certain of shelter.

He said: "Get in the car. We're turning back. We're making for Wychwood Forest. We'll eat on the way."

There was no time for discussion, for weighing up possible alternatives. The women had their own immense preoccupation. It must be for him to decide when to go and how to get there.

He had no real fear that they would again be attacked by the Painted Faces. That horror now seemed the fulfillment of his half-superstitious conviction at the start of the journey that they were destined for a tragedy as inescapable as its time and nature were unpredictable. Now it had come, had done its worst; it was over. Like an air-traveller, terrified of flying and expecting to crash each time his plane soared, he could rest knowing that the awaited disaster was behind him and that there were survivors. But he knew that neither Julian nor Miriam could so easily exorcise their terror of the Painted Faces. Their fear possessed the little car. For the first ten miles they sat rigid behind him, their eyes fixed on the road, as if expecting at every turn, at every small obstruction, to hear again the wild whoops of triumph, and to see the flaming torches and the glittering eyes.

There were other dangers, too, and the one over-riding fear. They had no way of telling at what hour Rolf had actually left them. If he had reached Xan, the search for them might even now be under way, the road blocks being unloaded and dragged into place, the helicopters wheeled out and fuelled to await the first light of day. The narrow side roads twisting between straggling, untamed hedges and broken dry-stone walls seemed, perhaps irrationally, to offer their best hope of safety. Like all hunted creatures, Theo's instinct was to twist and turn, to remain hidden, to seek the darkness. But the country lanes presented their own hazards. Four times, fearing the risk of a second puncture, he had to brake sharply at an impassable stretch of creviced tarmac and reverse the car. Once, soon after two o'clock, this manoeuvre was almost disastrous. The back wheels rolled into a ditch, and it took half an hour before his and Miriam's joint efforts got the Citizen back on the road.

He cursed the lack of maps but, as the hours wore by, the cloud-base cleared to reveal more clearly the pattern of the stars and he could see the smudge of the Milky Way and take his bearings from the Plough and the Pole Star. But this ancient lore was no more than a crude calculation of his route and he was in constant danger of getting lost. From time to time a signpost, stark as an eighteenth-century gallows, would rear up out of the darkness and he would make his careful way over the broken road towards it, half-expecting to hear the clank of chains and see a slowly twisting body with its elongated neck, while the pinpoint of light from the torch, like a searching eye, traced the half-obliterated names of unknown villages. The night was colder now, with a foretaste of winter chill; the air, no longer smelling of grass and sun-warmed earth, stung his nostrils with a faint antiseptic tang, as if they were close to the sea. Each time the engine was switched off the silence was absolute. Standing under a signpost whose names might as well have been written in a foreign language, he felt disorientated and alienated, as if the dark, desolate fields, the earth beneath his feet, this strange, unscented air, were no longer his natural habitat and there was no security or home for his endangered species anywhere under the uncaring sky.

Soon after the journey began the progress of Julian's labour had either slowed or stopped. This lessened his anxiety; delays were no longer disastrous and safety could take precedence over speed. But he knew that the delay dismayed the women. He guessed that they now had as little hope as he of eluding Xan for weeks, or even days. If the labour was a false alarm or was protracted, they might yet fall into Xan's hands before the child was born. From time to time, leaning forward, Miriam asked him quietly to draw into the side of the road so that she and Julian could take exercise. He, too, would get out and, leaning against the car, would watch the two dark figures walking backwards and forwards along the verge, would hear their whispered voices, and know that they were distanced from him by more than a few yards of country road, that they shared an intense preoccupation from which he was excluded. They took little interest and showed small concern about the route, the mishaps of the journey. All that, their very silence seemed to imply, was his concern.

But by the early morning Miriam told him that Julian's contractions had started again and were strong. She couldn't hide the triumph in her voice. And before dawn he knew exactly where they were. The last signpost had pointed to Chipping Norton. It was time to leave the twisting lanes and risk the last few miles by the main road.

At least they were now on a better surface. He had no need to drive in constant fear of another puncture. No other car passed them and, after the first two miles, his taut hands relaxed on the wheel. He drove carefully but fast, anxious now to get to the forest without delay. The petrol level was getting dangerously low and there was no safe way of filling up. He was surprised how little ground they had covered since the journey first began at Swinbrook. It seemed to him that they had been on the road for weeks: restless, unprovisioned, hapless travellers. He knew that there was nothing he could do to prevent capture on this surely final journey. If they came to an SSP roadblock there would be no hope of bluffing or arguing their way out; the SSP were not Omegas. All he could do was to drive and to hope.

From time to time he thought he heard Julian panting and Miriam's low murmur of reassurance, but they spoke little. After about a quarter of an hour he heard Miriam stirring in the back and then the rhythmic clink of a fork against china. She handed him a mug.

"I've held back the food until now. Julian needs strength for her labour. I've beaten up the eggs in the milk and added sugar. This is your share, I get the same. Julian has the rest."

The mug was only a quarter full and the frothy sweetness would normally have disgusted him. Now he gulped it down avidly, longing for more, feeling at once its strengthening power. He passed back the mug and received a biscuit smeared with butter and topped with a nugget of hard cheese. Never had cheese tasted so good.

Miriam said: "Two for each of us, four for Julian."

Julian remonstrated. "We must share equally"—but the last word was caught up in a gasp of pain.

Theo asked: "You aren't keeping some in reserve?"

"From a three-quarter packet of biscuits and half a pound of cheese? We need our strength now." The cheese and the dry biscuits had increased their thirst and they finished the meal by drinking the water from the smaller saucepan.

Miriam handed him the two mugs and the cutlery in the plastic bag and he placed them on the floor. Then, as if fearing her words might have implied a rebuke, she added: "You were unlucky, Theo. But you got us a car and it wasn't easy. Without it we wouldn't have stood a chance."

He hoped that she was saying, "We depended on you and you didn't fail us," and smiled ruefully at the thought that he, who had cared so little for anyone's approbation, should want her praise and approval.

And at last they were on the outskirts of Charlbury. He slowed down, watching out for the old Finstock station, the curve in the road. It was immediately after the curve that he must look for the right-hand track leading towards the forest. He was used to approaching it from Oxford and even then it was easy to miss the turning. It was with an audible sigh of relief that he drove past the station buildings, took the curve and saw on his right the row of stone cottages which marked the approach to the track. The cottages were empty, boarded up, almost derelict. For a moment he wondered whether one of them would provide a refuge; but they were too obvious, too close to the road. He knew Julian wanted to be deep in the forest.

He drove carefully up the track between untended fields towards the distant curdle of the trees. It would soon be light. Looking at his watch he saw that Mrs. Collins would have arrived to release the old couple. Even now they were probably enjoying a cup of tea, telling of their ordeal, waiting for the police to arrive. Changing gear to negotiate a difficult part of the rising track, he thought he heard Julian catch her breath and give an odd little sound between a grunt and a groan.

And now the forest received them with its dark

strong arms. The track became narrower, the trees closed in. On the right was a dry-stone wall, half demolished, its broken stones cluttering the path. He changed down into first gear and tried to keep the car steady. After about a mile Miriam leaned forward and said: "I think we'll walk ahead for a little while. It'll be easier for Julian."

The two women got out and, with Julian leaning against Miriam, made their careful way over the ruts and stones of the track. In the car's side lights a startled rabbit was for a moment petrified, then scampered before them, white-tailed. Suddenly there was an immense commotion and a white shape followed by another crashed through the bushes, just missing the bonnet of the car. It was a deer and her fawn. Together they lurched up the bank, tearing through the bushes, and disappeared over the wall, their hoofs clattering on the stones.

From time to time the two women stopped and Julian bent over with Miriam's arm supporting her. After the third time this had happened, Miriam signalled Theo to stop. She said: "I think she might be better in the car now. How much further?"

"We're still skirting open country. There should be a turning to the right fairly soon. After that it's about a mile."

The car shuddered on. The remembered turn

revealed itself as a crossroads and for a moment he was irresolute. Then he drove to the right, where the track, narrower still, sloped downhill. Surely this was the way to the lake and, beyond it, the remembered wood-shed.

Miriam called out: "There's a house, over to the right."

He turned his head just in time to see it, a far dark shape glimpsed through a narrow gap in the great tangled heap of bushes and trees. It stood alone on a wide sloping field. Miriam said: "No good. Too obvious. No cover in the field. Better press on."

They were now moving into the heart of the forest. The lane seemed interminable. With every lurching yard the path narrowed and he could hear the scratch and scrape of branches on the car. Overhead the strengthening sun was a white diffused light hardly visible above the tangled boughs of elder and hawthorn. It seemed to him, desperately trying to control the steering, that they were slithering helplessly down a tunnel of green darkness which would end in an impenetrable hedge. He was wondering whether memory had deceived him, whether they should have taken the left turn, when the path suddenly widened and opened on to a grassy glade. They saw before them the pale glimmer of the lake.

He stopped the car only yards from its edge and

got out, then turned to help Miriam half lift Julian from her seat. For a moment she clung to him, breathing deeply, then let go, smiled, and walked to the edge of the water, her hand on Miriam's shoulder. The surface of the pond—it was hardly a lake—was so thickly strewn with the green blades of fallen leaves and water weed that it looked like an extension of the glade. Beyond this green and shivering cover the surface was viscous as treacle, beaded with minute bubbles which gently moved and coalesced, broke apart, burst and died. In the patches of clear water between the weeds he could see the reflection of the sky as the morning mist cleared to reveal the opaque first light of day. Beneath this surface brightness, in the ochre depths, the sinews of water plants, tangled twigs and broken branches lay thickly encrusted with mud like the ribs of long-sunken ships. At the edge of the pond clumps of sodden rushes lay flattened on the water and in the distance a small black coot scurried in busy agitation and a solitary swan breasted her way majestically among the weeds. The pond was surrounded by trees growing almost to the water's edge, oak, ash and sycamore, a bright backcloth of green, yellow, gold and russet which seemed in the first light, despite the autumnal shades, to hold some of the freshness and brightness of spring. A sapling on the far bank was patterned with yellow leaves, its thin boughs and twigs invisible against the first light of the sun, so that it seemed as if the air was hung with delicate pellets of gold.

Julian had wandered along the edge of the lake. She called: "The water looks cleaner here and the bank's quite firm. It's a good place to wash."

They joined her and, kneeling, thrust their arms into the lake and dashed the stinging water over their faces and hair. They laughed with the pleasure of it. Theo saw that his hands had swilled the water into greenish mud. This couldn't be safe to drink even if it were boiled.

As they returned to the Citizen Theo said: "The question is whether we get rid of the car now. It may provide the best shelter we're likely to get, but it's conspicuous and we've nearly run out of petrol. It would probably only take us another couple of miles."

It was Miriam who answered. "Let it go."

He looked at his watch. It was just coming up to nine o'clock. He thought that they might as well listen to the news. Banal, predictable, uninteresting as it would probably be, to hear it was a small valedictory gesture before they finally cut themselves off from all news but their own. He was surprised that he hadn't thought of the radio before, hadn't bothered to turn it on during their journey. He had driven in such taut anxiety that the sound of an unknown voice, even the sound of music, would have seemed intolerable. Now he reached his arm through the open window and switched on the radio. They listened impatiently to details of the weather, information on the roads which were officially closed or which would no longer be repaired, to the small domestic concerns of a shrinking world.

He was about to turn off the set when the announcer's voice changed, becoming slower and more portentous. "This is a warning. A small group of dissidents, one man and two women, are travelling in a stolen blue Citizen car somewhere on the Welsh border. Last night the man, who is thought to be Theodore Faron of Oxford, forced his way into a house outside Kington, tied up the owners and stole their car. The wife, Mrs. Daisy Cox, was found early this morning bound and dead on her bed. The man is now wanted for murder. He is armed with a revolver. Anyone seeing their car or the three persons is asked not to approach them but immediately to telephone the State Security Police. The registration of the car is MOA 694. I'll repeat that number: MOA 694. I am asked to repeat the warning. The man is armed and dangerous. Do not approach."

Theo wasn't aware that he had switched it off. He was conscious only of the pounding of his heart and of a sick misery which descended and enveloped him, physical as a mortal illness, horror and self-disgust dragging him almost to his knees. He thought: If this is guilt, I can't bear it. I won't bear it.

He heard Miriam's voice. "So Rolf has reached the Warden. They know about the Omegas, that there are only three of us left. But there's one comfort, anyway. They still don't know that the birth is imminent. Rolf couldn't tell them the expected date of delivery. He doesn't know. He thinks Julian still has a month to go. The Warden would never ask people to look out for the car if he thought there was a chance they'd find a newborn child."

He said dully: "There is no comfort. I killed her."

Miriam's voice was firm, unnaturally loud, almost shouting in his ear. "You didn't kill her! If she was going to die of shock it would have happened when you first showed her the gun. You don't know why she died. It was natural causes, it must have been. It could have happened anyway. She was old and she had a weak heart. You told us. It wasn't your fault, Theo, you didn't mean it."

No, he almost groaned, no, I didn't mean it. I didn't mean to be a selfish son, an unloving father, a bad husband. When have I ever meant anything? Christ, what harm couldn't I do if I actually started to mean it!

He said: "The worst is that I enjoyed it. I actually enjoyed it!"

Miriam was unloading the car, shouldering the blankets. "Enjoyed tying up that old man and his wife? Of course you didn't enjoy it. You did what you had to do."

"Not the tying up. I didn't mean that. But I enjoyed the excitement, the power, the knowledge that I could do it. It wasn't all horrible. It was for them, but not for me."

Julian didn't speak. She came near and took his hand. Rejecting the gesture, he turned on her viciously. "How many other lives will your child cost before she gets herself born? And to what purpose? You're so calm, so unafraid, so sure of yourself. You speak of a daughter. What sort of life will this child have? You believe that she'll be the first, that other births will follow, that even now there are pregnant women not yet aware that they are carrying the new life of the world. But suppose you're wrong. Suppose this child is the only one. To what sort of hell are you condemning her? Can you begin to imagine the loneliness of her last years—over twenty appalling, endless years with no hope of ever hearing another live human voice? Never, never, never! My God, have you no imagination, either of you?"

Julian said quietly: "Do you think I haven't thought of that, that and more? Theo, I can't wish that she had never been conceived. I can't think of her without joy."

Miriam, wasting no time, had already pulled the suitcase and the raincoats from the boot and lifted down the kettle and the saucepan of water.

She spoke more in irritation than in anger: "For God's sake, Theo, take hold of yourself. We needed a car; you got us a car. Maybe you could have chosen a better one and got it at less cost. You did what you did. If you want to wallow in guilt, that's your affair, but leave it until later. OK, she's dead and you feel guilty, and feeling guilt isn't something you enjoy. Too bad. Get used to it. Why the hell should you escape guilt? It's part of being human. Or hadn't you noticed?"

Theo wanted to say: "In the past forty years there are quite a number of things I haven't noticed." But the words, with their ring of self-indulgent remorse, struck him as insincere and ignoble. Instead he said: "We'd better get rid of the car, and quickly. That's one problem the broadcast has settled for us."

He released the brake and put his shoulder to the back of the Citizen, scraping a foothold in the pebbled grass, grateful that the ground was dry and gently sloping. Miriam took the right-hand side and together they pushed. For a few seconds, inexplicably, their efforts were unsuccessful. Then the car began to move gently forward.

He said: "Give it a hard shove when I say the word. We don't want it stuck in the mud nose-first."

The front wheels were almost at the edge when he called out "Now," and they both pushed with all their strength. The car shot over the rim of the lake and hit the water with a splash that seemed to wake every bird in the forest. The air was clamorous with calls and shrieks and the light branches of the high trees shook into life. The spray flew upwards, splattering his face. The cover of floating leaves shattered and danced. They watched, panting, as slowly, almost peacefully, the car settled and began to sink, the water gurgling through the open windows. Before it disappeared, on impulse, Theo took the diary from his pocket and hurled it into the lake.

And then there came for him a moment of dreadful horror, vivid as a nightmare, but one which he could not hope to banish by waking. They were all there together trapped in the sinking car, water pouring in, and he was searching desperately for the handle, trying to hold his breath against the agony in his chest, wanting to call out to Julian but knowing that he dare not speak or his mouth would be clogged with mud. She and Miriam were in the back drowning and there was nothing he could do to help. Sweat broke out on his forehead and, clenching his wet palms, he forced his eyes from the horror of the lake and looked up at the sky, wrenching his mind from imagined horror back to the horror of normality. The sun was pale and round as a full moon but blazing with light in its aureole of mist, the high boughs of the trees black against its dazzle. He closed his eyes and waited. The horror passed and he was able to look down again at the surface of the lake.

He glanced at Julian and Miriam, half expecting to see on their faces the stark panic which must momentarily have transformed his own. But they were looking down at the sinking car with a calm, almost detached interest, watching the clustered leaves bobbing and bunching on the spreading ripples, as if jostling for room. He marvelled at the women's calmness, this apparent ability to shut away all memory, all horror in the concern of the moment.

He said, his voice harsh: "Luke. You never spoke of him in the car. Neither of you has mentioned his name since we buried him. Do you think about him?" The question sounded like an accusation.

Miriam turned her gaze from the lake and gave him a steady look. "We think of him as much as we dare. What we're concerned about now is getting his child born safely."

Julian came up to him and touched his arm. She

said, as if he were the one who most needed comforting: "There will be a time to mourn Luke and
Gascoigne. Theo, there will be a time."

The car had sunk out of sight. He had feared
that the water at the edge might be too shallow,
that the roof would be visible even under the
cover of reeds, but peering down into the murky
darkness he could see nothing but swirling mud.

Miriam said: "Have you got the cutlery?"

"No. Haven't you?"

"Damn, they're in the front of the car. Still, it
hardly matters now. We've no food left to eat."

He said: "We'd better get what we have got to
the wood-shed. It's about a hundred yards up that
path to the right."

Oh God, he prayed, please let it still be there, let
it still be there. It was the first time he had prayed
in forty years, but the words were less a petition
than a half-superstitious hope that somehow, by
the strength of his need, he could will the shed into
existence. He shouldered one of the pillows and
the raincoats, then picked up the kettle of water in
one hand, and the suitcase in the other. Julian
slung a second blanket round her shoulders and
bent for the saucepan of water only to have it
taken from her hand by Miriam, who said: "You
carry the pillow. I'll manage the rest."

Thus encumbered, they made their slow way up
the path. It was then that they heard the metallic

rattle of the helicopter. Half-imprisoned by the interlocking boughs they had little need for extra concealment but instinctively they moved from the path into the green tangle of the elder bushes and stood motionless, hardly breathing, as if every intake of breath could reach up to that glittering object of menace, to those watching eyes and listening ears. The noise grew to an ear-shattering clatter. Surely it must be directly overhead. Theo almost expected the sheltering bushes to shudder into violent life. Then it began to circle, the rattle receding then returning, bringing with it renewed fear. It was almost five minutes before the noise of the engine finally faded into a distant hum.

Julian said softly: "Perhaps they aren't looking for us." Her voice was faint and, suddenly, she doubled up with pain and grasped at Miriam.

Miriam's voice was grim. "I don't suppose they're on a joy-ride. Anyway they haven't found us." She turned to Theo. "How far is this wood-shed?"

"About fifty yards, if I've remembered rightly."

"Let's hope you have."

The path was wider now, making their passage easier, but Theo, walking a little behind the women, felt burdened by more than the physical weight of his load. His previous assessment of

Rolf's likely progress now seemed ridiculously optimistic. Why should he make his way slowly and by stealth to London? Why should he need to present himself personally to the Warden? All he required was a public telephone. The number of the Council was known to every citizen. This apparent accessibility was part of Xan's policy of openness. You couldn't always speak to the Warden but you could always try. Some callers even got through. This caller, once identified, once vetted, would get priority. They would tell him to conceal himself, to speak to no one until they'd picked him up, almost certainly by helicopter. He had probably been in their hands for over twelve hours.

And the fugitives wouldn't be difficult to find. By early morning Xan had known about the stolen car, the amount of petrol in its tank, had known to a mile how far they could hope to travel. He had only to stab a compass point in a map and describe a circle. Theo had no doubt of the significance of that helicopter. They were already searching by air, marking out the isolated houses, looking for the gleam of a car roof. Xan would already have organized the search on the ground. But one hope remained. There might still be time for the child to be born, as her mother wanted, in peace, in privacy, with no one to watch but the two people she loved. The search couldn't be quick; he had surely been right about that. Xan wouldn't want to come in force or to attract public attention, not yet, not until he could personally check the truth of Rolf's story. He would use only carefully selected men for this enterprise. He couldn't even be certain that they would hide in woodland. Rolf would have told him that that had been the original plan; but Rolf was no longer in charge.

He was clinging to this hope, willing himself to feel the confidence that he knew Julian would need from him, when he heard her voice.

"Theo, look. Isn't this beautiful?"

He turned and came up beside her. She was standing beside a tall overgrown hawthorn heavy with red berries. From its top bough there cascaded a white froth of travellers' joy, delicate as a veil, through which the berries shone like jewels. Looking at her rapt face, he thought: I only know it's beautiful; she can feel its loveliness. He looked beyond her to a bush of elderberries and seemed to see clearly for the first time their back glistening beads and the delicacy of the red stems. It was as if in one moment the forest was transformed from a place of darkness and menace, in which he was at heart convinced that one of them would die, into a sanctuary, mysterious and beautiful, uncaring of these three curious interlopers, but a place in which nothing that lived could be wholly alien from him.

Then he heard Miriam's voice, happy, exultant. "The wood-shed is still here!"

32

The shed was larger than he had expected. Memory, contrary to its custom, had diminished, not enlarged. For a moment he wondered whether this dilapidated, three-sided building of blackened wood, fully thirty feet across, could be the wood-shed he remembered. Then he noticed the silver birch to the right of the entrance. When he had last seen it the tree had been only a sapling, but now its branches overhung the roof. He saw with relief that most of the roof looked sound, although some of the planks had slipped. Many at the side were missing or jagged and the whole shed, in its lopsided, solitary decrepitude, looked unlikely to weather more than a few more winters. A huge wood-transporter, grained with rust, had sunk down askew in the middle of the glade, its tyres split and rotting and one immense wheel lying free beside it. Not all the logs had been carted away when the forestry finally ended, and one stack still remained neatly piled beside two huge felled trees. Their denuded trunks gleamed like polished bone and chunks and slivers of bark littered the earth.

Slowly, almost ceremoniously, they entered the shed, heads turning, anxious-eyed, like tenants taking possession of a desired but unknown residence.

Miriam said: "Well, at least it's a shelter and it looks as if there's enough dry wood and kindling here to make a fire."

Despite the thick surrounding hedge of tangled bushes and saplings and the rim of trees, it was less private than Theo had remembered. Their safety would have to depend less on the shed being unnoticed than on the improbability of any casual walker finding his way through the tangle of the forest. But it was not a casual walker he feared. If Xan decided to undertake a ground search in Wychwood it would only be a matter of hours before they were discovered, however secret their lair.

He said: "I'm not sure we ought to risk lighting a fire. How important is it?"

Miriam replied: "The fire? Not very at the moment but it will be once the baby's born and the daylight goes. The nights are getting cold. The baby and her mother need to be kept warm."

"Then we'll risk it, but not before it's necessary.

They'll be watching for smoke."

The shed looked as if it had been abandoned in some hurry, unless, perhaps, the workers had expected to return and had been prevented or told that the enterprise was now shut down. There were two stacks of shorter planks to the back of the shed, a pile of small logs and part of a tree trunk standing level which had obviously been used as a table since it bore a battered tin kettle and two chipped enamel mugs. The roof here was sound and the trodden earth soft with shavings and sawdust.

Miriam said: "About here will do."

She kicked and scraped the shavings into a rough bed, spread out the two raincoats and helped Julian to lie down, then slipped a pillow under her head. Julian gave a grunt of pleasure, then turned on her side and drew up her legs. Miriam shook out one of the sheets and placed it over her, covering it with a blanket and Luke's coat. Then she and Theo busied themselves setting out their store: the kettle and one remaining saucepan of water, the folded towels, the scissors and bottle of disinfectant. The small stock seemed to Theo pathetic in its inadequacy.

Miriam knelt beside Julian and gently motioned her on to her back. She said to Theo: "You may as well take a short walk if you feel like it. I'll be needing your help later, but not this minute."

He went outside, feeling for a second unreasonably rejected, and sat on the felled tree trunk. The peace of the glade enfolded him. He shut his eyes and listened. It seemed to him after a moment that he could hear a myriad small sounds, normally inaudible to human ears, the scrape of a leaf against its bough, the crack of a drying twig: the living world of the forest, secret, industrious, oblivious of or unconcerned with the three intruders. But he heard nothing human, no footfall, no distant sound of approaching cars, no returning rattle of the helicopter. He dared to hope that Xan had rejected Wychwood as their hiding place, that they might be safe, at least for a few more hours, long enough for the child to be born. And for the first time Theo understood and accepted Julian's desire to give birth in secret. This forest refuge, inadequate as it was, was surely better than the alternative. He pictured again that alternative, the high sterile bed, the banks of machines to meet every possible medical emergency, the distinguished obstetricians summoned from retirement, masked and gowned, standing together, because after twenty-five years there was a better hope of safety in their united memory and expertise, each one desperate for the honour of delivering this miraculous child, yet half-afraid of the terrifying responsibility. He could picture the acolytes, the gowned nurses and midwives, the anaesthetists, and beyond them, but dominant, the television cameras with their crews, the Warden behind his screen waiting to give the momentous news to an expectant world.

But it had been more than the destruction of privacy, the stripping-away of personal dignity, that Julian had feared. For her Xan was evil. The word had a meaning for her. She saw with clear and undazzled eyes through the strength, the charm, the intelligence, the humour into the heart, not of emptiness but of darkness. Whatever the future might hold for her child, she wanted no one evil to be present at the birth. He could understand now her obstinate choice and it seemed to him, sitting in this peace and quietness, to be both right and reasonable. But her obstinacy had already cost the lives of two people, one the father of her child. She could argue that good could come out of evil; it was surely more difficult to argue that evil could come out of good. She trusted in the terrible mercy and justice of her God, but what other option had she but to trust? She could no more control her life than she could control or stop the physical forces which even now were stretching and racking her body. If her God existed, how could He be the God of Love? The question had become banal, ubiquitous, but for him it had never been satisfactorily answered.

He listened again to the forest, to its secret life.

Now the sounds, seeming to increase as he listened, were full of menace and terror: the scavenger scurrying and leaping on its prey, the cruelty and satisfaction of the hunt, the instinctive struggle for food, for survival. The whole physical world was held together by pain, the scream in the throat and the scream in the heart. If her God was part of this torment, its creator and sustainer, then He was a God of the strong, not of the weak. He contemplated the gulf fixed between Julian and himself by her belief, but without dismay. He could not diminish it but he could stretch his hands across it. And perhaps in the end the bridge would be love. How little he knew her or she him. The emotion he felt towards her was as mysterious as it was irrational. He needed to understand it, to define its nature, to analyse what he knew was beyond analysis. But some things now he did know, and perhaps they were all he needed to know. He wished only her good. He would put her good before his own. He could no longer separate himself from her. He would die for her life.

The silence was broken by the sound of a groan followed by a sharp cry. Once it would have aroused his embarrassment, the humiliating fear that he would be found inadequate. Now, conscious only of his need to be with her, he ran into the shed. She was again lying on her side quite peacefully, and smiled at him, holding out her hand. Miriam was kneeling at her side.

He said: "What can I do? Let me stay. Do you want me to stay?"

Julian said, her voice as even as if there had never been the sharp cry: "Of course you must stay. We want you to stay. But perhaps you'd better build the fire now. Then it will be ready to light when we need it."

He saw that her face was swollen, the brow damp with sweat. But he was amazed at her quietness, her calm. And he had something to do, a job at which he could feel confident. If he could find wood shavings which were perfectly dry there was hope that he could light a fire without too much smoke. The day was practically windless, but even so he must be careful to build it so that no smoke blew into Julian's face or the face of the baby. A little towards the front of the shed would be best, where the roof was broken but close enough to warm mother and child. And he would need to contain it or there would be a danger of conflagration. Some of the stones from the broken wall would make a good fireplace. He went out to collect them, carefully selecting them for size and shape. It occurred to him that he could even use some of the flatter stones to produce a kind of funnel. Returning, he arranged the stones into a ring, filled it with the driest wood shavings he could find, then added a few twigs. Finally he laid flat stones across the top, directing the smoke out of the shed. When he had finished he felt some of the satisfaction of a small boy. And when Julian raised herself up and laughed with pleasure his voice joined hers.

Miriam said: "It would be best if you knelt at her side and held her hand."

During the next spasm of pain she gripped so hard that his knuckles cracked.

Seeing his face, his desperate need for reassurance, Miriam said: "She's all right. She's doing wonderfully. I can't make an internal examination. It wouldn't be safe now. I haven't sterile gloves and the waters have broken. But I'd estimate that the cervix is almost fully dilated. The second stage will be easier."

He said to Julian: "Darling, what can I do? Tell me what I can do."

"Just keep holding my hand."

Kneeling there beside them, he marvelled at Miriam, at the quiet confidence with which, even after twenty-five years, she exercised her ancient art, her brown and gentle hands resting on Julian's stomach, her voice murmuring reassurance: "Rest now, then go along with the next wave. Don't resist it. Remember your breathing. That's fine, Julian, that's fine."

When the second stage of labour began she told Theo to kneel at Julian's back and support her body, then took two of the smaller logs and placed them against Julian's feet. Theo knelt and took the weight of Julian's body, his arms clasping her to him under her breasts. She rested against his chest, her feet clamped hard against the two logs of wood. He looked down at her face, at one moment almost unrecognizable, scarlet and distorted, as she grunted and heaved in his arms, the next at peace, mysteriously wiped free of anguish and effort while she panted softly, her eyes fixed on Miriam, waiting for the next contraction. At these moments she looked so peaceful that he could almost believe that she slept. Their faces were so close that it was his sweat mingled with hers that from time to time he gently wiped away. The primitive act, at which he was both participant and spectator, isolated them in a limbo of time in which nothing mattered, nothing was real except the mother and her child's dark painful journey from the secret life of the womb to the light of day. He was aware of the ceaseless murmur of Miriam's voice, quiet but insistent, praising, encouraging, instructing, joyfully enticing the child into the world, and it seemed to him that midwife and patient were one woman and that he, too, was part of the pain and the labouring, not really needed but graciously accepted, and yet excluded from the heart of the mystery. And he wished, with a sudden surge of anguish and envy, that it was his child with which such an agony of effort they were bringing into the world.

And then he saw with amazement that the head was emerging, a greasy ball plastered with strands of dark hair.

He heard Miriam's voice, low but triumphant. "The head is crowned. Stop pushing, Julian. Just pant now."

Julian's voice was rasping like an athlete's after a hard race. She gave a single cry, and with an indescribable sound the head was propelled into Miriam's waiting hands. She took it, gently turned it; almost immediately, with a last push, the child slid into the world between his mother's legs in a rush of blood, and was lifted by Miriam and lain on his mother's stomach. Julian had been wrong about the sex. The child was male. Its sex, seeming so dominant, so disproportionate to the plump, small body, was like a proclamation.

Swiftly Miriam drew over him the sheet and blanket which covered Julian, binding them together. She said, "See, you have a son," and laughed.

It seemed to Theo that the decrepit shed rang with her joyful and triumphant voice. He looked down at Julian's outstretched arms and transfigured face, then turned away. The joy was almost too much for him to bear.

He heard Miriam's voice: "I'll have to cut the

cord, and later there'll be the afterbirth. You'd better light the fire now, Theo, and see if you can heat the kettle. Julian will need a hot drink."

He went back to his makeshift fireplace. His hands were shaking so that the first match went out. But with the second the thin shavings burst into flame and the fire leapt like a celebration, filling the shed with the smell of wood smoke. He fed it carefully with the twigs and pieces of bark, then turned for the kettle. But that moment brought disaster. He had placed it close to the fire and, stepping back, kicked it over. The lid came off and he saw with sick horror the precious water seeping into the sawdust and staining the earth. They had already used the water in the two saucepans. Now they had none.

The sound of his shoe striking the metal had warned Miriam. She was still busy with the child and, without turning her head, said: "What happened? Was that the kettle?"

Theo said miserably: "I'm sorry. It's appalling. I've spilt the water."

And now Miriam stood up and came over to him. She said calmly: "We were going to need more water anyway, water and food. I have to stay with Julian until I'm sure it's safe to leave her but then I'll go to the house we passed. With luck the water will be still laid on, or there may be a well."

"But you'll have to cross an open field. They'll see you."

She said: "I have to go, Theo. There are things we need. I have to take that risk."

But she was being kind. It was water they needed most and their need was his fault.

He said: "Let me go. You stay with her."

Miriam said: "She wants you with her. Now that the baby's born, she needs you more than she needs me. I have to make sure the fundus is well contracted and check that the afterbirth is complete. When that's done it will be safe to leave her. Try to get the baby to the breast. The sooner he begins sucking the better."

It seemed to Theo that she liked explaining the mysteries of her craft, liked using the words which for so many years had been unspoken but unforgotten.

Twenty minutes later she was ready to go. She had buried the afterbirth and had tried to clean the blood from her hands by rubbing them in the grass. Then she laid them, those gentle experienced hands, for the last time on Julian's stomach.

She said: "I can wash in the lake on my way. I could face your cousin's arrival with equanimity if I could be sure he'd provide me with a hot bath and a four-course meal before shooting me. I'd better take the kettle. I'll be as quick as I can."

On impulse he put his arms round her and held

her close for a moment. He said, "Thank you, thank you," then released her and watched as she ran with her long, graceful strides over the glade and passed out of sight under the overhanging boughs of the lane.

33

The baby had needed no encouragement to suck. He was a lively child, opening on Theo his bright unfocused eyes, waving his starfish hands, butting his head against his mother's breast, the small open mouth voraciously seeking the nipple. It was extraordinary that anything so new could be so vigorous. He sucked and slept. Theo lay down beside Julian and placed an arm over them both. He felt the damp softness of her hair against his cheek. They lay on the soiled and crumpled sheet in the stench of blood, sweat and faeces but he had never known such peace, never realized that joy could be so sweetly compounded with pain. They lay half-dozing in a wordless calm and it seemed to Theo that there rose from the child's warm flesh, transitory but stronger even than the smell of blood, the strange agreeable aroma of the new-born, dry and pungent like hay.

Then Julian stirred and said: "How long is it since Miriam left?"

He lifted his left wrist close to his face. "Just over an hour."

"She shouldn't take so long. Please find her, Theo."

"It isn't just water we need. If the house is furnished there are other things she'll want to collect."

"Only a few to begin with. She could always go back. She knows we'll be anxious. Please go to her. I know something's happened to her." As he hesitated, she said: "We'll be all right."

The use of the plural, what he saw in her eyes as she turned them on her son, almost unmanned him. He said: "They could be very close now. I don't want to leave you. I want us to be together when Xan comes."

"My darling, we will be. But she could be in trouble, trapped, hurt, waiting desperately for help. Theo, I have to know."

He made no further protest, but got up and said: "I'll be as quick as I can."

For a few seconds he stood silent outside the hut and listened. He shut his eyes to the autumn hues of the forest, to the shaft of sunlight on bark and grass, so that he could concentrate all his senses into listening. But he heard nothing, not even the sound of a bird. Then, almost leaping forward like a sprinter, he began pounding, past the lake, up the narrow tunnel of green towards the crossroads, leaping over the ruts and pot-holes, feeling the jar of the hard ridges under his feet, ducking and weaving beneath the low clutching branches. His mind was a tangle of fear and hope. It was madness to leave Julian. If the SSP were close and had captured Miriam there was nothing he could do to help her now. And if they were that close it was only a matter of time before they found Julian and her child. Better to have stayed together and waited, waited until the bright morning lengthened into afternoon and they knew that there was no hope of seeing Miriam again, waited until they heard on the grass the thud of marching feet.

But, desperate for reassurance, he told himself that there were other possibilities. Julian was right. Miriam could have had an accident, fallen, be lying there, wondering how long it was before he came. His mind busied itself with the images of disaster, the door of a pantry slamming fast behind her, a defective well-head which she hadn't seen, a rotting floorboard. He tried to will himself into belief, to convince himself that an hour was a very little time, that Miriam was busy collecting everything they might need—calculating how much of the precious store she could carry, what could be left until later, forgetting in her foraging how long those sixty minutes would seem to those who waited.

Now he was at the crossroads and could see, through the narrow gap and the thinner bushes of the wide hedge, the sloping field and the roof of the house. He stood for a minute catching his breath, bending to ease the sharp pain in his side, then plunged through the tangle of high nettles, thorns and snapping twigs into the clearer light of the open countryside. There was no sign of Miriam. More slowly now, aware of his vulnerability and of a deepening unease, he made his way across the field and came to the house. It was an old building with an uneven roof of mossy tiles and tall Elizabethan chimneys, probably once a farmhouse. It was separated from the field by a low dry-stone wall. The wilderness which was once the rear garden was bisected by a narrow stream spurting from a culvert higher up the bank over which a simple wooden bridge led to the back door. The windows were small and uncurtained. Everywhere was silent. The house was like a mirage, the longed-for symbol of security, normality and peace which he had only to touch to see vanish. In the silence the ripple of the stream sounded as loud as a torrent.

The back door was of black oak banded with iron. It stood ajar. He pushed it wider and the mellow autumnal sunlight splashed gold over the stone slabs of a passage leading to the front of the house. Again he stood for a second and listened. He heard nothing, not even the ticking of a clock. To his left was an oak door leading, he presumed, into the kitchen. It was unlatched and gently he pushed it open. After the brightness of the day the room was dim and for a moment he could see little until his eyes accustomed themselves to a gloom made more oppressive by the dark oak beams, the small dirt-covered windows. He was aware of a damp coldness, of the hardness of the stone floor and of a tincture on the air, at once horrible and human, like the lingering smell of fear. He felt along the wall for a light switch, hardly expecting, as his hand found it, that there would still be electricity. But the light came on, and then he saw her.

She had been garrotted and the body dumped into a large wicker chair to the right of the fireplace. She lay there sprawled, legs askew, arms flung over the ends of the chair, the head thrown back with the cord bitten so deep into the skin that it was hardly visible. Such was his horror that after the first glance he staggered over to the stone sink under the window and vomited violently but ineffectively. He wanted to go to her, to close her eyes, to touch her hand, to make some gesture. He owed her more than to turn away from the appalling horror of her death and vomit his disgust. But he knew he couldn't touch her and couldn't even look again. With his forehead hard against the cold stone, he reached up to the tap and a gush of cold water flowed over his head. He let it flow as if it could wipe away the terror, the pity and the shame. He wanted to throw back his head and howl out his anger. For a few seconds he was helpless, in the thrall of emotions which left him powerless to move. Then he turned off the tap, shook the water from his eyes and took hold of reality. He had to get back to Julian as quickly as possible. He saw on the table the meagre gleanings of Miriam's search. She had found a large wicker basket and had filled it with three tins, a tin-opener and a bottle of water.

But he couldn't leave Miriam as she was. This mustn't be the last vision he had of her. However great the need to get back to Julian and the child, there was a small ceremony he owed to her. Fighting terror and revulsion, he got up and made himself look at her. Then, bending, he loosened the cord from her neck, smoothed the lines of her face and closed her eyes. He felt the need to take her out of this awful place. He lifted her in his arms, carried her out of the house and into the sunlight, then laid her carefully down under a rowan tree. Its leaves, like tongues of flame, cast a glow on the pale brown of her skin as if her veins still pulsed with life. Her face now looked almost peaceful.

He crossed her arms on her breast and it seemed to him that the unresponsive flesh could still communicate, was telling him that death was not the worst thing that could happen to a human being, that she had kept faith with her brother, that she had done what she set out to do. She had died but new life had been born. Thinking of the horror and cruelty of her death, he told himself that Julian would no doubt say that there must be forgiveness even for this barbarity. But that was not his creed. Standing for a moment very still and looking down at the body, he swore to himself that Miriam would be avenged. Then he retrieved the wicker basket and, without a backward look, ran from the garden across the bridge and plunged into the forest.

They were close, of course. They were watching him. He knew that. But now, as if the horror had galvanized his brain, he was thinking clearly. What were they waiting for? Why had they let him go? They hardly needed to follow him. It must be obvious that they were very close now to the end of their search. And he had no doubt of two things. The party would be small and Xan would be among them. Miriam's murderers hadn't been part of an isolated forward search party with instructions to find the fugitives, leave them unharmed and send back word to the main party. Xan would never risk having a pregnant woman discovered except by himself or by someone he trusted absolutely. There would be no general search for this valuable quarry. And Xan would have learned nothing from Miriam, he was sure of that. What he was expecting to find was not a mother and child but a heavily pregnant woman still with some weeks to go. He wouldn't want to frighten her, wouldn't want to precipitate a premature labour. Was that why Miriam had been garrotted, not shot? Even at that distance he didn't want to risk the sound of gunfire.

But that reasoning was absurd. If Xan wanted to protect Julian, to ensure that she kept calm for the birth which he believed was close, why kill the midwife she trusted and kill her so horribly? He must have known that one of them, perhaps both, would go to seek her. It was only by chance that he, Theo, not Julian, had been faced by that swollen, protruding tongue, those bulging, dead eyes, the full horror of that awful kitchen. Had Xan convinced himself that with the child ready to be born nothing, however shocking, could really hurt it now? Or had he needed to get rid of Miriam urgently, whatever the risk? Why take her prisoner with all the consequent complications when one quick twist of cord could settle the problem for ever? And perhaps even the horror was deliberate. Was he proclaiming: "This is what I can do, what I have done. There are now only two of you left who are part of the conspiracy of the Five Fishes, only two who know the truth about the child's parentage. You are in my power absolutely and for ever"?

Or was his plan even more audacious? Once the child was born he had only to kill Theo and Julian and it would be possible to claim the baby as his own. Had he really in his overweening egotism convinced himself that even this was possible? And then Theo remembered Xan's words: "Whatever it is necessary to do, I shall do."

In the shed Julian lay so still that at first he thought she was sleeping. But her eyes were open and she still had them fixed on her child. The air was rich with the pungent sweetness of wood smoke, but the fire had gone out. Theo put down the basket and, taking the bottle of water, unscrewed the top. He knelt down beside her.

She looked into his eyes and said: "Miriam's dead, isn't she?" When Theo made no reply, she said: "She died getting this for me."

He held the bottle to her lips. "Then drink it and be thankful."

But she turned her head away, releasing her hold on the child so that if he hadn't caught the baby he would have rolled from her body. She lay still as if too exhausted for paroxysms of grief, but the tears gushed in a stream over her face and he could hear a low, almost musical moaning, like the keening of a universal grief. She was mourning for Miriam as she had never yet mourned the father of her child.

He bent and held her in his arms, clumsily because of the baby between them, trying to enfold them both. He said: "Remember the baby. The baby needs you. Remember what Miriam would have wanted."

She didn't speak but she nodded and again took the child from him. He put the bottle of water to her lips.

He took out the three tins from the basket. From one the label had fallen off; the tin felt heavy but there was no knowing what was inside. The second was labelled PEACHES IN SYRUP. The third was a tin of baked beans in tomato sauce. For these and a bottle of water Miriam had died. But he knew that was too simple. Miriam had died because she was one of the small band who knew the truth about the child.

The tin-opener was an old type, partly rusted, the cutting edge blunted. But it was adequate. He rasped open the tin, then wrenched back the lid and, cradling Julian's head in his right arm, began feeding her the beans on the middle finger of his left hand. She sucked at it avidly. The process of feeding her was an act of love. Neither spoke.

After five minutes, when the can was half

empty, she said: "Now it's your turn."

"I'm not hungry."

"Of course you're hungry."

His knuckles were too large for his fingers to reach the bottom of the tin, so it was her turn to feed him. Sitting up with the cradled child resting in her lap, she inserted her small right hand and fed him.

He said: "They taste wonderful."

When the tin was empty she gave a little sigh, then lay back, gathering the child to her breast. He stretched himself beside her.

She said: "How did Miriam die?"

It was a question he knew that she would ask. He couldn't lie to her. "She was strangled. It must have been very quick. Perhaps she didn't even see them. I don't think she had time for terror or pain."

Julian said: "It could have lasted a second, two seconds, perhaps more. We can't live those seconds for her. We can't know what she felt, the terror, the pain. You could feel a lifetime's pain and terror in two seconds."

He said: "My darling, it's over for her now. She's beyond their reach for ever. Miriam, Gascoigne, Luke, they're all beyond the Council's reach. Every time a victim dies it's a small defeat for tyranny."

She said: "That's too easy a comfort." And then, after a silence: "They won't try to separate us, will they?"

"Nothing and no one will separate us, not life nor death, nor principalities, nor powers, nor anything that is of the heavens nor anything that is of the earth."

She laid her hand against his cheek. "Oh, my darling, you can't promise that. But I like to hear you say it." After a moment she asked: "Why don't they come?" But there was no anguish in the question, only a gentle bewilderment.

He reached out and took her hand, winding his fingers round the hot, distorted flesh amazed that he had once found it repulsive. He stroked it but he didn't answer. They lay motionless side by side. Theo was aware of the strong smell of the sawn wood and the dead fire, of the oblong of sunlight like a green veil, of the silence, windless, birdless, of her heartbeats and his own. They were wrapped in an intensity of listening which was miraculously devoid of anxiety. Was this what the victims of torture felt when they passed through the extremity of pain into peace? He thought: I have done what I set out to do. The child is born as she wanted. This is our place, our moment of time, and, whatever they do to us, it can never be taken away.

It was Julian who broke the silence: "Theo, I

think they're here. They've come."

He had heard nothing but he got up and said: "Wait very quietly. Don't move."

Turning his back so that she couldn't see, he took the revolver from his pocket and inserted the bullet. Then he went out to meet them.

Xan was alone. He looked like a woodman with his old corduroy trousers, open-necked shirt and heavy sweater. But woodmen do not come armed; there was the bulge of a holster under the sweater. And no woodman had stood blazing with such confidence, such an arrogance of power. Glittering on his left hand was the wedding ring of England.

He said: "So it is true."

"Yes, it's true."

"Where is she?"

Theo didn't answer. Xan said: "I don't need to ask. I know where she is. But is she well?"

"She's well. She's asleep. We have a few minutes before she wakes."

Xan threw back his shoulders and gave a gasp of relief like an exhausted swimmer emerging to shake the water from his eyes.

For a moment he breathed hard; then he said calmly: "I can wait to see her. I don't want to frighten her. I've come with an ambulance, helicopter, doctors, midwives. I've brought everything she needs. This child will be born in comfort and safety. The mother will be treated like the miracle she is; she has to know that. If she trusts you, then you can be the one to tell her. Reassure her, calm her, let her know she has nothing to fear from me."

"She has everything to fear. Where is Rolf?"

"Dead."

"And Gascoigne?"

"Dead."

"And I've seen Miriam's body. So no one is alive who knows the truth about this child. You've disposed of them all."

Xan said calmly: "Except you." When Theo didn't reply he went on: "I don't plan to kill you, I don't want to kill you. I need you. But we have to talk now before I see her. I have to know how far I can rely on you. You can help me with her, with what I have to do."

Theo said: "Tell me what you have to do."

"Isn't it obvious? If it's a boy and he's fertile, he'll be the father of the new race. If he produces sperm, fertile sperm, at thirteen—at twelve maybe—our female Omegas will only be thirty-eight. We can breed from them, from other selected women. We may be able to breed again from the woman herself."

"The father of her child is dead."

"I know. We got the truth from Rolf. But if there was one fertile male there can be others.

We'll redouble the testing programme. We've been getting careless. We'll test everyone, the epileptic, deformed—every male in the country. And the child may be a male—a fertile male. He'll be our best hope. The hope of the world."

"And Julian?"

Xan laughed. "I'll probably marry her. Anyway, she'll be looked after. Go back to her now. Wake her. Tell her I'm here but on my own. Reassure her. Tell her you'll be helping me to care for her. Good God, Theo, do you realize what power is in our hands? Come back on the Council, be my lieutenant. You can have anything you want."

"No."

There was a pause. Xan asked: "Do you remember the bridge at Woolcombe?" The question wasn't a sentimental appeal to an old loyalty or the tie of blood, nor a reminder of kindness given and taken. Xan had in that moment simply remembered and he smiled with the pleasure of it.

Theo said: "I remember everything that happened at Woolcombe."

"I don't want to kill you."

"You're going to have to, Xan. You may have to kill her too."

He reached for his own gun. Xan laughed as he saw it.

"I know it isn't loaded. You told the old people that, remember? You wouldn't have let Rolf get away if you'd had a loaded gun."

"How did you expect me to stop him? Shoot her husband in front of her eyes?"

"Her husband? I didn't realize that she cared greatly about her husband. That isn't the picture he so obligingly gave us before he died. You don't imagine you're in love with her, do you? Don't romanticize her. She may be the most important woman in the world but she isn't the Virgin Mary. The child she is carrying is still the child of a whore."

Their eyes met. Theo thought: What is he waiting for? Does he find that he can't shoot me in cold blood, as I find I can't shoot him? Time passed, second after interminable second. Then Xan stretched his arm and took aim. And it was in that split second of time that the child cried, a high mewing wail, like a cry of protest. Theo heard Xan's bullet hiss harmlessly through the sleeve of his jacket. He knew that in that half-second he couldn't have seen what afterwards he so clearly remembered: Xan's face transfigured with joy and triumph; couldn't have heard his great shout of affirmation, like the shout on the bridge at Woolcombe. But it was with that re-membered shout in his ears that he shot Xan through the heart.

After the two shots he was aware only of a great silence. When he and Miriam had pushed the car into the lake, the peaceful forest had become a screaming jungle, a cacophony of wild shrieks, crashing boughs and agitated bird-calls which had faded only with the last trembling ripple. But now there was nothing. It seemed to him that he walked towards Xan's body like an actor in a slow-motion film, hands buffeting the air, feet high-stepping, hardly seeming to touch the ground; space stretching into infinity so that Xan's body was a distant goal towards which he made his arduous way held in suspended time. And then, like a kick in the brain, reality took hold again and he was simultaneously aware of his own body's quick motion, of every small creature moving among the trees, every leaf of grass felt through the soles of his shoes, of the air moving against his face, aware most keenly of all of Xan lying at his feet. He was lying on his back, arms spread, as if taking his ease beside the Windrush. His face looked peaceful, unsurprised, as if he were feigning death but, kneeling, Theo saw that his eyes were two dull pebbles, once sea-washed but now left for ever lifeless by the last receding tide. He took the ring from Xan's finger, then stood upright and waited.

They came very quietly, moving out of the forest, first Carl Inglebach, then Martin Woolvington, then the two women. Behind them, keeping a careful distance, were six Grenadiers. They moved to within four feet of the body, then paused. Theo held up the ring, then deliberately placed it on his finger and held the back of his hand towards them.

He said: "The Warden of England is dead and the child is born. Listen."

It came again, that piteous but imperative mew of the new-born. They began moving towards the wood-shed but he barred the path and said: "Wait. I must ask his mother first."

Inside the shed Julian was sitting bolt upright, the child held tight against her breast, his open mouth now suckling, now moving against her skin. As Theo came up to her he saw the desperate fear in her eyes lightening to joyous relief. She let the child rest on her lap and held out her arms to him.

She said with a sob: "There were two shots. I didn't know whether I should see you or him."

For a moment he held her shaking body against his. He said: "The Warden of England is dead. The Council is here. Will you see them, show them your child?"

She said: "For a little while. Theo, what will happen now?"

Terror for him had for a moment drained her of courage and strength and for the first time since the birth he saw her vulnerable and afraid. He whispered to her, his lips against her hair.

"We'll take you to hospital, to somewhere quiet. You'll be looked after. I won't let you be disturbed. You won't need to be there long and we'll be together. I shan't leave you ever. Whatever happens, we shall be together."

He released her and went outside. They were standing in a semicircle waiting for him, their eyes fixed on his face.

"You can come in now. Not the Grenadiers, just the Council. She's tired, she needs to rest."

Woolvington said: "We have an ambulance further down the lane. We can call up the paramedics, carry her there. The helicopter is about a mile away, outside the village."

Theo said: "We won't risk the helicopter. Call up the stretcher-bearers. And get the Warden's body moved. I don't want her to see it."

As two Grenadiers immediately came forward and began dragging at the corpse, Theo said: "Use some reverence. Remember what he was only minutes ago. You wouldn't have dared lay a hand on him then."

He turned and led the Council into the woodshed. It seemed to him that they came tentatively, reluctantly, first the two women, then Woolvington and Carl. Woolvington didn't approach Julian but took a stand at her head as if he were a sentry on guard. The two women knelt, less, Theo thought, in homage than from a need to be close to the child. They looked at Julian as if seeking consent. She smiled and held out the baby. Murmuring, weeping, shaken with tears and laughter, they put out their hands and touched his head, his cheeks, his waving arms. Harriet held out a finger and the baby grasped it in a surprising grip. She laughed and Julian, looking up, said to Theo: "Miriam told me the newborn can grip like that. It doesn't last very long."

The women didn't reply. They were crying and smiling, making their silly happy sounds of welcome and discovery. It seemed to Theo a joyous, female camaraderie. He looked up at Carl, astonished that the man had been able to make the journey, was still managing to stay on his feet. Carl looked down at the child with his dying eyes and spoke his Nunc Dimittis. "So it begins again."

Theo thought: It begins again, with jealousy, with treachery, with violence, with murder, with this ring on my finger. He looked down at the great sapphire in its glitter of diamonds, at the ruby cross, twisting the ring, aware of its weight. Placing it on his hand had been instinctive and yet deliberate, a gesture to assert authority and ensure protection. He had known that the Grenadiers would come armed. The sight of that shining symbol on his finger would at least make them pause, give him time to speak. Did he need to wear it now? He had all Xan's power within his grasp, that and more. With Carl dying, the Council was leaderless. For a time at least he must take Xan's place. There were evils to be remedied; but they must take their turn. He couldn't do everything at once, there had to be priorities. Was that what Xan had found? And was this sudden intoxication of power what Xan had known every day of his life? The sense that everything was possible to him, that what he wanted would be done, that what he hated would be abolished, that the world could be fashioned according to his will. He drew the ring from his finger, then paused and pushed it back. There would be time later to decide whether, and for how long, he needed it.

He said: "Leave us now," and, bending, helped the women to their feet. They went out as quietly as they had come in.

Julian looked up at him. For the first time she noticed the ring. She said: "That wasn't made for your finger."

For a second, no more, he felt something close to irritation. It must be for him to decide when he would take it off. He said: "It's useful for the present. I shall take it off in time."

She seemed for the moment content, and it might have been his imagination that there was a shadow in her eyes.

Then she smiled and said to him: "Christen the

baby for me. Please do it now, while we're alone. It's what Luke would have wanted. It's what I want."

"What do you want him called?"

"Call him after his father and after you."

"I'll make you comfortable first."

The towel between her legs was heavily stained. He removed it without revulsion, almost without thought, and, folding another, put it in place. There was very little water left in the bottle, but he hardly needed it. His tears were falling now over the child's forehead. From some far childhood memory he recalled the rite. The water had to flow, there were words which had to be said. It was with a thumb wet with his own tears and stained with her blood that he made on the child's forehead the sign of the cross.